DUAL THERAPY

Elvis Bray

ISBN: 1545385300
ISBN 13: 9781545385302

Other books by Elvis Bray

The Presence of Justice

This book is dedicated to the men and women I served with for thirty-five years at the Mesa Police Department and Mesa Community College

I am proud to get the opportunity to review author, Elvis L. Bray's second book, "Dual Therapy". His first book, "The Presence of Justice" was a terrific, well written mystery that I thoroughly enjoyed. I have been looking forward to his second writing. Bray brings his many years of law enforcement experience into his writings. This assisted him in creating a very intriguing mystery that will hold your attention to the very last page. His knowledge of police investigative techniques and court procedures helped create a novel about an experienced homicide detective and a complicated investigation involving a serial murderer.

Guy Meeks
Retired Mesa City Chief of Police

CHAPTER ONE

I woke to a phone vibrating on my nightstand. A red haze shown above the eastern horizon through my window as raindrops flowed gently down the panes. I was hot, sweaty, and my heart pounded in my chest. I answered my cell phone, "Storm Harrison."

"Storm, where the hell are you? I've been calling you for half an hour."

"I'm at home, Charlie. What time is it?"

"It's 6:30."

I yawned trying to shake myself awake. "It's Saturday, Charlie, my day off. What do you want?"

"We have another body."

I took a deep breath and slowly let it out. "Shit, Charlie, not today. Call Pomush or handle it yourself."

"I'll deal with it if you want, but Pomush is on vacation, remember? I got the call from Lieutenant Fowler and he said to call you."

"Damn it, I really don't need this today. I'm not feeling well. Can't you take care of it?"

"I'll try."

There was a short pause and I fooled myself into thinking maybe I'd be able to go back to sleep.

"She's sixteen, raped and murdered."

I sat on the edge of the bed and ran fingers through my hair with the phone to my ear. Charlie Blakely was new to homicide and assigned to me for training. Tall, blond, handsome, he was eager to learn and had an eye for detail. Someday he would see the bigger picture and make a great detective. But for now he was as green and innocent as the son of a Mormon Bishop that he was. I thought about the other three victims as he waited for my answer.

"Storm... you still there?"

"Yeah, I'm here, Charlie. What's your location?"

"At the apartment complex on the corner of 32nd Street and Academy Blvd."

"All right, give me a quick brief." I took a deep breath and forced myself upright.

"The victim's mother is a divorced nurse who works nights at the hospital. She discovered her daughter's body when she came home from work this morning. The mother's a mess and had to be sedated."

"Yeah, I know how that feels."

Charlie ignored my comment. "It looks like the girl was strangled in the living room and dragged into her bedroom where she was raped. There's a feces trail all the way to the bedroom."

I felt sick to my stomach. I stumbled, caught myself and knocked an empty beer bottle off the nightstand. "Secure the scene and keep the reporters at bay. I'll be there in twenty minutes."

Being a homicide detective for the Colorado Springs Police Department had its perks. Most murders were solved within the first 24 hours. You work your butt off for a couple of days and then spend the next week or two doing interviews and completing the never-ending paperwork. There was lots of overtime involved but I was off most weekends, although I'm always subject to call. I have to keep that in mind when having a few. If I show up drunk at a crime scene, I'll be back on patrol working the graveyard shift. Not good for a single man's social life, as if I had one. But these murders have been going on for a few months now and we don't have any suspects.

Snow-covered Pikes Peak glowed in the distance, promising another fine spring day on the eastern slopes of the Rocky Mountains. A robin's egg colored blue sky shone through patches of evaporating white clouds. New leaves budded on the tree branches and flowers flourished in the planters. The air was fresh and clean and the morning rain had stopped before I arrived on the scene.

The apartment complex looked like a zoo. It was two stories and the victim's apartment was on the bottom floor facing a large grass area. Residents and curiosity seekers crowded the lawn in front of the victim's apartment. Reporters and news vans cluttered the parking lot while a news helicopter circled overhead. I parked across the street, gargled mouthwash, spit in the shrubs, and walked in on foot.

Side-stepping the reporters, I made it under the crime scene tape before anyone recognized me and started asking stupid questions. A uniformed officer guarded the door. While signing the crime scene log, I heard a familiar voice behind me. "Detective Harrison, is this the same guy that murdered the other three girls?"

The voice belonged to Connie Mason, a reporter for Channel 10. She covered most murder cases and hated my guys for not answering her questions. We had a history that went back to the days when she was still a writer for the newspaper. I smiled at the camera and gave her my standard reply, "No comment." She frowned, wrinkled her cute little freckled nose and flipped me off as I entered the apartment and closed the door behind me.

Maggie Hawthorn, the best crime scene technician in the department's Identification Bureau, stood just inside the apartment fiddling with her equipment. She insisted on processing all murder scenes even if they occurred on her days off. As wide as she was tall, she wore her hair in a crew cut and treated make-up like the plague, avoiding it at all cost. "Where the hell have you been, Storm? I'm almost finished here and you look like crap."

"I love you too, Maggie." I surveyed the room. A broken lamp on the floor next to the sofa indicated a struggle. The smell of feces and death hung in the air like a fog next to a sewage plant.

Maggie put her camera in its case and closed it. "I'm serious, big guy. You need to get some sleep. You're killing yourself."

"I've thought about it, Maggie, but I'm fine now. I got a good night's sleep for a change."

She stared at me as if she wasn't sure if I was joking or not. "You couldn't tell it by looking at you. Have you been hitting the booze?"

"A little," I said. "I need to take a look around, Maggie."

She placed her hands on her wide hips and gave me a threatening stare. "Go ahead but don't touch anything. I'm going to get this creep's DNA this time if I have to process the whole damn apartment complex. I want you out of here in five minutes. And don't push it."

Following the feces smear from the living room to the bedroom, I was careful not to disturb anything. I eased around the corner into the hall and made my way to the first bedroom on the right. The odor was stronger now and I wished I had worn a mask.

The body hung halfway off the bed, face down with her buttocks propped up on a pillow. Her head was turned facing me at an unnatural angle. Her skin was smooth and pale with her blue eyes wide open staring up at me. She looked more like a porcelain doll than a real person. While looking at her, I thought about the other three victims, all about her age, pretty, raped and strangled. She reminded me of a beautiful young lady who had died in my arms years ago and still haunts my dreams.

My mind drifted back to an alley twelve years ago where she had died. I could almost see this little girl's lips mouthing the words, *"Help me, please help me!"* I knew it wasn't real but the image made me sick. I tried to hold it together but was losing it. As my stomach churned, I stepped into the bathroom across the hall and puked in the sink.

"Damn you, Storm!" Maggie yelled from the family room. "You're screwing up my crime scene."

I closed the bathroom door and locked it. Feeling light-headed, I could hardly stand up. I sat on the floor in front of the toilet feeling as if I might puke again. Opening the lid, I dry-heaved several times. Sweat beaded on my forehead.

I heard Maggie jiggle the door handle. "Storm, unlock the door!"

"Go away, Maggie."

I thought she had left until I heard her try to open it again. "Are you all right?" This time, she sounded concerned.

"I'm fine. Just give me a minute."

"Darn you," I heard her mutter, and then there was silence.

My head throbbed, my chest hurt and I could hardly breathe. It felt as if I were catching the flu. Wrapping my arms around the toilet, I dry-heaved again and again. I laid my head on my arms to rest. After a few minutes, I felt better and started to stand up. I was about to flush the toilet when I noticed something that appeared to have gotten hung up when it was flushed previously. "Maggie, get in here!"

She tried to open the door to no avail. I crawled over and unlocked it for her. She saw me on the floor and yelled, "Storm, hold on. I'll call 911."

"No Maggie. I'm all right. I want to show you something."

"What?"

"In the toilet," I said pointing downward. "Look in the toilet."

She moved next to me and looked down. "I don't see anything."

"Come down here with me and tell me what you see."

Maggie got on her hands and knees beside me. Shaking her head, she said, "I hope no one catches us like this. We'll never be able to stop the rumors."

I smiled and pointed in the toilet, "Look under the drain at the very back. What is that?"

She tilted her head to the side and stared inside. She put on rubber gloves, reached her hand into the water and very slowly pulled out a condom. She held it up in front of her at arm's length. It had a knot tied at the top and appeared to have semen in it. Maggie looked at me, smiled, and looked back at the condom. Then she broke into an old Joe Cocker song. "You are so beautiful to me."

Her voice was coarse from years of smoking Camel cigarettes. She sang off key and couldn't hit any note higher than a C if her life depended on it. I patted her on the shoulder. "Maggie, you have the voice of an angel."

Smiling, she stood, still holding the condom almost reverently. "I think my work here is almost complete." She was still humming *You are so beautiful* as she exited the bathroom.

Rising to my feet, I viewed myself in the mirror. Not only did I feel like crap, I looked like crap. My pale face, uncombed hair and unshaved stubbles gave me the appearance of a homeless man. I needed some fresh air.

My stomach was still churning as I walked out the back door of the apartment and dry heaved into some bushes.

"That bad, huh? I didn't think anything could rattle the great Storm Harrison."

Angry that I'd been caught, I turned towards the source of the annoying voice. "I've got the flu, Connie. Don't get any closer or you'll catch it."

She looked as if she didn't believe me but took a step backwards anyway. "How about a statement for the cameras, Storm? You owe me."

"Don't hold your breath. I don't owe you a damn thing." I walked around Connie and headed for my car.

I dialed Charlie's cell phone. He answered after the first ring. "Charlie, are you still at the apartment complex?"

"Yeah, I'm in the office getting the names and numbers of the residents."

"Have you come up with any witnesses yet?"

"Not yet. I've talked to the all the neighbors around her apartment that were home last night and came up empty. I haven't talked to the maintenance crew and they don't have a night watchman."

"I'm not feeling well, Charlie. I'm going home. Call someone out if you need any help. Contact everyone in the complex if you can. Call me when you have the preliminaries."

"You got it, boss. Are you all right?"

"I think I'm coming down with something. And stop calling me boss."

As soon as I hung up, I hit another number on my speed dial. Doctor Robert Martin answered on the second ring. "Doc, this is Storm, I need to see you."

He normally doesn't work on weekends but scheduled an appointment for me later that afternoon. I drove home, crawled into bed and pulled the covers up over my head.

CHAPTER TWO

Doctor Martin is the psychiatrist for the City of Colorado Springs Police Department. We knew each other long before either of us worked for the city. He had been assigned to my army unit when we crossed the border into Iraq from Kuwait during Desert Storm. He was a colonel at the time studying troops under fire as part of the government's program investigating the causes of PTSD. I was a new recruit just out of basic training. We developed a mutual respect and friendship for each other that lasted all these years.

His office was located at the rear of his private residence. I entered through the back door, laid on his sofa and closed my eyes. He ignored me and lit his pipe. After a few moments, he said, "I'm not a mind reader, Storm. Are you going to tell me why you're here, or are you going to just lay there wasting the city's money?"

I ignored the question.

"Are you having nightmares again, Storm?"

"Doc, remember when we were in Iraq and those snipers had us pinned down?"

"Of course. We couldn't move and were waiting for a helicopter to come put rockets into the window they were firing from. The temperature hovered well above 100 degrees and flies and ants ate us alive. A sniper's bullet grazed your shoulder and you cussed him like a sailor, calling his mother all kinds of nasty names."

"Yeah, and do you remember what you asked me?"

"I don't recall."

"After I cursed him out, you asked me if I felt better."

"Ah yes, and I believe you said, 'Hell no!' "

"That's right, and you asked me what would make me feel better. I told you I'd feel great if I killed that son-of-a-bitch."

"Yes, then you jumped up like a mad man and ran toward the building where the snipers were concealed. You fired your weapon on full auto, screaming at the top of your lungs. I should have had you committed for that."

"Probably. I hated that shithole. Do you remember what happened next?"

"Sure, you ran up the stairs, got into a firefight with those snipers and killed all three of them."

"Yes, and I felt better. Much better."

Doc nodded. "Yeah, and they gave you the bronze star with valor, when they should have court-marshaled you for disobeying an order."

I grinned. "They would have if you had told them the truth." I could still hear his words in my head. *"Harrison, stay where you are and keep your head down and that's an order!"*

Doc took a drag on his pipe and grinned. "You've never learned to listen to me. So what does Iraq have to do with why you're laying on my couch today?"

"I think the bastard that killed Julia is back. I have a hunch he's the same guy that is killing these girls. There was another one this morning and it's my fault. I should have killed him. Next time I won't hesitate."

Doc looked at me with pity in his eyes. He took a deep breath. "You're assuming a lot of guilt that doesn't belong to you."

"Don't lecture me, Doc. If I had killed him when I had a chance, these girls would be alive today. So yeah, it is my fault."

"What do you need from me, Storm?"

"I need to know why he kills these girls so I can get into his head and figure out his next move."

"The *why* question is something I can't answer. It's like asking why Jeffery Dahmer killed those boys and ate them. Why did Robert Benjamin Smith line up four women and a three-year-old little girl in a circle and shoot them in the head? Why did a bunch of hippie kids with no prior criminal records kill Sharon Tate and four other people and then cut her baby out of her womb? Why did Jim Jones lead 900 of his followers in a mass murder plot? Why did Hitler kill six million men, women and children because they were Jews? I don't think any of these killers could answer the questions, *why*."

"If I could understand how his thought process works then I might be able to catch him."

"You don't want to go there, Storm. It is a black hole that isn't good for your soul. It would be like falling in a well, turning darker and darker the further down you go, and never knowing when you'll hit the bottom." He paused to study me for a moment. "Your nightmares are back, aren't they?"

"Yeah. They started right after these killings began."

"What makes you think it's the same guy?"

"Just a gut feeling. There are too many similarities."

Doc paused, took more notes while considering my answer. "But you still don't know his name or who he is. How are you going to kill him?"

"Slowly, Doc. I'm going to find him and I am going to kill him very slowly. He will suffer for killing those girls and for what he's put me through."

Doc took more notes. "You know the death penalty is also a slow way of dying."

"Too slow and not enough suffering. A waste of tax dollars and there's always a chance some sorry-ass defense attorney would get him off on a technicality. Look what happened to OJ Simpson."

Doc emptied his pipe in his ashtray and started scraping the bowl with his pocketknife. "You're starting to worry me, Storm. They'll arrest you if you kill him like that."

"So what? I'd sleep well in prison and wouldn't have these nightmares."

Doc took more notes but didn't say anything. After a few minutes, I asked. "So what do you recommend?"

"I recommend you find yourself a girlfriend, get laid and lay off the booze. That's what I'd do. Relax a little and have some fun. You're working too hard and developing whiteout."

"What the hell is 'whiteout'?"

"Sperm up to your eyebrows." Doc smiled at his own joke.

He wrote me another prescription for something knowing I would never fill it. "Take these and get some rest, Storm. And call me if you need to talk."

I nodded, took a deep breath and left.

CHAPTER THREE

I parked my car in the rear parking lot of The Oak Barrel, an upscale bar and restaurant located below the Alamo Building in downtown Colorado Springs. It's known for fine food and great service to overpaid lawyers and yuppies. Many judges and attorneys dine there because it's located next to the County Court House.

I walked down several steps and entered the bar. Three-piece suits were the norm and I wasn't wearing a tie. Very few detectives dined here because it was too expensive and most cops couldn't afford it. Besides, police officers don't like drinking with attorneys. I don't like drinking with them either but drinking with cops gets me into trouble. They're always trying to hook me up with some police groupie. The last thing I need right now is a woman in my life. The last groupie I dated was a reporter and that was disastrous.

To tell the truth, I couldn't afford to eat here either, but I liked seeing how the other half lived. Normally, I have a drink or two and head home.

I found a seat at the far end of the bar where I could watch the door and see anyone coming in. The bartender brought me a Bud without having to ask.

"Hey, Pete. How's it going?" Pete was an ex-cop who had to retire after being shot three times.

"I'm all right, Storm. How are you doing?"

"Lousy!" I nursed my beer, minding my own business when Pete nodded towards the door. "Trouble's coming."

Glancing at the mirror, I saw Connie Mason walking toward me intent on ruining my evening. She was with an older fat guy wearing a gray suit and tie. I looked for an exit sign out the back, but it was too late. She and the fat man wended their way towards me before I could escape.

"Connie," I said without standing.

She smiled and introduced me as a homicide detective for the Colorado Springs Police Department. She identified her companion as Don Fibler, her boss at the TV station. He offered his hand and I ignored it. "Storm and I are old friends," Connie told him, "but he won't answer my questions about these recent homicides."

"Don't you believe the public has a right to know about these murder cases, Detective Harrison?"

"Of course I do, Mr. Fibber. But I'm always busy when Connie sticks her microphone in my face." *And I know where I'd like her to stick it.* "Besides, we have public information guys for answering questions."

Mr. Fibler frowned and corrected me. "The names' Fibler, *not Fibber.*"

"Sorry," I replied, though I was anything but.

"You know those public information guys don't know crap until they read your reports," Connie said. "By then, the story is stone cold."

"I wouldn't know. I've never worked in that department. Maybe you should call the Chief about that."

"Can I quote you on that?" asked Connie.

"I'd rather you never quote me again." I stood. "Nice to meet you Mr. Fibber." I dropped a ten on the table and left.

As I walked away I heard Mr. Fibler say, "He's a rude son-of-a-bitch."

Knowing I'd made a good impression on him lifted my spirits. I went to the outside patio, which was separated from the main dining by a glass wall. I sat at a table with my back to the far wall with a view of the door to the restaurant.

A good many cases are resolved at The Oak Barrel by their attorneys, sealing the fate of unsuspecting clients. While scanning the room, I noticed an angel sitting at the outside bar having a drink with a gray haired loudmouthed fossil. She wore a blue skirt with four-inch heels and a bright white blouse with buttons that stretched at the center of her breasts. Her diamond earrings sparkled like Christmas lights. I didn't see a wedding ring but an expensive looking watch lay snug against her wrist. She reminded me of Robin Meade from CNN.

The man she was with reminded me of Aristotle Onassis, or maybe the guy who makes those Dos Equis beer commercials. Whatever he was selling, she wasn't buying. She was turned on her bar seat facing the man and I could see her reflection in the mirror. I recognized her from somewhere but couldn't come up with a name. She saw me in the mirror and held her stare to let me know she knew I was watching her. I looked away.

After a few moments, the fossil dropped a hundred dollar bill on the bar and left taking his lizard hide shoes, Rolex watch and three-piece suit with him. The Angel picked up her drink, turned on her stool and faced me. She smiled and I smiled back. I still couldn't place her. After a moment, she downed her glass of wine and walked over to my table. "You don't remember me do you?"

I stood. "You look familiar but for the life of me, I can't remember your name or where I know you from."

"I'm disappointed, Detective. I must not have made much of an impression on you."

I didn't know how to answer her.

She removed my business card from her purse and handed it to me. "We met on a houseboat at Lake Powell a few summers ago when I was a law student. You gave me this and said if I called you'd buy me a beer."

My heartbeat accelerated. "Katy... Katy Taylor at Lake Powell during spring break. Oh yeah! There is no way I could forget you."

Back then, Katy was dating some hotshot lawyer who walked around like he had a dime stuck up his ass and was afraid he'd drop it. I liked her at first sight, so he didn't like me. He thought I was hitting on her, which I was. He was a total jerk and I couldn't understand what she was doing with him. That was four years ago.

"Of course I remember you. How could I forget? You look different with clothes on . . . I, I mean all dressed up."

"Maybe your memory isn't as bad as I thought. Do I look better or worse without my bikini?"

"You're beautiful either way."

"Good answer. I see you haven't changed much. Is your offer still good?"

"By all means, have a seat." I pulled out the chair next to me and she sat. I flagged down a waiter and Katy ordered a beer.

"What was your friend at the bar trying to sell you?" I asked.

Katy smiled. "A job. He owns a business in Denver with a branch office in this building."

"Are you going to accept?"

"Not a chance. I like the job I have. Besides, the guy I was with on the houseboat works for him."

Katy nodded towards Connie Mason. "Who's the woman you were talking to inside the bar?"

Connie was glaring at us. "Oh, she's a hooker and that's her pimp. She offered me a job too."

She nudged me with her shoulder. "No she's not. They don't let hookers in here. What kind of job did she offer you?"

"It had to do with sex. But she wanted too much."

"No she didn't." Chuckling, she took a sip of her beer and licked her lips. "How much did she want?"

"Two dollars. I offered a buck fifty but her pimp wouldn't budge."

She laughed again, shaking her head. "Liar." Her brow furrowed as she looked at Connie. "She resembles that news commentator on TV."

"Who? Robin Mead?"

"No, silly. Robin Mead has dark hair. She's a blonde."

"I bet it's not real." *I know it's not.*

Katy had the body of a playboy bunny, a quick wit and a great sense of humor. We could have had a lot of fun on that houseboat if it hadn't been for the tight-ass lawyer she was with. We had a few more drinks making small talk while catching up since the summer we met on the houseboat.

I glanced at Connie who was still watching us. She was talking on her cell phone and looked upset.

It was time to leave. "Katy, how would you like to go somewhere and have dinner with me?"

She wrinkled her nose. "Sure, but what's wrong with this place?"

"I never eat at a restaurant that serves prostitutes. Besides, I know a place that serves great Vietnamese food."

"All right. I've never tried it, but I'm game. Let's go."

As soon as Connie saw me paying the bill, she hurried out the front door. I didn't want to get caught in an ambush so I slipped the waiter a twenty, flashed my badge and asked him to show me a back way out of here. We followed him down a hallway and through the kitchen to an emergency exit, which led to the alley on the north side of the bar. I walked Katy to the rear parking lot where my car was parked.

"What about my car?" Katy asked.

"I'll bring you back to get it after dinner."

I drove around to the front of The Oak Barrel where a News truck was parked. Connie stood on the sidewalk next to the truck with a microphone in her hand. A crowd of people had gathered around her.

Katy pointed at Connie. "See, she is the news commentator I told you about."

Connie recognized my car and stared at me. "Wave," I said. As we drove by, Katy waved, Connie frowned, and I smiled.

"I think she likes you."

"I don't think so or she would have taken the buck fifty."

She laughed and backhanded me in the arm. "And I think she would do it for free. How long have you known her?"

"Who? Her? I've never seen that woman before in my life."

"You're starting to sound like Bill Clinton." Katy smiled and placed her hand on mine. "It's all right, Storm. She's BK."

"BK. What's that?"

"Before Katy. Now tell me about her."

"There's nothing to tell. I gave her the best two minutes of her life and she can't get over it, that's all."

"A whole two minutes?"

"Oh, she's not upset about that. She's pissed because she asked me how it was and I replied, 'no comment.' "

Katy laughed, "You're so full of it." She caught me off guard by asking, "Do you think she would be better than me?"

I answered, "No comment," and got a short jab to my ribs. "Ouch, I mean, not even close! That hurts."

"Wimp!"

Katy didn't say anything for a while but I felt her watching me. She broke the silence. "Storm, I don't remember you being so...." She paused so I interrupted her, "Crazy?"

"No, that's not the word I'm looking for."

"Funny."

"No. And you're not as funny as you think you are."

"Okay, then what?"

"I'm not sure. But you seem different."

With confidence fading, I answered. "Sorry, I guess I'm not very good company anymore."

"What's going on, Storm. What are you hiding from?"

"Nothing. I'm just not sleeping very well lately, that's all. It's these little girls getting killed. I'm not sure I'm up to the task of catching this guy."

"Not from what I hear. You have a reputation of bringing good solid cases to the courts."

"You can't bring them to court if you can't identify them. And, we don't always catch them. This guy has killed three young girls and we aren't any closer to catching him now than when he killed the first one. Another girl is going to die soon if we don't find him and there's nothing I can do about it."

"That's not your fault. I'm sure you're doing all you can."

"It might be my fault. I think this guy may have killed another girl a long time ago. I had a chance to kill him then, but didn't."

"That's not your fault either. Those decisions are made in a split second. It's impossible to make the right choice every time under those conditions."

"It wasn't like that. I made a conscious decision not to kill him."

"Storm, I still don't… " I cut her off.

"Katy, I really don't want to talk about it, or about work. I'm trying to get away from the job."

She dropped the subject and I drove to my favorite restaurant located in a corner strip mall on the outskirts of town called Wong's Express. This time we were the ones overdressed. The restaurant owners are Twee and Harlum Wong. Twee was born and raised in Vietnam and Harlum was from Hong Kong. Their food is a combination of both cultures. The place is always crowded with no news media or prostitutes allowed and many of their customers don't even speak English.

"It smells wonderful," Kate said as we entered.

The owners, Twee and Harlum met us at us at the door. Twee grabbed me by the arm. "We no see you in a while. Where you go Mr. Hairson?"

"Busy, Twee. These investigations are keeping me on the run."

Harlum replied, "I see you bring daughter. Very good."

Twee smiled at Katy and said, "Tell em' he still have to eat. I want him to be my sugar daddy."

"No way, Twee." I replied. "You already married the Wong man."

We all laughed and Twee led us to our table.

"They're funny." Katy said after they left. "What do you normally order when you come here?"

"I like the sweet and sour house cat and flied lice."

She nudged me in the ribs again. "They don't serve cat here."

I made a note to myself to move to the other side of her for the rest of the evening or slow down with the jokes. My ribs were killing me. "They don't? I'm going to stop bringing them my road kill. I hate being lied to." I covered my ribs.

"Seriously, Storm, you're ruining my appetite. What's good?"

"You'll like anything on the menu. Order whatever you want and you won't be disappointed."

I watched her franticly searching the menu for cat. When she didn't find any, she ordered something from the vegetarian menu. We had a great meal, or at least I did and Katy seemed content. We ordered a couple glasses of wine with names neither of us could pronounce. After dinner, I drove Katy back to The Oak Barrel to pick up her car. She pointed to a newer looking silver Mercedes and I stopped next to it. "When can I see you again?" I asked.

"Who said you're going to see me again?"

"I'm going to see you again even if I have to get a warrant."

"Now that's funny. If you can get a judge to sign it, you can walk upstairs to my office and serve it."

"Your office is in the Court Building?"

Katy smiled. "Yes, on the 4th floor just above the courthouse."

"Don't tell me you're a defense lawyer."

Katy smiled. "Yep. My office is on the 4th floor just above the courthouse."

"Please don't tell me you're a defense attorney."

"Nope, a prosecutor. The jerk I was with on the houseboat is a defense attorney."

"Figures. I assume you're not together anymore?"

Katy grinned, "Defense attorneys and prosecutors don't usually see thing in the same light. Besides, he's an ass."

That answered one of my questions. "You know, if I have to come arrest you, I'll have to frisk you. Department policy." Hope soared when the idea of that didn't appear to deter her. "So when can I see you?"

"I think I'll hold out for the warrant. I've never been frisked before." She leaned over and kissed me on the cheek and handed me one of her business cards. "Thanks for dinner, Storm. Call me."

She got into her car and drove off into the night leaving me standing in the parking lot in awe.

CHAPTER FOUR

K aty kissed Dr. Robert Martin on the cheek when she walked into his office. "Hi, Doc, it's a lovely day, isn't it?"

He peeked outside at overcast skies threatening rain and shut the door. "Good morning, Katy. Want some coffee?"

"I'll get it." She walked through the door connecting his office to his home and helped herself to a cup of coffee, bringing him one as well. "Been busy?"

"Not really," Doc said. "I try not to see patients on weekends unless it's an emergency. I had a call yesterday morning, but put him off until later in the day."

"Must have been important."

"No, he's an old friend. He's been having trouble sleeping. Why are you in such a great mood this morning?"

"I don't know. Maybe it's because I met someone last night."

"Oh?" Doc glanced at her over the top of his glasses.

"Hmm. I had a date last night." She couldn't keep from smiling.

"Well, this is a surprise. It's been a long time since you've dated anyone.

"More of a surprise to me than to you. But, I may have made a professional enemy."

"Oh really. And who might that be?"

"Connie Mason. I may have pissed her off."

"Connie? I thought you two were on good terms. Want to talk about it?"

"Of course. That's why I'm here."

Doc raised his eyebrows and gave Katy one of his questioning looks. "Do you want to talk to Uncle Robert or Dr. Martin?"

Katy closed her eyes and took a deep breath. "Uncle Martin will do."

Doc Martin smiled and walked to his file cabinet to put her file away. He laid his notepad and pen on his desk, took his coffee and sat on the couch next to his niece. "All right then, Uncle Martin at your service, Miss Taylor. How may I be of assistance?"

"I ran into an old acquaintance last night. When I first noticed him, he was talking to Connie Mason. She didn't look happy when I left with him. I don't need enemies in the press."

He peered at Katy over the top of his glasses. "What happened?"

Stalling, she took a drink of her coffee and licked her lips while she decided how much she wanted to explain. "We went to a little Vietnamese restaurant and had dinner. I had a great time and was totally relaxed. I may have embarrassed myself a little by over-drinking and might have given him the wrong impression. Totally out of character for me."

"What does that have to do with Connie Mason?"

"She stared at us the whole time we were together at The Oak Barrel. I think they may have dated."

Doc nodded. "How do you feel about this guy?"

Katy looked down at her lap. "I'm not sure. It's a little complicated. I met him a few of years ago at Lake Powell when I was still dating Chas Woods. But I really liked him. He gave me his card and told me to call him sometime. Being in a relationship, I'm surprised I even kept his card. Anyway, I saw him on television the other night and started thinking about him."

"Did you meet him before, or after your incident at college?"

"Just prior. Maybe a month."

"What was he doing on TV?"

"He's a homicide detective here in Colorado Springs. He's working on the murders of those young girls. I thought you might know him."

Doc took off his glasses. "Maybe. Do you want to tell me his name?"

"Storm Harrison."

Dr. Martin choked on his coffee and coughed to clear his throat. "Yes. I'm aware of Detective Harrison."

"Really? What can you tell me about him?"

"Not a whole lot. We served together in Iraq before he joined the police department."

Katy leaned forward in her chair. "Seriously? It's a small world, isn't it? I didn't know he was in the Army. Did you know him well?"

"No, not really. He was a raw recruit and I just happened to go into Iraq with his unit when I was doing PTSD research. He reminded me of our service together during one of my classes. Let's get back to your date last night. What happened?"

"Not much. We went to dinner and I got a little tipsy."

"Tipsy as in intoxicated?"

"A little. You know I don't drink often, but I drank a cocktail, a beer and two glasses of wine last night. I got a little lightheaded."

"That doesn't sound like you, young lady. Knowing you like I do, I bet it was on an empty stomach."

"I hadn't eaten lunch but we had a nice dinner. I normally cut myself off after a couple of drinks, but not last night. I was having too much fun."

"Were you intimate with him?"

"You're not supposed to ask me that," she said, shocked and a little embarrassed.

"I can if you're asking for professional advice. I'm a therapist and you can't have it both ways. I'm concerned about you."

"Just be my uncle today. And no, I didn't sleep with him. I just kissed him goodnight, gave him my card and told him to call me."

"So you like this detective, do you?"

Katy smiled and raised her eyebrows. "Maybe."

"I'll take that as a yes." Doc smiled.

Katy clinched her teeth and wrinkled her nose. "Not good, right?"

"I'm not here to judge you, sweetheart. I'm here to listen and to give you professional advice if you want it. And I'm glad you dipped your toe back into the dating pool."

"I know." Katy paused, "But I didn't intend to kiss him."

Doc took her hand. "Nothing bad happened and you feel good about the date. That's an improvement if you ask me."

"He asked to see me again. I didn't know what to tell him. He's the first man I've felt completely at ease with since the incident. I really enjoyed myself."

Doc looked Katy in the eye. "Do you think you're ready for a relationship?"

"I'm not sure. I'm concerned about what he might think of me when he finds out what I did."

Doc paused for a moment pondering her statement. "Knowing Storm, I think he'd be proud of you. He must have made quite an impression on you."

Katy shook her head. "Oh, I'm not sure what I think. He's handsome, fun, quick-witted and has a relaxed confidence about him. Overall, he left a good impression on me. It's difficult to put into words."

"How do you feel about him this morning?" Doc asked

"I'm a little embarrassed to say this, but I hated to see the night end or to see him leave. I might have gone home with him if he'd asked. I can't imagine what he's thinking of me right now."

Doc looked up. "Do you want to see him again?"

"I think so. I hate one-time dates. But I'm not sure I'm ready for this yet. I don't know how I would have reacted if he had touched me."

"Has he called you?"

"He left a message on my work phone. I didn't give him my cell number. I'm not sure if he'll call back."

"If he's already called you once, he'll call you again."

Katy licked her lips. "I'm not so sure. He acted as if he liked me and I believed he was sincere. But you can never tell which head is doing the thinking when it comes to men. As far as I know, he may already be in a relationship. I'll let him make the next move."

Doc smiled. "I think you're doing the right thing. And he'll call. Just prepare yourself if he doesn't. This all happened very quickly and he may need time to think about it. Be patient, he may be confused about your intentions as well."

Katy gave Doc a hug. "Thanks for talking to me. I gotta run."

"Anytime. You're my favorite niece."

"I'm your only niece." Katy looked at her watch. "I've got some things to do at the office. See you at the Broadmoor for dinner?"

"I wouldn't miss it. I thought you didn't work on Sundays."

"Normally I don't. But I have a big trial starting tomorrow morning and one of my bosses agreed to go over my opening statement with me."

"I see. Well keep me informed about Storm, will you?"

"Certainly. I'm anxious to see how this plays out."

CHAPTER FIVE

Bright cloudless skies followed me to work the next morning. The weather in Colorado has always been unpredictable and if you didn't like the way it was, all you had to do was wait a few hours and it would probably change.

I arrived late. Conversations and ringing phones could be heard as other employees went from place to place in a hurry. I felt like I was behind the eight ball this morning but no one got excited about the hours a homicide detective keeps. My boss, Lieutenant Jerry Fowler, watched me from the hallway as I walked in. "Good morning, Lieutenant," I said.

He studied my face for a moment before turning and walked down the hall with me. "Are you still sick?"

"No. Who said I was sick?"

"Charlie and Maggie both did."

"I wasn't feeling well Saturday, but I'm fine now."

"Step in my office and close the door." He walked past me, entered his office and sat at his desk.

I hate closed-door meetings. I followed him in and pulled the door shut behind me. He didn't offer me a seat.

"Have you seen Doc Martin lately?"

"Yeah, yesterday. Why?"

"You still having those nightmares?"

"That's none of your business," I said. We locked eyes for a moment. "You wouldn't even know I was seeing him if I hadn't told you."

Chastened, he looked down at his desk, tapping his fingers on the file in front of him. "You're right, Storm, that isn't any of my business, unless it affects your work." Then to change the subject, he asked, "How are you coming with this latest murder case?"

"I'll let you know after I talk to Charlie and Maggie. We may have found DNA evidence."

I suspected Jerry wasn't satisfied with our conversation and that he wanted to say something else. He watched me for a moment then nodded. "That's good, we need a break." He turned towards the window. "Keep me informed?" He waved with the back of his hand ending the meeting.

I wasn't sure if he wanted me to keep him informed about the murders or about my visits with Doctor Martin. I knew Fowler was under a lot of pressure to solve this case before the body count got any higher. But I wasn't falling for his bullshit. He wasn't a bad guy and normally was easy to work for. I went by the break room, got a cup of coffee and took it to my office.

The light on my office phone was blinking, indicating I had messages. I pushed back a stack of reports to make room for my coffee cup and sat down. Most of the messages were from Connie Mason. Since I wasn't interested in anything she had to say, I deleted those and listened to the rest. Maggie had left a message saying she wanted to see me.

I located Maggie in the lab, bent over a microscope. Her flowered dress made her rear end look like the back of a delivery truck full of nursery plants. She noticed me when I sidestepped around her.

"Good morning, sweetheart." I said, "Have you missed me?"

She looked up at me and stuck her pencil behind her ear. "Hell no, and don't 'sweetheart' me. What do you want, Harrison?" She looked me up and down and smiled. "How are you feeling?"

"Better. Thanks for asking."

She squeezed my hand, "Okay, what do you want, darlin'?"

"You called me, remember? Did you find any DNA?"

Maggie grinned. "I'm good. Tell me I'm good, Storm."

"You're the queen of the lab and the best looking woman I have ever known."

She slugged me on the arm. "Don't patronize me, fool. And to answer your question, yes I found DNA."

I took her head in my hands and kissed her on the forehead. She slapped my hands away.

"Stop that, you're going to ruin my reputation," she said while glancing furtively around the lab to see if anyone was watching.

I smiled and rubbed my hands together. "So, what do you have for me?"

"I found DNA and I'm sure it belongs to our suspect. He's getting sloppy."

"How do you know it's his?"

"Because Charlie asked the victim's mother if she had been with anyone who could have thrown a condom down the toilet and she said 'no way'. The little girl was a virgin prior to the rape and I found traces of her feces on the outside of the condom."

"I love you, Maggie. How long before we get the results back?"

"I put a big rush on it. We may get it back today if we're lucky."

I gave her a big bear hug and she frowned. "Get your ass out of my lab before you break something." She turned her attention back to her work. "And keep your cell phone on. I'll call you if I hear anything."

Charlie Blakely looked exhausted sitting at his desk. I figured he hadn't screwed anything up or Jerry would have said something. "Hi, Charlie, how's it going?"

"Not bad. How are you feeling?"

"Good."

"That's a relief. I'm over my head and could use your help."

"You're doing fine, Charlie. Did you hear Maggie found DNA?"

"Yeah. Maybe now we can nail this asshole."

Charlie's preliminary report didn't reveal much that I didn't already know. He had done a good job interviewing the employees and residents of the apartment complex. No one seemed to have seen or heard anything unusual the night of the murder. The girl's mother left for work at 10:45 p.m. She claimed her daughter had gone to bed before she went to work and she didn't see anyone or anything suspicious while leaving the apartment complex. When she arrived home around 7:15 the next morning, she discovered her daughter's body.

"Charlie, we're going to have to re-interview the mother in a few days after the shock and medication wear off."

"I know. I ran criminal history checks on all the employees of the apartment complex. None of them have any history that would warrant suspicion. I compiled a list of all of the victim's teachers so they could be interviewed. I secured the victim's cell phone and placed it into evidence. I'll check it this morning to see who she has been talking to."

"Thanks, you're doing a great job." Scanning the top of the report, I noticed the victim's name, Julie Gardner, and it hit me like a brick. I couldn't believe it. I've been haunted all these years by a girl named Julia and now there's another victim with almost the same name. My guts knotted and I felt my blood pressure rising. *I'll kill that bastard.* I needed to clear my head.

"Charlie, I'm going to take a break."

"You sure you're feeling all right? You look pale."

"I'm fine. I just need a minute. I'll be right back."

With coffee cup in hand, I hurried outside and sat on a bench in the shade next to the building to collect my thoughts. I watched a small bird building a nest in a nearby tree and listened to the distant thunder. Huge clouds hung high above the landscape and a cool breeze carried the smell of fresh flowers and cut grass through the break area. I thought about Katy and felt like calling her, but I didn't want to bother her at work.

Glancing up at the thunderclouds building overhead, I noticed Jerry Fowler watching me from his office window on the third floor. We looked at each other for a few moments before he turned away. I finished my coffee, returned to my office, and continued reading reports. Charlie came in and sat down. His eyes were red with bags under them. He looked spent. "Have you gotten any rest, Charlie?"

"Yeah, a little."

I doubted he had slept more than a few hours.

My cell phone rang and the caller ID indicated it was Maggie. I held up my hand to Charlie and answered it. "Hi, Maggie."

"Storm, are you still in the building?"

"Yeah, what's up?"

"I got the DNA results back."

"Hold on a minute, Charlie's here. I'm putting you on speaker phone." I switched it over so we both could hear. "Okay, go ahead."

"I have good news and bad news."

"Did you get a match?"

"Kind of."

"Kind of my ass! Did you or didn't you, damn it?"

"Hold your horses, Storm. We got a match, but you aren't going to like knowing who it is."

"You're killing me with suspense, Maggie. Just give me the name so I can go arrest the prick."

"I don't have a name."

"What are you talking about? You said you had a match."

"The DNA matches the guy who killed Julia in the alley."

I didn't comprehend what she was saying at first, and then it hit me. The bastard that slit Julia's throat twelve years ago was the same person who's been killing these little girls.

"Storm, are you still there?"

"Yes, I'm here, Maggie."

"You okay?"

I took a deep breath. "Not really. And you're starting to sound like my mother."

"What are you thinking about?"

"That I should have killed that bastard when I had a chance. I'll kill him nice and slow when I find him."

"Sorry," Maggie said, "Call if you need anything."

"Thanks."

I disconnected the call. Charlie looked at me. "Is that your Julia?"

"Yeah." My eyes burned with anger and I turned away so he couldn't see my face.

"I'm so sorry, Storm."

"Don't be. I'll kill him the next time I see him."

"I didn't hear that."

I pondered my conversation with Maggie, and then turned to Charlie. "Go home and get some sleep," I told him. "There's nothing you can do here today. I don't want to see your face until tomorrow morning."

Once he'd gone, I called Doc. "Can I see you?"

"Sure. Stop by after work. Is there anything in particular you want to discuss?"

"Yeah. I want to kill someone."

"Do you want me to stop you?"

"I doubt if you could." I disconnected and stared at the police drawing pinned to my office wall.

CHAPTER SIX

I t rained most of the day, which left the city smelling like wet asphalt and fresh pine. I arrived at my appointment on time and made myself comfortable on Doc's couch without saying anything. I stared silently at the ceiling thinking about what I wanted to say after all that had happened during the last twenty-four hours. Doc Martin picked up his pen and notepad. After a couple of minutes he broke the silence. "Well?"

"The guy who killed Julia Moore is the same one who's killing these girls. Maggie matched his DNA to both homicides."

Doc flipped back in his notes. "Until yesterday I hadn't seen you for three months."

"Yeah, I know."

"At Saturday's meeting, you said your dreams had returned. How many have you had?"

"Seven. . . maybe eight."

"Why didn't you call and make an appointment earlier?"

"I don't know. After twelve years, I thought the worst was over. I thought I could control them, but I can't."

"When was the last time you had a nightmare?"

"Saturday. But, it wasn't really a dream. When I was at the crime scene, the body appeared to be talking to me. I became nauseated and threw up after seeing her. Hell, Doc, I can't even do my job right anymore. I think I'm losing my mind."

"People don't have nightmares when they're awake. Tell me what happened."

"I thought the corpse was mouthing, '*Help me, please help me.*' I got sick, went home and went to bed."

Doc put his pen down. "Has anything unusual happened to you within the last twenty-four hours that may have contributed to this vision?"

"Is that what you call it when a dead person talks to you?"

"You didn't hear her speak, did you?"

"No, but her lips were moving."

"You had an illusion. Your mind relived an exact moment. Your overwhelming guilt for not being able to save Julia allowed your mind to see the vision. I'm not trying to minimize what happened to you. It was real in your mind. You saw her mouth moving, but it didn't. It wasn't real."

I thought about what he said and it made sense. I saw a flashback of that exact moment Julia died twelve years ago when I was just a dumb rookie.

"What are you thinking about now?"

"About what you said. Is this like Post Traumatic Stress Disorder the guys get after coming home from the war?"

"It's the same. You don't have to be in a war zone to suffer from PTSD."

"And you think this was caused by my own guilt?"

"How much guilt has to do with PTSD is still a mystery. It seems to be a common denominator among many patients within my studies. But, it's hard to get soldiers to admit they feel guilt. Many patients claim they don't feel guilty at all. There's still a lot we don't understand about the subject."

I didn't say anything for a long time.

"How do you feel at this moment?" Doc asked.

"I'm all right. Do you think the nightmares will stop if I can get rid of the guilt?"

"I believe they will. But I'm not sure."

"Good, then there's hope."

"Yes," Doc said as he looked at his notes. "Has anything unusual happened to you in the last day or so?"

"No, except I feel responsible for these girls' deaths."

"Just because you didn't catch the guy doesn't make you responsible for anything he is doing now. Is there anything else going on in your life that I should know about?"

"Not really."

"Are you sure?"

"Like what?"

"Anything out of the ordinary."

"I had a date last night but that wouldn't have anything to do with these dreams."

"Perhaps not. But dating is unusual for you. How long has it been since you've went out with anyone?"

"Not counting Connie Mason, twelve years."

"Why haven't you been dating?"

"Would you want to be with someone knowing you might wake up in the middle of the night screaming like a mad man?"

"I'm not sure how anyone would react to something like that. You've never been violent during these dreams, have you?"

"No, but I still wouldn't want anyone seeing me like that."

"Tell me about the girl."

"Nothing to tell really. I met her a couple of years ago. I ran into her last night and took her to dinner."

Doc frowned. "Why now? What is so different about this girl?"

"I don't know. I've only gone out with her once."

Doc paused to write a few notes. "Have you ever considered hurting anyone?"

"Only the guy who killed Julia."

"Have you ever had a desire to hurt yourself?"

I sat up and shook my head. "No." Doc Martin looked relieved but I wasn't sure if he believed me or not.

"Does this girl know about these dreams?"

"No. That's not the kind of thing you usually share on a first date."

"Did you have a nightmare last night while sleeping with her?"

"Good try, Doc. But I didn't say I slept with her. And if I did, I wouldn't kiss and tell."

"If I remember right, you told me you were intimate with Connie Mason."

I rolled my eyes. "That's different. I was drunk."

Doc lifted his eyebrows. "Sorry, I must have misunderstood."

"And for your other question, no I didn't sleep with her. But, when I got home, I slept like a baby."

Doc jotted down more notes. "Are you planning on seeing her again?"

"I'm not sure. I'm going to call her when I'm finished here. Hopefully we'll see each other tonight."

"These dreams could possibly become a problem if you keep dating. If you really care about this girl, tell her about the nightmares and why you're having them."

I looked at the floor and thought of Katy. "That wouldn't be an easy thing for me to do. I hate talking about it, even to you. I wish they would just go away."

"I don't think that's going to happen for a while. She'll deserve to know before you get too involved. I believe she would be supportive if she cares about you at all. Just tell her the truth before she finds out the hard way. Or, don't sleep with her."

I didn't like that option.

"If I see her again, and I believe she has feeling for me, I'll tell her."

"I think you're doing the right thing. But, I must caution, love is a two edged sword. Take it slow."

"You're starting to sound like a marriage counselor, Doc. Are we done?"

"I don't know. What do you think?"

"I think we'll be done after I kill that prick."

Doc studied me for a full minute before answering. "That is not a healthy thing to be considering."

"I'll stop saying it then. Are we done now?"

"For now, but I want to see you again, and soon. Keep me informed."

I was getting a headache by the time I left his office. Sometimes I wonder why I even bother seeing him. I wouldn't even talk to him if I didn't like him so much.

After getting to my car, I called Katy's office. She answered this time. "Hi, Katy. Are you hungry or do I have to come serve you with this warrant?"

Katy laughed, "You don't have a warrant." ·

"I can get one. I know judges in low places."

"Don't you ever stop?"

"Katy, if I have to come arrest you, I'll have to cuff and frisk you. Department policy."

"Ok, Storm. I'll come along peacefully."

"Good, where do you want to meet?"

"Are you familiar with The Flamingo?"

"Yeah, sure, I know where it is."

"I'll meet you there in an hour."

"I'll be there."

CHAPTER SEVEN

The Flamingo was a swanky Chicago-style joint located on Tejon Street. It boasted old-school vibes and a pianist who looked like Liberace. Eating there could drain your wallet faster than a pickpocket. But I wasn't going to say that to Katy.

The Liberace impersonator was banging on the piano, wearing Elton John style of glasses when I walked in. The clientele was mostly doctors, lawyers, and stockbrokers. A lot of them walked around like they were celebrities looking for someone to ask for their autograph. I looked for Katy's old boyfriend, but he wasn't there.

Katy stood near the bar talking to a couple of men in three-piece suits. She wore a navy blue dress with a slit up the side, a wide white belt, three inch white heels and a pearl necklace. She was well dressed for a county attorney and fit right in. As usual, I was underdressed. Katy saw me, excused herself and walked over to me. She didn't seem to notice my attire.

"Hi, Storm. I have a table reserved." She waved to the maître'd, who escorted us to a corner table. Katy ordered a wine I couldn't pronounce the name of and I ordered a beer. My beer cost more than I usually pay for a six-pack and Katy's wine was double what I'd normally pay for a whole bottle. I was glad it was happy hour prices.

When the server took our order, Katy chose a chicken salad that cost more than a whole chicken plus the cost of all the eggs it would have produced during its lifetime. I ordered a hamburger and the waiter rolled his eyes when he wrote it down.

Katy seemed to have gotten better looking overnight. Although she's good for my ego, if we keep dining in places like this, I may have to get a second job. I frowned at the thought. Katy looked at me as if she wanted to ask a question. "What?" I asked.

"What are you thinking about?"

"About you."

"Oh?" Her smile urged me to continue.

I leaned over and looked her in the eyes. "I'm thinking about how gorgeous, sweet, loving, and kind you are and what a great sense of humor you have. Did I miss anything? Oh yes, and you have a cute nose and a perfect body."

Katy shook her head. "You're so full of it."

I grinned and she placed her hand on mine.

"I'm glad you called, Storm. How was your day?"

"Not good, but they seldom are when you're working homicide."

Katy paused for a moment, a serious look on her face. "So, where do we go from here?"

"I'm hoping to go to your place."

She narrowed her eyes. "Is that all men think about?"

"Nope, sometimes we think about sports. But not right now."

"You know you're insane, don't you?"

I crossed my eyes. "That's what my therapist tells me."

Katy shook her head. "What am I going to do with you?"

After paying the tab, we left the restaurant and I followed her to her house.

Large oak and pine trees created tunnels over the street where she lived. Most of the houses were built in the early 1900s with close proximity to downtown Colorado Springs.

Her home consisted of two stories plus a basement and had been recently remodeled. The driveway ran past the house to an unattached two-car garage at the rear. An old coal chute attached to the side of the house had been padlocked.

It surprised me that Katy could afford living here. She had been attending law school when I first met her and young attorneys didn't usually make a lot of money, especially working for the County Attorney's Office.

I parked in the side driveway. We walked around to the front and up three steps to a large raised front porch. When we entered the house, Katy turned off the alarm and re-locked the deadbolt. "Make yourself at home," she said. "I have to get out of these heels."

I watched her climb a large hand-carved wood staircase leading upstairs. A large rock fireplace sat in the corner of the family room to my left. Antique furniture decorated the house and it smelled of fresh lemon furniture polish. The ceilings were ten feet high.

Katy re-appeared a few minutes later wearing cut-off jeans, sandals, and a shirt tied around her waist. Her blonde hair hung below her shoulders and she displayed a great tan.

I followed her into the kitchen. An antique hand-cranked telephone was mounted on the wall. I picked up the receiver and heard a dial tone. "Does this thing work?"

"Sure, it's a reproduction. I don't use it much but needed a landline for the security system. I had it hooked up at the same time."

I returned the receiver to its hook.

"Beer or wine?" she asked.

"Beer."

Katy took a beer from the refrigerator, removed the cap and handed it to me. She poured herself a glass of wine. I made a toast. "To good friends and old times." We both took a swallow.

A small door off the kitchen was padlocked. "Where does this door lead?" I asked.

"To a hidden staircase." She retrieved a key from the top of the refrigerator, unlocked the padlock and opened the door. A narrow steep stairway led up to the second floor and down into the basement. "The stairs were installed as a way for the maids to move around the house without being noticed when the original owner entertained guests," Katy said. "They could either go to the basement to add coal to the furnace or upstairs without ever being seen."

The one going upstairs had an electric seat mounted to the handrail. "What's that for?" I asked.

"When the owner got too old to walk up and down the main stairway, he had the lift chair installed so he could go up to his bedroom."

Katy showed me the rest of the downstairs and we retreated to the family room. Using a remote, Katy turned on the gas log fireplace. The fire looked and sounded like the real thing.

We sat on the sofa gazing into the flames. "You still like rounding up the bad guys?" she asked.

"Yeah, but I'm getting tired of it."

"Really? I had the impression you loved your job."

I took a sip of my beer. "I like putting criminals in prison but it seems I've been spending more time in court than working cases lately."

"I assume seeing all those dead bodies isn't good for your morale either."

I paused for a moment. "It's the children that get to me."

Katy sipped her wine while studying my face. I'm not normally shy but I felt insecure under her gaze. That had never happened to me before.

"I've seen you on TV a few times while watching the news," Katy said. "You've lost weight since we were at Lake Powell."

"I haven't been sleeping well lately."

"The reporters must love you for all those, 'No comment' statements you keep giving them."

"They're a pain in the ass. You can't trust any of them."

"Amen to that," she said as she lifted her glass.

"You have to deal with reporters much?"

"Sure, especially on big cases."

"What ever happened to your boyfriend, old what's his name? If I remember right, he insisted on everyone calling him Chas."

"Yes, Charles Woods, and he is younger than you are. He's a defense attorney now. Why, you're not jealous of him are you?"

"I certainly am not."

"Are you sure?"

"You've got to be kidding. How could anyone be jealous of a guy who wears a swimsuit from Victoria's Secret and looks like an advertisement for a half off sale?"

Katy grin was devious. "He looked pathetic, didn't he?"

"It might not have been so bad if his midsection hadn't matched the Fat Tire beer he drank. What a puss!"

"That was pretty bad, wasn't it?"

"Bad. Are you kidding me? I bet he had to wax himself before putting that swimsuit on."

Katy laughed so hard that she spilled wine on the front of her shirt and had tears in her eyes.

"I couldn't see what you saw in the guy. I'm not surprised Sir Charles became a defense attorney."

She laughed even harder when I called him, Sir Charles. "Yes, and you and 'Sir Charles' are bound to butt heads someday. When you do, ask him if he waxes himself."

"I might just do that. But why do you think we'll butt heads?"

"He's defending murder cases now."

"Any I should know about?"

"No, I don't think so, but it's only a matter of time. And I know he was jealous of you. I'm sure he can't wait to get you on the witness stand."

"Where does he work?"

"He has an office in the building above The Oak Barrel. That was his boss you saw me talking to in the tesraurant. I think Chas was the reason his boss was trying to hire me. And Chas is the reason I'd never consider working there.

"I assume the two of you aren't friends anymore."

"I dumped him as soon as we got back to law school. It's a matter of morals, or the lack thereof. Besides, you're right, he is a self-centered jerk."

Things were looking up from my point of view. Katy stood to get us another round of drinks. I decided to take the direct approach. When she returned I asked, "What do you think of me?"

She didn't answer right away. "I'm not sure what to think. I thought about calling you after I dumped Chas. But I was busy with law school. And, I had other concerns at the time."

"So why now? What changed? Break up with someone recently?"

"No, I haven't been seeing anyone."

"Then why didn't you call me after you and Charles broke up?"

Katy hesitated as if she didn't want to answer that question. "It's complicated."

When someone tells me that, I know they're usually lying. It could mean anything like, "I was pregnant," or "My parents were going through a divorce." If I were a woman, when Katy asked about Connie Mason, I would have said, "It's complicated." But instead, I said, "I gave her the best two minutes of her life." I lied. But Katy didn't want to talk about Connie. She just wanted to know about our relationship. So whatever was complicating Katy's life that made her not want to call me will just have to wait until she wants to tell me.

"Are you disappointed I didn't call? Or is it just your curious detective nature?"

"I'm disappointed."

"Sure you are."

I assumed she was just avoiding my question. "So what do you think of me now?"

"I have to admit, Storm, I've thought of you often since that summer on the lake."

"Then you should have called. I was devastated when you didn't." I gave her my best sad puppy face.

"Oh, how romantic," she said. "I thought detectives were supposed to be hard asses."

I smiled. "We are. But we're also human."

Katy emptied her glass and licked her lips, pausing before she answered. "I like your sense of humor, your smile, and your honesty. You have confidence without being pretentious. And you use humor to hide your serious side. To tell you the truth, I wished I hadn't been with Chas when we first met. My life may have been different."

"Just my luck. Defense attorneys are always getting in my way."

"He's not in your way now," she said. Reaching over, she took my hand.

She had doubt in her voice and longing in her eyes. I leaned over and kissed her. She kept her eyes closed a little longer than normal and when she opened them she said, "I see you haven't lost your confidence. No one has ever kissed me that soon in a relationship before."

"That's because you've been dating fools." I kissed her again. "And we've already wasted four years."

I hadn't dated in over a year but I felt completely at ease with Katy. We talked about anything and everything, told lighthearted jokes and laughed a little harder after each drink. My laugh wasn't the only thing getting harder. It didn't appear she was used to drinking and she was getting a little tipsy. I kissed her lips and moved down to her neck and then to her cleavage. I softly caressed her breast. When she pulled away, I thought she'd stop me. Her expression held both expectation and fear. She stood up, pulled me from the couch and led me into the kitchen. She filled her wine glass and handed me a fresh beer, then took my hand and guided me upstairs to her bedroom.

Antique oak furniture surrounded an ornate queen size four-poster bed that looked as old as the house. Oil paintings decorated light tan walls and long flowing curtains covered the windows. Plush rugs accented the wood floors and the room smelled of roses.

She never stopped smiling as she as she made a toast, "To wasted years." She drank her wine down, sat the glass on the nightstand and started getting undressed. I followed her lead.

The next morning I awoke naked and alone. Sunlight showed through long curtains and soft music played in the background. For a moment I wondered if I was dreaming. I hadn't slept that well in years. Katy walked into the room with nothing on but a smile and a see through negligee, I knew it wasn't a dream.

"Good morning, Storm."

"Come over here and pinch me so I know you're real."

"I'll do better than that." She knelt on the bed and kissed my stomach, my chest and worked her way up to my lips. She slid into bed next to me and snuggled in my arms. It wasn't long before we were fast asleep.

When I woke, Katy was talking to someone on the phone, telling them she wasn't going to breakfast this morning. She came back to bed and we made small talk. She told me about a big case she was working on where a stepfather had been molesting his stepdaughter for years until his wife caught him and almost killed him with a golf club. The woman beat him half to death before the police got there. Katy was trying to get him fifteen years in prison.

We talked about the homicides I was working on. I gave her a quick rundown. I considered telling her about the nightmares but the timing didn't seem right.

"We better get to work or we'll both be out of a job," she said as she slipped out of bed. A moment later I heard the shower running. I joined her, thus delaying us even further. Katy got out of the shower before I did. I stood under the hot water until it started getting cold. "I wish we could just call in sick and spend the day together," I said while getting dressed.

She ignored me. Her hair was already dry, she was dressed and she'd put on makeup. "I'll fix you something to eat while you're getting ready."

I got dressed, combed my hair and went downstairs. Katy handed me an egg sandwich and a large cup of coffee, kissed my cheek and whispered in my ear. "I'm sorry I have to go, I'm going to miss you today."

"I'll miss you too," I said as I walked her to her car and kissed her goodbye.

I drove out of her driveway a few minutes later and called her. "I had the best night of my life. Thank you."

"Me too," she said. "And thanks for calling. It means a lot to me."

CHAPTER EIGHT

A cold spell descended on Colorado Springs and the weatherman predicted snow this evening. On the way to work, I saw geese flying south. Maggie was working in the lab when I arrived.

"Hi, darlin', are we still friends?"

She turned, faced me and smiled. "You know I love you, Storm. What do you want?"

Wanting to make sure she meant it, I said, "Thanks, I love you too. Have you lost weight?"

"Maggie beamed while glancing down at her round physique. "Well, yes I have. Almost ten full pounds. Thanks for noticing."

Actually, I hadn't noticed. "Is Sam working today?"

"I haven't seen him but I have him on speed dial. Want me to call him?"

"Please. Tell him I have work for him."

Sam Coffman was a local sketch artist on contract with the city. He draws suspects for the police department. He's an art instructor at the community college and a master at his craft. I first met him when he drew Julia's killer for me many years ago. I look at the old drawing pinned to my wall every day because I never want to forget that face.

I returned to my office and shuffled through the stacks of paperwork on my desk looking for a copy of an old report I knew was there somewhere. My thoughts were interrupted by a phone call from Sam. "Hey, Storm. Maggie said you needed to see me. What's up?"

"Do you remember the first drawing you did for me?"

Sam paused for a moment. "Yeah, what about it?"

"I need you to draw some more sketches of that same suspect."

"You saw him again?"

"No, but he's back. He's killed at least four more young girls. We got a match of his DNA. I want you to make drawings of what you think he might look like today. He had a beard when I saw him but I want renderings with and without a beard. I want one with and without a mustache. I'd also like one of him with a hat, a cap, and with sunglasses. Think of any possible way he might be disguising himself today and draw him that way. Sam, no matter what he might look like, I want to be able to identify him when I see him again."

"You mean, if you see him again, don't you?"

"No, I mean when. He's still here and I'm going to find him."

"And I guess you want these drawings today?"

"Yesterday would be better, but I'd rather have quality than speed. Get them to me as soon as you can."

"You got it."

Ending the call, I stared at the drawings on my wall. *So you're still alive and you're still killing. You won't be for long, I'm coming for you and this time, I'm going to kill you very slowly.*

Wanting to etch his face deep into my memory, I decided to visit the alley where I had first seen the suspect. Parking in the same parking spot as I had twelve years ago, I entered the small corridor that ran along the side of the Pike Peaks Theater leading to the rear alley, which ran east to west behind the Wyndham Grand Hotel and then south into the alley where Julia was murdered.

It hadn't changed much. The dumpsters were still there. I didn't see any rats but knew they were permanent residents, watching me from the shadows. Standing where I stood on that frightful night, old memories haunted my mind. The dumpster that Julia was murdered behind looked the same. I could almost hear her pleading from the grave. I broke out in a cold sweat and my heart rate increased. The foul pungent smell of burnt grease and rotten tomatoes radiated out of the dumpster where I had thrown my pistol that long ago night. It turned my stomach. My fists were clenched with the onslaught of dreaded memories.

A sound drew my attention to an apartment above. A young woman holding a child watched me through a dirty gray spider-infested window. I waved, she didn't. The hot tone on my police radio sounding snapped me back to reality.

The dispatcher broadcasted a bank robbery in progress at the Vetra Bank of Colorado. It was located just around the corner, about a block south of my location. I heard sirens in the distance as I ran down the alley toward the bank. When I got to the street just north of the bank, I stopped to catch my breath. Two police officers were hidden behind their patrol cars on the other side of the street with their guns drawn pointing at my side of the street. I flashed them my badge and radio so they knew I was a police office and they acknowledged me by nodding.

Peeking around the corner, I saw a large man wearing a ski mask holding an older gentleman around his neck. The robber had a pistol pointed at the man's head. He half pulled, half dragged the man backwards crossed the street from the bank to my side of the street. They sidestepped in my direction along the wall of the U.S. Olympic Committee Building.

The gunman wore a sleeveless shirt. His biceps were the size of my thighs. Tattoos covered every inch of exposed skin. He yelled to the officers across the street to back off or he would blow the banker's head off. I held my position and watched as more officers took up positions around the bank and the multi-story parking garage next to it. Civilians coming out of the parking lot and restaurants were in danger. The officers shouted at them to get back. More police cars arrived and blocked off both ends of the street. A SWAT sniper set up on the roof of the parking lot across the street. A news van stopped in the alley across the street from me. Connie Mason and a cameraman stepped out and started filming. I had to admit they had balls. But they were likely to get themselves shot.

The robber walked in my direction, facing the other side of the street. He kept yelling at the officers to back off. I turned my police radio off so it wouldn't give my position away. The bad guy kept his back to the wall and held the banker in front of him as he inched his way along the building towards me. It took several minutes for him to get close. When he got to the alley, I stepped out behind them and placed my pistol behind his ear. "Don't move or you're dead!" I thought about pulling the trigger but decided against it because the bullet might hit the banker or someone across the street.

He glanced back over his shoulder at me. "You better put that gun down or I'm going to blow this guy's head off."

"No you won't. Put your gun down or I'll kill you where you stand."

The banker was shaking so badly, I thought he was going to pass out.

"You don't understand, fool," the suspect said. "I'm a bad man and I'll kill him as sure as I'm standing here. Put your gun down or I kill him now!" he yelled.

I smiled at him. "No you won't, because if you do, I'll blow your brains all over the street. Like Dirty Harry said, 'make my day'."

For the first time I saw fear in his eyes. I pressed my gun harder into his temple. "Well?"

"You're a crazy motherfucker!" he yelled.

I kept smiling and in a quiet calm voice replied, "My therapist tells me that all the time. So what's it going to be, dickhead?"

He looked across the street at the officers in SWAT gear and up at the sniper on the roof pointing a rifle at him. He glanced at the officers blocking off each end of the street.

"You're one fucked up dude!"

He pointed his gun up in the air, took his finger off the trigger and released the hostage. The old man stumbled, then ran across the street and took cover behind the officers. I reached around and took the gun and placed it in my waistband. "Now, let's see what a bad man looks like." I pulled his mask off and pushed my weapon back against his temple. He had a shaved head with swastika tattoos on both sides of his neck. "You don't look so tough. You look like a Nazi wimp."

He turned his head to the side and stared at me with one eye.

"They say your life flashes before your eyes when you know you're going to die. See any flashes yet?"

"Hey...hey, what are you doing?" he said. "You can't shoot me. What the hell is wrong with you? You're a cop."

"Sure I can, I'm crazy, remember. Anything flashing?"

"You're bluffing. You don't want to shoot me. I got a wife and kids. Come on, officer."

"On your knees!" I ordered.

He slumped down on his knees and covered his head with his hands. "Hey man, what are you doing? Don't shoot me."

"Why not? You're a badass, right?"

I put more pressure on his head shoving it downward with my pistol. He started shaking. I think he believed he was about to die.

"I'm going kill you, you sorry prick." I said.

I pushed the gun harder into the side of his head. He curled into a ball and started mumbling to himself. I saw a wet spot on the sidewalk under him.

"Guess you're not so tough. You just pissed your pants."

I felt a hand on my shoulder and heard the voice of Sergeant Jim Pomush. "Don't do it, Storm. He's not worth it."

I lowered my weapon and handed Pomush the suspect's gun, then I holstered my pistol. As soon as the robber was cuffed, I walked across the street to where the news truck blocked the parking garage's entryway. Connie Mason spoke rapidly into her microphone. As I passed, she stopped talking and followed me down the alleyway.

"Detective Harrison, can you give us an update on what's going on."

"No comment," I replied and kept walking.

I proceeded south past the parking garage to the Colorado Springs Pioneer Museum. Katy stood on the sidewalk in front of the courthouse across the street. She ran to meet me and grabbed my arm. "They are broadcasting the robbery on live television. Are you all right, Storm?"

"Yeah, I'm fine. Let's get out of here. Where's your car?"

"In the rear parking lot."

We crossed the street, walked to the rear of her office, got into her car and drove away.

"Where do you want to go?" she asked.

"How about Wong's?" I turned off my radio and phone. "I need a drink."

Katy called her office and told them she wouldn't be in for the rest of the day. When we got to Wong's, I ordered a Crown Royal on the rocks and she ordered a martini. Twee Wong approached our table and pointed towards the bar. "Mr. Hairson, you on TV."

The big screen behind the bar was broadcasting a re-run of the robbery scene. Connie's voice could be heard as the film rolled: *"Detective Storm Harrison of the Colorado Springs Police Department is holding the bank robber at gunpoint and the suspect is holding a gun to the banker's head."*

Watching myself on television, I questioned my own sanity. I looked a lot calmer than I'd felt. What in the world was I thinking? Watching Connie Mason follow me down the sidewalk asking me if I would give her a statement and me saying, "No comment," made me feel better.

Other customers were staring at us. It was time to leave. I asked Twee for our bill. "Lunch on me, Mr. Hairson. You do good work."

I dropped a twenty on the table and we left. When we got to Katy's car, I asked, "Where are we going?"

Katy smiled. "Yoga lessons at my house! You need to chill out."

CHAPTER NINE

B ill Walker, a robbery detective, followed me into my office. We'd worked a few cases together when someone got waxed during a robbery.

"Good morning, Storm. How you feeling this morning?" He took a seat.

"Great. What's up?"

"I'm working on the report from yesterday's bank robbery. I need to ask you a few questions."

"No problem."

"Where'd you go yesterday when you left the robbery scene? I looked for you but no one knew where you were."

"I was late for my yoga class."

"Yoga?" He looked at me as if I was nuts. "Are you serious?"

I recorded my interview with Det. Walker so I could remember what I had told him when writing my supplemental report. He asked normal routine questions and I kept my answers short and sweet like I was planning to do on my report. I didn't want to get anything mixed up that some smart assed attorney could trip me up on later. Before leaving, Bill asked one final question. "Did you hear the suspect had two outstanding warrants for murder?"

"No, I didn't. Too bad I didn't kill the prick."

Bill smiled, "Some of us out there thought you were going to, and so did the suspect. He's convinced you're insane."

"Maybe he's right."

I spent the rest of the day completing the never ending reports and drinking coffee. Often I've wished police work was more like the movies, no paperwork and no reporters. Connie Mason called at least ten times. I ignored her calls and didn't listen to any of her voice messages. With most of what had to be done completed, I decided to call it a day. Lieutenant Fowler approached me as I was locking my office. "You going home, Storm?"

"I was. You need something?"

"I need to talk to you in my office."

We went to his office and he motioned for me to have a seat and told me to close the door. He made a phone call. "We're ready," he said and hung up. I declined his offer of coffee. Police Chief Henderson came into the room and took a seat next to me and said, "That was quite a situation you got yourself into yesterday."

"No one got hurt, that's all that matters." I replied.

Lieutenant Fowler intervened, "Why don't you tell us about it. The Chief is getting a lot of questions from the press about the incident."

"Not much to tell. I got the jump on the guy and he didn't have much choice but to let the banker go and give himself up."

"How did you end up in that alley anyway?" asked Fowler.

"I was in the alley about a block north when the call came out on the radio. It was quicker to run to the bank than it was to go back to my car and drive around. Just lucky, that's all."

Chief Henderson glanced over at Fowler and then asked, "What did you say to the suspect?"

"I told him to drop the gun or I'd kill him. That's about all there was to it. He let the banker go and gave me his weapon."

"Some people thought you were going to kill the suspect."

"I wanted him to believe it so he'd do what I wanted."

Chief Henderson paused for a minute staring at me. "The banker is a friend of mine, Storm. He painted a far more dramatic story than you are."

"It's a lot more intense when someone is holding a pistol to your head."

Chief Henderson smiled. "I assume you're right about that. The banker thinks you're nuts."

"Is he filing a complaint?" I asked.

"Hell no. He wants to give you a medal or something for saving his life. He'll probably nominate you for officer of the year."

"So, what's the big deal then?"

"It's been aired on national television, Storm," said Lieutenant Fowler. "It is a big deal. You did a great job out there."

I directed my next comment to Chief Henderson. "Any of us would have done the same thing in my position. I was just lucky to be at the right place at the right time. I don't want to make this into something it's not. I was just doing my job."

Chief Henderson rose and shook my hand. "Good job, Storm. We needed some positive press after being hammered with these little girls getting killed. Connie Mason is requesting a press release and wants you to be there."

"I'll do it if I'm ordered to, but I'd rather sit it out if you don't mind."

"I'd like you to be there, but I won't make it an order. You deserve that much. If you change your mind, the press conference will be in front of the police station in an hour."

"I'll pass, sir. I have yoga lessons."

They both looked at me as if I had just told them I was gay. I knew they were disappointed about me not attending the press conference, but screw 'em. I don't get paid to babysit reporters. That's why they're getting the big bucks. Besides, I had a cold beer to attend to.

CHAPTER TEN

The next morning I was talking to Jim Pomush in the break room. He is the sergeant over the detective division and my immediate supervisor. He had just returned from a vacation to the Holy Land the day I arrested the robbery suspect. He could be anal at times but has a great eye for details. His good mood was short lived when he received a call from Lieutenant Jerry Fowler saying he needed to see Jim in his office.

"I'll see you later, Storm. I've got a feeling my vacation is over."

Jerry Fowler had his chair back to his desk looking out the window at the city below when Jim Pomush entered his office.

"Hi, Jerry. Miss me?" asked Jim Pomush as he walked in.

Jerry turned to face him. "Yes, I did. How was the vacation?"

"We had a wonderful time."

"Have a seat, Jim," Jerry said as he pointed to the empty chair. "I'd like to hear about it sometime. But right now I need you to do something for me you're not going to like."

"All right. Let's hear it?"

"I want you to take over Storm's murder cases."

"Why would you want me to do that? Storm is as capable as I am. Better maybe... well, not better, but just as good."

"I'm not asking, Jim, it's an order."

Jim and Jerry had known each other for a long time and considered each other good friends. Jerry had never given Jim a direct order before. He knew there had to be a damn good reason. "All right, Jerry, what's going on?"

"You remember the Julia Moore murder twelve years ago in the alley behind the drug store?"

"Of course I remember it. I investigated the case and it's never been solved."

"He's back."

"Who's back?"

"Julia Moore's killer is back. He's the same guy that's killing these little girls that Storm's investigating."

"Really. I investigated Julia's murder and the case was never solved. How many victims are there now, three?"

"No, four. Storm is investigating another murder that happened while you were on vacation. I want you to take control of all of them. I'll be putting together a task force to assist you."

Jim stared at the table for a moment shaking his head. "Storm is not going to like this."

Jerry took a deep breath. "I'm not sure how he'll feel. He looks exhausted most of the time and seems to be having mood swings. I'm not sure if his head is on straight."

"Why do you say that? He did a damn good job at that robbery scene."

"Yeah, but he also walked out of that last murder scene and told Charlie to handle it. Claimed he wasn't feeling well. I want to lighten his load and keep a close eye on him."

"Hmm, that doesn't sound like Storm. Charlie has never worked a homicide by himself before."

Fowler waved him off. "Charlie did fine. In fact, I'm going to give him a commendation when this is over. He took on a lot more responsibility than I expected of him."

Jim had the feeling his boss hadn't told him everything. "I really don't like being on Storm's bad side. So what's the real reason you want me to take over his investigations?"

"That's just the point. Storm's too hardheaded and this case is too personal. I'd hate to think what he might do to the suspect if he finds him before we do."

Jim considered that and nodded. "You're right, Boss. He might kill him the first chance he gets. The County Attorney would be all over it like stink on shit. Then we'd be investigating Storm."

"Yep, and the Police Department would have a lawsuit on their hands to boot. We don't need the bad publicity or the headaches. We need a good clean trial to get this asshole convicted and on death row."

"I'll take care of Storm," Jim said.

"How are we going to handle him?"

"I am going to schedule a meeting for tomorrow morning. I'll tell everyone you ordered me to take the lead on all five cases. We could use some extra help from the robbery detail to assist us. Storm will work directly with me. I'll make it clear that I'm in charge of all the investigations. Behind the scene, the other detectives will know not to feed Storm information unless it's cleared through me. We'll keep him a few steps behind our suspect until we catch the guy. Once the suspect is safely behind bars, I'll loosen the restrictions on Storm."

Jerry sat back in his chair. "Knowing Storm, he won't like it."

"I'm sure he won't, but he'll do as I say or I'll suspend him for his own good."

CHAPTER ELEVEN

When Storm got to the office, he found a memo taped to his door stating that Lieutenant Fowler had scheduled a meeting and for all homicide and robbery detectives to report to the briefing room. Rumor had been going around that Fowler was putting a task force together to help catch the suspect who has been killing the girls. Storm was sure Fowler had different ideas about what to do with the guy once we caught him, but we'd work that out when it happens.

There were five detectives already at the meeting room when I entered. Chief Henderson walked in with Lieutenant Fowler. Sam Coffman followed them carrying two boxes that he set on the table. A tall guy in his mid-fifties with gray hair and glasses came in and took the seat next to me. He looked like an older version of Howie Long. His short flattop haircut screamed ex-special forces. I assumed he must be FBI because I didn't recognize his face or the name on his ID tag.

Chief Henderson addressed the men in the meeting. "Good morning gentlemen."

We returned his greeting in unison.

"I can't overemphasize how important this investigation has become. We need to catch this killer soon. I have authorized as much overtime as needed for the case. If any of you have planned vacations, cancel them until this guy is off the street. Bodies are piling up and it's up to us to stop him."

He waited for comment. When none was forthcoming, he continued. "I have ordered Lieutenant Fowler to put Sergeant Pomush in charge of this investigation. We need only one engineer driving this train and I want this investigation to stay on track until the murderer is in jail. Is that understood?"

No one said anything. I knew I had just been derailed. I wondered who had made that decision. Chief Henderson had never before dictated how an investigation would be conducted. *I had a bad feeling about this.*

The chief continued. "I've asked the FBI to assist us and see if we can get a read on this guy."

"This is Ted Wohler, a criminal profiler from the FBI." He pointed to the man sitting next to me. "Storm will be working with Ted since he's the only person who has seen or talked to the suspect."

The chief looked at me and then continued. "Lieutenant Fowler has sent a bulletin out to other agencies to see if anyone else has had any murders with the same MO or matching DNA. As far as we know, this guy killed his first victim here in Colorado Springs twelve years ago. He has now murdered four more girls in the last three months. We don't know if he moved away after that first killing and continued killing somewhere else, or if he stayed here all the time and just started killing again. We have to find him fast or the body count will continue to climb. We don't want that on our consciences."

I don't know how much more my conscience can stand.

"If there are no questions, I'll turn this meeting over to Lieutenant Fowler."

No one raised their hand to ask a question, so the Chief left the room.

"Gentlemen, you heard the Chief," said Lieutenant Fowler. "That wasn't a request. It was a direct order. You have no idea how much pressure he is under to get this guy off the street."

I have a good idea and it isn't anything compared to the pressure I'm feeling.

"For the guys that are not up-to-date on the investigation, Sergeant Pomush will brief you after the meeting." He pointed to the two boxes on the table. "Those contain the reports of the murders we know he's committed thus far. I expect each of you to familiarize yourself with them so you know what we're up against."

I feel a headache coming on.

Lieutenant Fowler continued, "Sam's going to post the sketches he drew of the suspect on this wall." He pointed behind him. "He will explain them and tell you what the suspect might look like today. No one has seen him in the last twelve years that we know of. We matched his DNA from his first killing to the one three nights ago. We are reasonably sure he is responsible for all four recent murders because the MO is the same. Any questions?"

I raised my hand.

"Yes, Detective Harrison?"

"How are we going to work the investigations?"

"We will no longer work the murders as five separate crimes. We will treat them as one large investigation divided into five parts. Pomush will be in charge of all of them. He will advise you what he expects each of you to do to help the overall investigation. I expect all of you to follow his lead. If he asks you to do something, take the request as if it were coming from me. Anyone unwilling to cooperate with Sergeant Pomush will be removed from the case."

I felt Jerry was making that comment for my benefit. The question now was how tight were the reins going to be?

Fowler continued, "We may be getting two more detectives from burglary to assist us but I don't know who they are yet. Any other questions?"

There were plenty, but this wasn't the time to ask them knowing I wouldn't get a straight answer anyway.

Fowler ended the meeting. "Take a fifteen minute break and Pomush will get back to you for further instructions. I need to talk to him in my office for now."

It was going to be a long day so I took four Excedrin when I got back to my office. Knowing people considered me a loose cannon didn't bother me, but no one had ever interfered with any of my cases before. Julia's murder must have played into their decision.

I called Maggie on her office phone. She answered and stated she would call me back in a minute and hung up on me. My cell phone rang a second later.

"Why did you call my cell, Maggie?"

"Because I didn't want to use the office phone. What's up?"

"They're trying to pull the rug out from under me. Have you heard anything?"

"Sorry, Storm, I can't feed you any information. That's why I called your cell. Shit runs downhill and I need this job."

"Well how do they expect me to do my job while cooped up in the office?"

"You'll have to ask Pomush. I'll let you know if they lower the red flag."

Maggie hung up on me again. I knew she had already said more than she should have and I didn't want to jeopardize her job. I would have to get my answers from Jim Pomush.

At times, I felt as if Katy and Doc Martin were the only ones keeping me from going insane. I'd resign if I thought it would help me catch this guy or stop the nightmares, but it would only lessen my chances at either one.

I saw Jim Pomush walk by and I followed him to his office.

"Got a minute, Jim?"

"Sure have a seat."

"Do you mind if I shut the door?"

"I'd rather you didn't. I've only got a few minutes. I have to start giving the men their assignments."

The fact that Jim Pomush didn't want me to close his door spoke volumes. Our offices were not soundproof by any stretch of the imagination. He wanted witnesses in case I went off on him. His third day back from vacation and I could already see the blood veins bulging in his neck. He wasn't having a great day either. He pulled a bottle of aspirins out of his desk and downed four. I wondered how to approach him, knowing he hated this as much as I did. Jim had a family to support and needed the overtime homicide provides more than I did, and he couldn't afford to jeopardize his position.

"Well, let's have it, Storm?"

"I just wanted to know what I could do to help with the investigation."

"Storm, I just walked in. I haven't even had a chance to look at your last report yet. Get with the FBI guy and see how you can assist him. Let me get up to speed and I'll get back to you tomorrow."

Jim had to know I wasn't serious and he knew we couldn't talk with his door open. I had the feeling he had been instructed to keep me in the dark as much as possible. Maybe I was being paranoid. This case was way too personal and I couldn't let it go. It appeared that I was going to be the FBI's gopher for now.

I located Ted in the Task Force meeting room. He was reading Julia Moore's case. He didn't talk much, which was fine as far as I was concerned. We had major differences. He wanted to get into the suspect's head and I just wanted to put a bullet in his head. He spent the day reading the murder investigation reports while I started five different profiles on our victims to see what they had in common. Catching this guy would be my salvation and I needed to stay in the game or I wouldn't have the slightest chance of catching him.

All five victims were white females between the ages of thirteen and sixteen years old. All had been raped, strangled and sodomized except Julia. She had her throat cut because of me and he couldn't sodomize her because I'd interrupted his plans. I listed their names, ages, addresses, schools, hair color, weight, churches, clubs and events they attended on a large white board. A recent photo of each girl was placed above her information. The older girls looked much younger than they were and if I didn't know the difference, I would think they were all the same age. Our suspect liked them young. I listed their parents' name and job descriptions. All of the girls had been killed in their homes or apartments and all lived with a single mom except victim number one who was a runaway.

I placed a map of the city on another wall and stuck red pins at the location of the murders. I used blue pins to mark the victim's schools, yellow for their churches and so on. I listed the dates of the murders. They were about a month apart except for Julia. If we were lucky, he might not kill again for another three weeks.

Ted came in to look at the maps. "Good job. Now we need to find anything those girls have in common that we haven't listed. Somehow the suspect knew where these girls lived and that they only had a single parent. How did he know that?"

"Good question. I don't think he picked them randomly. He had to have some availability to their information."

"So who would have that information?"

"Their doctors or dentists, their schools, their churches maybe. Who else?"

Ted studied the maps. "I know there are more places we haven't thought of yet, but they'll come to us. Usually when we're sleeping."

Not when I'm sleeping.

"Why don't we call it a day, Storm? We'll clear our heads and finish this tomorrow. We can review the new information as we get it."

As I was driving out of the parking lot, Katy called. "Are you hungry?"

"Starving. But I need a drink worse. It's been a long day."

"Good, I'm buying. Meet me at The Oak Barrel."

"What are we celebrating?"

"I won my case today. He'll get at least fifteen years for molesting his stepdaughter."

"Congratulations. I'll be there in twenty minutes."

"What's wrong?" she asked. "You sound bummed."

"I'm not sure. We'll talk about it when I see you."

CHAPTER TWELVE

K aty ordered escargot for our appetizers. My ego wouldn't let me admit that I had never eaten them before. I thought she was getting back at me for the jokes I made about eating cat at Wong's. I slipped one in my mouth and to my surprise it wasn't bad. I ate two just to prove my bravery. I had no idea how much a bottle of Chateau Montelena Estate Cabernet Sauvignon cost, but I liked the way it sounded as it flowed off of Katy's lips when she ordered it. While staring at the menu, I couldn't help noticing the prices. I searched the menu, looking for something that I could actually afford.

"May I order for you?" Katy asked.

"Sure, I can't find the road-kill section."

Katy smiled and ordered something I couldn't pronounce. It was a wonderful dinner and although the tab was more than my car payment, I gallantly picked it up anyway.

"Oh no you don't," Katy said as she snatched it out of my hand. She didn't even flinch as she signed the credit card receipt. The tip alone was more that I normally pay for a meal.

"Let's go to your home, Storm. I want to see how you live," Katy said as we walked out of the restaurant.

She seemed surprised when I said, "All right," without hesitation. I gave Katy my address and she followed me to my house. I live in the back of a cul-de-sac in a quiet neighborhood next to the park in the center of town. My home has three bedrooms, two bathrooms, a maintenance-free front yard and big shade trees in the back. It has a shop where I keep my tools, motorcycle, snow skies, backpacking and hunting equipment.

We parked in the garage and walked inside. I was relieved that my cleaning lady had been there.

"I'm surprised, Storm. This is not what I expected," Katy said as we walked in.

"What did you expect?"

"I don't know, a half-eaten pizza sitting on the counter and maybe an empty beer can or two." She walked to the fireplace and ran her finger over the mantle, checking it for dust. "I think you keep a cleaner house than I do."

"It's easy to keep it clean when I sleep over all the time."

She frowned. "I hope that wasn't the case before I met you."

"That was BK."

She smiled and picked up the opened Bible on the fireplace mantle. "Do you read this?"

I answered. "What transgressions have you committed? What is your sin?"

Katy looked at the opened page then looked back at me. "I'm impressed."

"It keeps me sane."

"I should read the Bible more often. Maybe we can read it together."

"Maybe we should." *God help us both!*

Katy asked to see the rest of the house. I showed her the living room, kitchen, and bedrooms. When we got to the master bedroom, I said. "This is the ballroom." She didn't seem to think that was funny.

We went out to the rear deck and sat watching the birds in the birdbath, while we drank wine and made small talk. After we turned in, I had a hard time going to sleep. There was a killer out there somewhere looking for his next victim and I couldn't help wondering if he would strike again tonight. I fell asleep with a restless mind.

Around 3:00 a.m., I sat up in bed screaming. "Don't die, please don't die."

Katy grabbed me, trying to shake me awake. "Wake up, Storm. It's a dream. Wake up, wake up!" She reached over and turned on the lamp.

My heart pounded in my chest, I felt disoriented and covered in sweat. I tried to catch my breath. "I'm sorry . . . I'm sorry."

Katy held me, stroking my back in a soothing rhythm. "It's all right, Storm."

I knew she couldn't possibly understand and I didn't know how to explain these dreams to her. I hoped she would forgive me.

"How long have you been having these nightmares?"

"For twelve years now."

"Storm, I know someone who can help you."

"I thought I did too. But I now believe I have to help myself."

"Do you want to talk about it?"

"I owe you an explanation, but I need a little time to think about it? This isn't easy for me."

"Sure, but I want to help you. Okay?" She cradled me in her arms until we fell back to sleep.

When my alarm sounded, I woke up alone. I panicked, thinking Katy had gone. The smell of frying bacon confirmed she hadn't. Slipping on my robe, I walked into the kitchen. Katy greeted me with a smile, a kiss and a hot cup of coffee. "Good morning. Are you hungry?"

I felt loved and wanted. "Yes I am. I thought you'd gone."

"And leave the most wonderful man I've ever met? Sorry, you're stuck with me now."

I took her in my arms and held her tight. She kissed me on the forehead and said, "We'll get through this together. If you want to talk, I can call off work."

She deserved an explanation, but I wasn't ready. "Not now, but I will. Can you give me a little time, please?"

"All right, Storm, but I want to help."

After breakfast, she put the plates in the sink and grabbed her purse. "I have to run or I'll be late. Will I see you tonight?"

"Do you have to leave so early?"

"I've got to go home, shower and get dressed. It takes a woman a lot more time than it does a man." She kissed me goodbye and hurried out the door.

I picked up the phone and hit speed dial. Doc answered on the first ring, "You're up early, Storm. What's going on?"

"I'd like to see you. It's important."

"I'm already meeting someone this morning but I can see you later."

"Can I come after work?"

"Sure. I'm available all afternoon."

Doc Martin sat in his favorite spot next to the windows overlooking the lake at the Broadmoor Hotel's main dining room. He was early for his lunch date with Katy who hadn't arrived yet. He called Storm Harrison on his cell phone. "Hey, Storm, this is Doc."

"What's up?"

"Just wanted to check to see how you're doing."

There was a slight pause. "I'm fine, Doc."

"Are you sure?"

"Yeah, but thanks for thinking of me."

"Are you sure there isn't anything you want to discuss?"

"No, not now, I'm kinda busy. And I need to cancel our appointment. I have something I need to do first. I'll get back to you."

"Please do. I'm worried about you," Doc said and hung up.

Katy arrived, kissed Doc on the cheek and took a seat. "Who were you talking to?"

"A client," Doc said. "What's so important in your life that it couldn't wait?"

"You know Storm Harrison, the guy I told you I've started dating."

"Of course, your knight in shining armor. What about him?"

"We were together again last night."

"He sounds like a horn dog."

Katy grinned. "No, just a typical man."

The waiter came and took their lunch orders.

After he left Dr. Martin asked, "So what's the emergency?"

"Storm is having nightmares. He woke up at 3:00 a.m. screaming, 'Don't die! Please, don't die!' It scared the hell out of me."

Doc took a small notebook and pen from his shirt pocket and wrote some notes. "Was he violent or did he try to harm you?"

"No, just the opposite. He apologized several times. I think he was ashamed and frustrated."

"How did he act this morning?"

"When he woke and I wasn't in bed, he thought I had left him. But after seeing me fixing breakfast, he acted as if nothing happened. I asked him if he wanted to talk about it and he said he would, but he needed time."

"Are you going to keep seeing him?"

"Of course. I really care about him and want to help him."

"I swear people fall in love a lot faster these days than they used to."

"I didn't say I was in love, Doc, but I need your help. I want him to see you."

Doc put his notebook away, took a drink of his coffee and looked at Katy. "That could be tricky. Treating two people who are involved with each other can be very difficult. Revealing confidential information about each other is unprofessional and unethical."

"You can tell him anything about me you need to, it's all right."

"No it's not, and I won't."

Katy stared at her plate and didn't respond. Doc studied her emotions and felt she was desperate. "I can recommend someone else for him if you'd like."

"No, Doc. I've tried others and you were the only one that helped me. He needs you."

"I'll think about it, Katy. This is a very unique situation."

Katy paused for a moment. "I know, we could both come in for therapy at the same time."

"Dual therapy. Normally that only happens with spouses. I'll give it some thought but he would have to agree. Wait until he tells you what's causing his nightmares. Then if you still want me to see both of you, we can talk about it. But you'll have to tell him about your incident first. I wouldn't want him to come in blindsided."

CHAPTER THIRTEEN

I t was time to face my demons. I picked up Italian takeout and
a bottle of red wine and met Katy at her house. We sat on her
front porch on the swing and ate dinner; sipping wine and watching a peaceful world go by. Children played in their front yards as
mothers walked their baby carriages down the sidewalk and fathers
mowed their lawns. The kids acted as if they didn't have a care in
the world and it reminded me of a happier time. The sounds of
children laughing, birds chirping and the wine calmed my soul
and put me at ease. It wasn't going to be easy reliving Julia's story
and I wasn't sure what feelings it might trigger.

"A penny for your thoughts?" Katy said as she placed her hand
on mine.

"I need to tell you about my nightmares so you'll know what
you're getting yourself into."

"Are you worried? Because if you are, I want you to go see Dr.
Robert Martin. He can help you."

I almost choked on my wine. "Doc Martin? How do you know
him?"

"He's my uncle."

"And he didn't tell you that I'm already seeing him?"

"Of course not," Katy said with a surprised look on her face. "I had no clue. I've been seeing him too." Katy studied me for a minute. "Are you worried about discussing this?"

"No, are you?"

"Not at all. I love you."

I looked into her beautiful sea blue eyes. "Katy, I've loved you since the moment I first saw you."

She smiled, and pulled my hand up to her cheek. "Let's talk about us. I have confessions of my own."

We went into the family room and sat on the couch. She hit the remote and fire started in the fireplace. Katy filled our glasses with wine and kissed me.

"I'm not sure where to start," I said.

"Let's start with Dr. Robert Martin," Katy said. "It appears we each have a history with him. You go first."

"I was in Kuwait, and when the war started, my unit was one of the first to cross the border into Iraq."

"You didn't tell me you were in the military."

"It's not something I talk about a lot. Anyway, a few days prior to leaving Kuwait, an Army colonel came to talk to us. It was Doc Martin. He was doing a study on Post Traumatic Stress Disorder for the Army. He attached himself to our unit to study the effects of war on the men."

"My father and Doc Martin were roommates at West Point." Katy said, "My mother is Doc's sister, and that's how she met my dad."

"Doc's full of surprises," I said. "I'm going to have a word with him about hiding his niece from me all this time."

Katy laughed. "Uncle Robert has always been very protective of me. I guess there's a lot I don't know about him or my father. "

Katy refilled our wine glasses and I continued. "Four days later, we were lined up ready to cross into Iraq and Colonel Martin stood right beside me in full battle fatigues. He had a .45 pistol on his hip and a laptop computer in his hand. I asked him if he intended on going with us and he said he didn't want to miss the action. Doc told me to never salute him because he didn't want to get picked off by a sniper."

"Didn't he have a rifle?" Katy asked.

"Nope, he carried a lot of extra ammo for his pistol. But I never saw him draw his pistol. He had that computer fired up all the time. I'd be hunkered down half scared to death and he'd be pecking away on his computer as calm as a cucumber. Strangest thing I ever saw."

"I always thought Uncle Robert was a brave man."

"Brave hell. He had balls of steel."

Katy laughed. "I knew there had to be a reason he never had children."

We both laughed. She got a faraway look in her eyes. "What are you thinking about?"

"I'm thinking about my dad. I've never given much thought about what he experienced during the war. He never talked about it."

"It's not something you bring up at a party or talk to your kids about."

"You're right. Uncle Robert and my dad both served in Vietnam and neither one ever said anything about what that was like."

Excusing myself, I went to the bathroom. Katy opened another bottle of wine and when I came back, I said, "I respected Doc Martin more than any soldier I ever knew."

"What brought you and Doc together this time and what caused the nightmares?"

"After the war, I joined the Colorado Springs Police Department. After completing the police academy, I was assigned the graveyard shift working the downtown area. We had a lot of burglaries in the older business section at that time. I had a hard time staying awake during the early morning hours. One morning around 3:00 a.m., I walked into an alley to check for unlocked doors or evidence of forced entry into the back of the buildings. It was a dark moonless night with thick clouds threatening rain. The alley was quiet except for the scurrying of rats and a few papers blowing around. Once in a while I could hear the faint sounds of a radio or TVs from the apartments located above the stores." I paused for a moment and took a deep breath.

"I heard a scuffing sound behind one of the dumpsters. Pointing my flashlight towards the sound, I saw a figure hiding in the shadows. I yelled, 'Police Officer, don't move,' while pulling my service weapon and moving forward. No one answered. When I got closer, I saw a man holding a young girl with a large hunting knife at her throat. He had knelt down behind her, holding her mouth so she couldn't scream. Her blouse was torn open and her bra was showing. I ordered him to drop the knife. He said to lower my gun or he would slice her throat. I told him that if he hurt the girl I'd blow his brains out. He moved his hand from her mouth and lifted her up by the waist to help conceal himself. The girl had tears streaming down her cheeks and she was begging me to do as he said. She kept saying she didn't want to die. I moved forward trying to get a clear shot at the bastard but he was too well hidden behind her. He swore he'd kill her if I got any closer. I moved forward to within six feet and he cut her on the side of her neck. The girl panicked and begged me to please do as he said. I knew he'd kill her if I didn't do something fast."

I paused to collect my thoughts while staring into the flames. "You want to stop?" Katy asked.

"No." I shook my head. "I want to get this over with. I lowered my pistol and asked him what he wanted me to do. He told me to back up and I did. While holstering my gun, I held the transmit button down on my police radio so other officers could hear us. He wouldn't know they were listening as long as the button was pressed. I told him to leave the girl alone and I'd let him go. He said to give him my pistol. I told him that would never happen. He said if I'd throw my gun in the dumpster, he'd let her go.

"The girl pleaded for me to throw my gun in the dumpster. Tears streamed down her face as she begged me again and again to do what he wanted. She kept saying over and over that she didn't want to die. Blood had already soaked the front of her shirt.

"I thought if I threw my gun in the dumpster he'd let her go. Then I could stop the bleeding and get her to a hospital while the other officers searched for the suspect."

Katy asked, "Did you think she would bleed to death?"

"I wasn't sure. There was a lot of blood. I promised not to chase him if he'd just let the girl go. He said if I'd drop my gun in the dumpster, he'd let her live. As soon as he heard the thud of my gun hit the bottom of the dumpster, he cut her throat from ear to ear, dropped her and ran down the alley. The bastard knew I would try to save the girl instead of chasing him."

Tears smeared Katy's mascara. I paused. "You okay?" I asked.

She got a tissue and blew her nose. "I'll be all right. Go ahead."

"I ran to the girl while screaming for paramedics over the radio. I held her in my arms trying to stop the bleeding. The blood ran through my fingers and into my lap. She couldn't speak because of her throat was cut. Her mouth was moving. I think she was saying, '*Help me, please help me,*' but there were no words, just a gurgling noise as she drowned in her own blood. All I could do was hold her in my arms and stare into her eyes watching her die."

"Oh, Storm, that's horrible," Katy said. She was visibly shaking and I put my arm around her.

"I can still see and smell her blood when I'm having those nightmares. I still hear those gurgling sounds as she begged me to help her."

I held Katy until she stopped shaking and then continued. "When I looked up several officers were staring at me. I'll never forget the sergeant's words, 'Storm, you know better. NEVER give up your weapon!'"

"But you didn't have a choice."

Staring at the floor, I took another deep breath. "Yes I did and he was right. I had a choice and I made the wrong one. The paramedics had to pry her out of my arms. The whole area had been surrounded by police officers within a couple of minutes. But they didn't find the guy. He was never seen again. And now he's back killing these little girls again and it's all my fault."

Tears streamed down Katy's cheeks. I held her tight against me.

"Storm, I'm so sorry, I had no idea."

"I was suspended during the proceedings that followed. After the internal investigation had been completed, a hearing was scheduled to decide my fate. I had violated department policy by giving up my weapon. Being a rookie, they could terminate my employment without cause. The Fraternal Order of Police hired an attorney to represent me. Everyone, including me, thought I would be fired."

"What happened?"

"My attorney hired Doc Martin to speak on my behalf. He arrived at the hearing and introduced himself. He never mentioned that he knew me or that we had served together in the war."

"Did you know he would be there?"

"No. I knew someone would be coming but I had no idea it would be him. Doc told the board that any police officer in that situation would do what I had done, no matter how much training we received. He said the human brain would automatically put more importance on a little girl begging for her life versus any instruction we'd received in a classroom. He estimated that nine out of ten seasoned police officers would have done the same thing under the same set of circumstances. He presented case studies and written testimonies from some of the most respected psychiatrist in the world. By the time he'd finished, he had everyone in the room, except one, convinced that I hadn't done anything wrong. His last statement hit them like a brick when he asked, 'If the suspect hadn't killed the girl and let her go, would we be here today?'

"When no one answered," Doc said, 'No we wouldn't. You would have given him a medal for saving her life. Most of you would have done the same thing Officer Harrison did if you had been in his shoes'.

"You could have heard a pin drop when Doc closed his files and sat down. No one spoke for a few moments. The attorney representing the city asked for a vote from the committee. Every one of them voted to find me not responsible for Julie's death. I was cleared and reinstated to duty."

Katy asked, "Who was the person not convinced?"

"Me."

CHAPTER FOURTEEN

Snow covering Pike's Peak heralded the end of summer. Soon the leaves would turn yellow, red, and orange and purple. The cool crisp air smelled of pine and fresh baked bread from the local bakery down the street from the police station. Fall was my favorite time of the year and reminded me of Paul Simon's song Kodachrome. Winter was just around the corner and the crazies were out in force.

Dead end leads and self-confessed suspects without a clue filled my days. I became bored and anxious. Wiley Hinton, a man from the local nut house, came to the station and confessed. He wore overalls with a cowboy hat and hadn't shaved in weeks. His right eye twitched as he spoke through yellowed teeth. He sat in my office and said very seriously, "My 'other self' sneaks out at night and kills them girls."

"I see. Mr. Hinton, can you describe the girls you have killed?"

"I'm sorry, you'll have to ask my 'other self' to get that information. He's evil and won't tell me anything."

A homeless black man named Willy Keys asked the women in the lobby to watch his cart with all his belongings while he spoke with me. His hair was full of lice and his tennis shoes were wrapped with duct tape. He smelled up my office as he wrote a full confession to the killings. It contained the basic information anyone who read the newspaper would know. Claiming he used a kitchen knife to kill the girls, he demonstrated by lifting up his shaggy head and making a cutting action across his neck with his hand. He didn't know any details but insisted he was the killer.

"Mr. Keys, can you explain why you sodomized the girls after they were dead?"

Looking confused, he asked, "Is that some type of religious ceremony?"

After I explained what sodomized meant, he jumped up and down and called me a "homo-pervert," and stomped out.

The other detectives out beating the bushes were as frustrated as I was. We weren't any closer to finding our serial killer today than we were last month. Fowler pressured us for information for patrol, but we didn't have anything new to give them. Spending my evenings with Katy while the rest of the Task Force worked overtime was the only thing keeping me sane.

Ted Wohler completed the profile of our suspect and briefed us. "The killer is a light skinned African American about 35 to 40 years old. He is around six two and weighs about 210 lbs. He's a pedophile who can't get sexually aroused with mature women. I believe the killer strangles the girls as he climaxes to get his kicks from their death spasms. I can't explain why he sodomizes the girls after they're dead. I'm sure of one thing, he won't stop until he is either caught or killed. You should concentrate your search on places where young girls hang out. I believe the suspect will place himself in contact with as many young girls as possible. I suggest health clubs, malls, movie theaters, schools, parks, the YWCA or even churches. We will have another dead body on our hands any day now if the killer keeps to his MO of killing once a month."

Moans could be heard around the room. Guys were shaking their heads and throwing their notes in the trashcan on the way out. We all expected some great revelation coming from the FBI. I wondered how much they were paying him to research our files and tell us what we already knew. There wasn't much useful information from him.

Fowler was talking on the phone when I got to his office. He looked tired and had bags under his eyes. I waited for him to hang up and knocked on his door.

"What do you want?" he snapped.

"I want to talk to you. But, if it's a bad time, I'll come back."

"No, have a seat, Storm. I'm sorry for taking it out on you. I'm having a bad week. What do you need?"

"You can take this straightjacket off me for one thing. I'm going nuts staring at the walls all day. It's not doing anyone any good having me sitting on my hands. Besides, Ted's completed his profile."

Fowler leaned back in his chair and rubbed his chin. "Pomush needs someone here during the day in case any fresh leads come in. What do you have in mind?"

"If it's all right, I'd like to stay on days, but I want to beat the bushes a little. If we get any leads, I'll still be available to follow them up."

"What's your plan?"

"I want to hit the schools, parks, malls, YWCA, local gyms and any other place this guy might be lurking around. I'll show everyone I come in contact with the drawings and see if I get lucky. I know he's still out there, I can feel it in my bones."

"Hell, Storm, those drawings are on television every night. If anyone recognizes him, they'll call us."

"Little girls don't watch the news, Lieutenant."

Jerry put his pen down and rubbed his temples. "Maybe you're right. We're not making any progress the way we're going. But, if you get any leads, you call Pomush right away. I don't want to hear about any John Wayne shit. You hear me?"

"Loud and clear, boss."

Getting out of the office was a relief. With a hundred copies of Sam's drawing, I stopped by the Bell Bar Gym located on the first floor of an old three-story brick building in the downtown area. The upper floors are rented apartments, which are commonplace in downtown Colorado Springs. I didn't see anyone resembling the suspect so I contacted the gym manager and showed him the drawings. He didn't recognize the guy. He showed the drawings to several of his employees with the same results. I left copies and my business cards and asked him to post the picture in the gym.

I visited every high school and junior high in the downtown area. No one at the schools recognized the guy in the drawings. The principals were cooperative and wanted to help catch this guy. They all assured me they would post the drawing around the schools.

There are three YWCA's in Colorado Springs. I headed for the one farthest from the police station and worked my way back to the one in the downtown area on Nevada Way. I stopped at the first two with negative results and left drawings at both locations. It was getting late so I decided I'd call it a day and finish up tomorrow. My sixth sense told me I was getting close to this guy.

CHAPTER FIFTEEN

Doc Martin answered on the second ring. "I've been expecting you to call, Storm. Want to stop by for a little chat?"

"Yeah, if it's convenient. I'm just leaving work."

He was grinning like a possum eating shit when I walked into his office.

"How long have you known, Doc?"

"Katy told me shortly after you started dating her."

"When in the hell were you going to tell me she was your niece?"

"I'm not sure. I had a lot of issues to consider, both professionally and personally after finding out my favorite patient was dating my niece. When Katy told you she knew someone who could help you, she was referring to me. She called me the morning she found out about the bad dreams. That complicated the situation."

I had mixed emotions about these new revelations. Doc had known Katy all of her life. In a way I felt betrayed by him for not telling me Katy was his niece. From a professional standpoint, I knew he was in a difficult situation. I wanted to know more about her.

"What can you tell me about Katy?"

"Her father, John Taylor, was an Army Doctor. We attended West Point together and became best friends. I introduced him to my sister, Beth, and they got married right after we graduated. I was their best man."

I thought about that for a moment. "She's never spoken of her parents."

"They're both deceased. Katy is their only child."

"How did they die?"

"In a plane crash. After her father retired from the Army, he worked as a surgeon in the private sector. Beth was also a medical doctor. After Katy graduated from high school, John and Beth traveled to third world countries giving aid to people who couldn't afford medical care. While flying to a small village in Peru, their plane crashed into a mountain during bad weather, killing all four doctors on board plus the pilot."

I realized just how little I knew about Katy. I felt like a jerk and made a commitment to myself to find out as much about her life as possible.

"Where do we go from here, Doc?"

"That's up to you and Katy. You're both adults and I'm only here to help. But remember, Storm, blood is always thicker than water. And you're not the only one with personal problems. She's my niece, but I love her like a daughter."

"Do you want to expand on that?"

"No. She'll tell you when she's ready."

CHAPTER SIXTEEN

Like Vegas, The Colorado Springs Police Department never sleeps. There's always something going on in the station's lobby day and night. The main difference is what happens at the police department often ends up in court, on the pages of the local newspaper and TV, and sometimes a major story on national primetime news.

It's a top story when a girl gets raped and murdered. But when there's a serial killer involved, it's national news and you find yourself in the crosshairs of every reporter in the country. The bigger the crime the tighter the microscope you're under and the louder the criticism or praise, depending on how lucky or unlucky you get. All good detectives learn not to pay much attention to headlines or local TV when working major cases. They know there's no such thing as, "off the record," when talking to reporters. I learned the hard way that it is never smart to sleep with a reporter.

I parked my black Dodge Charger in the employee's three-story parking garage and walked into the building at 6:30, an hour prior to my normal starting time. I had a feeling that Fowler had unpleasant plans for me and I'd hoped to get a heads up on what those plans were before he arrived.

I went to my office and checked my e-mails. Only one caught my eye and it said: "Task Force Meeting 0700." I wrote my reports as one by one the detectives arrived for work, helped themselves to coffee and fired up their computers. When Charlie arrived, he waved and stuck his head in the door.

"What's going on with the Task Force?" I asked.

"Not sure, everyone has been tight-lipped so far."

"Any new leads on our suspect?"

"Not that I'm aware of. We'd better get to the meeting."

I walked into the Task Force room at 7:00 a.m. There were seven name cards on the table. I sat in front of the one with my name on it and Ted Wohler took the seat next to me.

We had five full time homicide detectives including Pomush, but one was tied up in court. Fowler assigned a couple of detectives from other departments to assist us. He handed us keys to the room. "Don't let anyone in that isn't on the Task Force."

He turned the meeting over to Pomush, who started the meeting by introducing each of us by name and title, including the department to which we were currently assigned. He matched everyone with a partner and gave us our assignments. I assumed he put me with Ted because I was the only person who had ever seen the suspect and to keep a close eye on me.

Pomush assigned each of the other teams to one of the murder investigations reports and told them to go over the cases with a fine-toothed comb. He wanted them to find any possible leads that we may have missed the first time around and follow up on them. My responsibility was to bring Ted up-to-date on all the investigations and provide him with any relevant information he needed to do his job. In other words, I was still his gopher.

Pomush and his team would attempt to locate local sex offenders in the area and find out who they're hanging with. Dirt bags always have a way of finding each other. I took Ted to my office and we spent the next few hours going over the reports. What he wanted most was information about my contact with the suspect and his current MO's.

Just before noon I called Katy to see if she was available for lunch. We met at The Famous Restaurant and again, I was still underdressed. Katy wore a tight blue dress with four-inch f-me-heels. Everyone noticed her, no one noticed me. I needed to go shopping.

I ordered a five-dollar sandwich, which cost fifteen and Katy opted for a chicken sandwich. Again, they charged her for the whole chicken.

"We should take the afternoon off and go practice yoga," I suggested.

"I'll take a rain check. How's work going?"

"I've been sentenced to house arrest until further notice."

Katy smiled. "I thought working with the FBI would be interesting."

"You've been watching too much TV."

We made happy hour plans at The Oak Barrel after work. When I asked for the bill, the waiter told us someone had picked up our tab. He pointed to a man in a double-breasted pinstriped suit sitting in a booth with a sleazy-looking blonde at the other end of the restaurant. Chas Woods waved.

"Let's go say hello," Katy said.

"Let's not."

"Where are your manners, Storm? Besides, I want to meet your old girlfriend."

"Oh, the hooker. I wouldn't think they'd let her in here. Ouch!"

When we got to their table, Chas stood. "Hi, Katy. I assume everything is copasetic." *Of course it is, she's with me!*

"Life's wonderful, Chas."

He introduced Connie Mason to us, oblivious to the fact she and I knew each other. Katy said hello and I didn't. Chas offered me his hand. "Hello, I'm Chas Woods, you look familiar." *He damn well knew who I was.*

I shook his hand but didn't thank him for buying lunch. "Hi, Charles, Storm Harrison."

"Oh yes, the police officer."

"Homicide Detective."

I'd never seen Connie looking uncomfortable before now.

Chas said, "I haven't had the pleasure of seeing you in court yet. I've seen you on TV. Aren't you working the serial murders of those young girls?"

"I'm part of the Task Force working the case."

He handed me his card. "Give me a call sometime and I'll buy you a drink."

I didn't commit or offer to buy him one.

"Thanks for buying our lunch," Katy said.

I tossed his card on the table on the way out. Katy grinned at the exchange. When we got outside, she asked, "You're not jealous are you?"

"Jealously is the fumes of small hearts. Besides he's BS."

"BS?"

"Before Storm."

"She's a cute girl. Do you think he knows you guys have a history?"

"I doubt it. And she's still not worth two dollars." Ouch, ribs again. I reminded myself to start wearing my bulletproof vest when dining with Katy. She kissed me goodbye and I returned to my office feeling better.

The afternoon was just as boring as the morning and I couldn't wait to get out of the office. I met Katy at The Oak Barrel restaurant after work for happy hour and we ate there. She kept looking around, as if searching for Connie, who never showed. After we left the restaurant we went to her house where she changed into something more comfortable. We sat on her front porch with my arm around her, drinking wine and watching the sunset. I didn't have a care in the world and was at peace. Katy looked at me and said; "I guess it's my turn at show and tell." She took my hand and led me into the house.

We went into the family room and turned on the gas log fireplace. Once we settled in with fresh glasses of wine, Katy began to speak in a soft voice. "After meeting you at Lake Powell, I returned to law school. Chas had already graduated and moved to Colorado Springs to take a job offer with a well-respected law firm. I was living by myself in a small house off campus and spent most of my spare time studying and going to a local gym, trying to stay in shape."

"Were you and Chas still an item?"

"No, not really. We were never serious and the trip to Lake Powell was the only vacation I ever took with him. He kept calling and e-mailing me but I seldom answered. I'd already decided we were not made for each other before I left the lake."

"What did you see in him in the first place?"

"Chas has a brilliant legal mind. He was a big shot on campus and graduated Summa Cum Laude. Everyone knew he was going to be a big time attorney someday."

"Why did you decide to stop dating him?"

"Chas treated me well, but not other people. He always acted as if he was a little better than they were. His arrogance wore thin quickly and he was very jealous. He knew I was flirting with you at the lake and wasn't happy with you being there."

"I'm glad I don't have his jealous traits."

Katy smiled, not buying my bullshit. She continued with her story.

"About a month after I returned to school, I woke up in the middle of the night with a naked man wearing a hood standing beside my bed. I started to scream but he placed his hand over my mouth and put a large kitchen knife to my throat. He said if I screamed, it would be the last sound I ever made. He told me we were going to have a little fun and then he'd leave. If I cooperated, he said he wouldn't hurt me. I was scared to death and nodded that I would do as he said. He took his hand off my mouth but kept the blade of the knife close to my face. He was really big and built like Arnold Schwarzenegger. I slept in the nude, so all he had to do was throw the sheets off and climb on. I waited for the inevitable or an opportunity."

Katy reached for a tissue and blew her nose. "I was so scared, I was shaking. He got on top of me and fondled my breasts and vagina with his fingers but he never inserted himself. He didn't have an erection and was talking to himself saying things like, "Come on baby, you can do it. Get in there." He fumbled around for a few minutes trying to insert his limp dick inside me. I saw him lay the knife on the bed while he used both hands trying to force himself inside me. I reached under my pillow and grabbed my .32 revolver, placed the barrel next to his temple and pulled the trigger twice. Both rounds entered his brain. He looked up at me surprised and then collapsed on my chest. I pushed him off and called 911."

"I'm so sorry, Katy. I had no idea. I assume they didn't charge you with a crime."

"No. I was his third victim and the other two women hadn't survived. He worked at the gym where I was a member and had taken so many steroids he couldn't get it up."

Katy's eyes filled with tears. I held her for a long time and felt her shaking. I stroked her hair to calm her.

She looked up at me, "That's the reason I never called you. I left school and came to live with Uncle Martin for the rest of the semester. I returned to school the next year and lived in the women's dorm with a classmate until graduation. I was too frightened to be alone or sleep by myself. After graduation, I came back to Colorado Springs and lived with Doc again." She took a sip of wine.

"I got a job with the county attorney's office but was too afraid to move into the house I had inherited from my parents. Uncle Martin treated me until I got the nerve to move here. I saw you on the news several times and kept thinking about you. I didn't want to be alone and hadn't been with a man since the attempted rape. I didn't trust anyone but couldn't stop thinking about us on the boat and how I felt safe around you. That's when I ran into you. I'm glad I had the nerve to talk to you."

"Did you have nightmares?"

"No. I'm glad I killed him. That's why I understand how you feel about wanting to kill the guy who's raping and killing those girls. I wouldn't blame you if you did."

I thought about the twists and turns our lives had taken. I worried about Katy. We drank another glass of wine and went to bed where we made love, and I thanked God for her and Doc Martin.

CHAPTER SEVENTEEN

When I arrived at work, Ted Wohler was sitting in my chair with his feet on my desk talking on his cell phone. He wore mirrored sunglasses, giving me the feeling he was watching me even when he wasn't looking in my direction.

"Someone using your desk this morning, Ted?"

He stood and used a sweeping motion with his hand inviting me to sit as if ushering a customer to a table at a fancy restaurant. I sat down to check my phone messages. Ted stepped out into the hallway all the time talking into his cell. When he finished, he returned and popped himself into the spare chair.

"Sorry, about that, Storm. But, I've got something you'll want to hear."

"Not until after I've had my coffee," I said as I got up to leave.

"Oh yeah. We've got a guy who claims he knows your murder suspect."

That got my attention and I sat back down.

"What do you have?"

"The FBI has a guy in the federal pen who claims he's seen the guy you're looking for in Denver. He said he'd talk to you if you promise to put in a good word for him when he comes up for parole."

"Who is he and what's he in for?"

"His name is Freddie Millsap. He was a school teacher in Denver who was caught sending child porn over the Internet."

I rubbed the back of my neck and shook my head. "I'm not sure I want to help a pervert get out of jail."

"Don't worry about it. He won't be up for parole for another ten years and I'm betting he won't last that long. He's already had his throat cut once and is being kept in isolation for his own protection. That's why he'll do anything to get out as soon as possible."

"Yeah, and I bet he'd say anything to get out too. Why do you think he'd square with me?"

"Because he sang like a bird when we nailed him and all his info was reliable."

A misting rain followed me up US Route 285 to the federal prison on a foggy Tuesday morning. Freddie Millsap was being held in the Englewood low-security Federal Correctional Center located ten miles southwest of Denver. His roommates include Rod Blagojevich, former governor of Illinois who was convicted of wire fraud, extortion, and bribery, and Rafael Cordenas, a former high-ranking member of the Gulf Drug Cartel, Jared Fogle, the spokesman for Subway who pled guilty to crossing state lines to engage in illicit sexual conduct with minors and receiving child pornography and former USC professor, Walter Lee Williams, who flew to the Philippines in 2010 to have sex with underage boys he'd met online.

The prison was a modern sandstone pink windowless building with high fences topped with razor wire. A large US flag hung proudly from a tall flagpole. Footsteps echoed off a polished floor being mopped by an inmate as I was escorted to the interview room by two guards. The inmate stepped to the side and faced the wall with his head down as we passed.

Freddie sat at a metal table bolted to the floor. A pink scar ran down the left side of his neck from his ear to the bottom of his Adam's apple. He couldn't have weighed a buck twenty soaking wet. I sat across the table from him in the gray block room with my notebook and a small tape recorder.

"I'm Detective Harrison from the Colorado Springs Police Department," I said without offering him my hand.

"I know who you are. I've seen you on television." His eyes were set close and magnified because of the thick lenses.

"I hear you might have some information for me."

He took a deep breath, his balding head shinning from the overhead lights, his wire-rimmed glasses sitting firm against his long nose. "I don't have a name but I seen the guy you're looking for in Denver at one of those adult shops that sells dirty magazines and movies"

"Do you think he's still there?"

"Maybe, because he wasn't buying. He was selling."

"Selling what?"

Freddie looked around as if someone might hear him and then whispered, "Pictures of little girls."

"Tell me about them." He kept his eyes downward and picked at his nails as he spoke.

"The girl in the photo was white, nude and had a penis stuck in her. You couldn't see the guy's face she was with but he had her propped up with her legs spread real wide. He had another photo where she was bent over and he was doing her from the back. The girl looked like she was unconscious or on drugs. Dead maybe, I don't know."

"How old was this girl?"

"I'm guessing twelve or thirteen, real pretty." Freddie looked up at me and raised his eyebrows.

"Could you tell what race the guy in the photo was?"

"Not really. He had dark skin. Could have been a Negro, Indian or Mexican. He was in his late thirties, medium build."

I studied him for a long time trying to decide if he was telling me the truth or not. He wouldn't look me in the eye. The little hair he had left on the sides of his head was salt and pepper and his eyebrows were gray, making the forty-year-old look well over fifty.

"What, you don't believe me?" he said. "Give me a polygraph test if you want to. I'm telling you the truth, man."

I took the digital recorder out of my shirt pocket, sat it on the table and pressed the record button. "All right, then start from the beginning and tell me everything you got."

Freddie looked at the tape and leaned back away from the table. "You going to speak up for me when I come up for parole?"

"If your information turns out to be reliable, I'll stand up for you."

"What if the information is good but it's the wrong guy?"

"If you tell me the truth, I'll stand up and tell them you tried to help me get this killer off the street."

"All right here's what happened." He leaned forward and put his bony elbows on the table. "There's an adult book store in Denver called *The Romantic* that sells dirty magazines and DVD's. A skinny white guy named Phillip works there. He sells photos out of the back of his car when the owner's not around. The owner is a big fat guy, but I don't think he knows Phillip is selling illegal stuff. You'll have to go there late at night when the owner is not around if you want to buy from Phillip. I paid him a hundred bucks for several color photos of a little girl about ten years old."

"What was the girl doing?"

Freddie ran his finger along his bottom lip. "She was naked and playing with herself."

I wanted to reach across the table and rip his heart out, but I just sat there looking at him. "Go ahead."

"Once, when I went there, Phillip was talking to the guy you're looking for at the back door. They didn't see me come in. They went into the rear parking lot to Phillip's car, but left the back door standing open. I stayed inside watching them. The guy handed Phillip some photos and Phillip paid the guy a handful of money and came back inside. I ducked around the corner and walked back to the front of the store so it looked like I had just come in. Phillip tried to sell me the photos he had just purchased. The girl was limp and looked dead or at least passed out. I wouldn't buy them because they freaked me out."

"Did you tell the FBI about this?"

"No," Freddie said shaking his head.

"Why not?"

"Because they didn't ask. All they were interested in was the Internet photos, and if I had taken any of them."

"Did you?"

Freddie folded his hands in his lap and hung his chin to his chest but didn't answer. "You know I've read the report don't you?" I lied. "Tell me about the photos you took."

He spoke as soft as a child and I strained to hear him. "My daughter."

"How old was she?"

"Six years old." He teared up and held his hands out, palms up. "I know, man. I'm sick," he said looking up at me for the first time. "I'm taking treatment in here. I'm reading the Bible. I'm trying to help you. What do you want from me?"

I wondered how much damage he had done to his daughter and how long it would take her to fully recover, if ever. I also didn't think he would change. Feeling sorry for him was something I couldn't do. But the description he gave me matched my suspect and I believed his story about the guy in Denver.

—≺+≻—

The next evening, I drove to Denver in the darkness while lightning lit up thunderclouds high above the Rocky Mountains. Traffic on I-25 was heavy even at 10:00 p.m. When I got off the freeway, I grabbed a burger and fries before driving to the older part of town. *The Romantic* had XXX following the name on the sign above the building. It was located on East Colfax Avenue among liquor stores, dive bars and pawnshops. Hookers stood near the curb with short skirts that barely covered their panties. Their red lipstick looked as if a blind man had applied it and their six-inch heels appeared to hurt their feet. They smiled at the cars driving by and homeless men sat alone beside buildings drinking from containers concealed in paper sacks.

With a two-day growth of beard and way out of my jurisdiction, I tucked my Glock neatly under my jacket and parked on a dark side street. With my windows down, I watched *The Romantic* with binoculars. The air was still and moist and smelled of rain. Dry lightning flashed in the western sky.

A fat guy wearing a round brimmed straw hat sat next to the cash register smoking a cigar. His Hawaiian shirt was half unbuttoned and a thick gold chain hung around his plump neck. A skinny white guy that matched the description Millsap had given me assisted a customer looking at videos on the far wall.

I exited my car and walked past the front window. The customer came out onto the sidewalk carrying a brown paper bag tucked under his arm. He cut down the side alley next to the store and entered the small parking lot at the back. I followed him, but kept walking until he had driven away. I went back to the parking lot and found two cars parked near the back door. They matched the vehicles Freddie had described to me. I returned to my car and adjusted the mirror so I could see anyone leaving the alley. It was 11:30 pm before the owner pulled out of the alley heading my way. The skinny white guy, I assumed was Phillip, stayed to attend the store.

Lightning streaked across the northern sky in a spider-webbed pattern as the first raindrops hit my windshield. Thunder followed a few moments later. The smell of rain on blacktop filled my nostrils as a cool breeze blew raindrops into my car. I rolled up the window, got out and locked the doors. I zipped up my windbreaker and walked across the street. Phillip was reading a magazine at the counter and looked up at me when I entered the store. He had a diamond earring in his left ear. His face was thin and he had a long nose and soft blue eyes. There were no other customers. I went to the magazine rack and thumbed through a few, hoping he'd come talk to me, but he didn't. I approached the counter and asked him where the younger girls were located. Without looking up, he pointed with his thumb to the far wall on his right.

The first magazine I picked up contained photos of Asian girls with no pubic hair and small boobs holding dolls or sucking their thumbs. They appeared to be 16 to 17 years old. Many Asians look young for their age and I figured they were probably 18 or older and just trying to look younger. I took the magazine to the counter and paid Phillip for it. When he handed me my change, I slid a hundred dollar bill across the counter and put the change in my pocket. "I prefer white girls and a lot younger."

He pushed my money back towards me. "Sorry, that's as young as we have here buddy."

I left the hundred on the counter and added a fifty next to it. "I heard you might have something a little younger."

He frowned and looked behind me at the front door as if he expected the police to be busting in at any minute.

"You heard wrong. Try The Pigeon Store on the next block. Maybe they'll have what you're looking for."

"A friend told me I might find what I'm looking for here."

"He told you wrong," he said as he pushed the money closer towards me. Figuring he smelled a cop, I picked up my money, shoved the magazine under my arm and walked outside into the rain. After putting the magazine in my car, I walked around the block and entered the alley from the far end to get to the rear parking lot. A large hedge along the back of the lot hid the store from the houses behind it. There was a chain link fence behind the hedge separating the properties. I slid into a break in the shrubbery to conceal myself among the leaves, broken wine bottles, trash and discarded condoms. It smelled of rotting leaves, urine, and dog shit. I pulled the hood over my head and settled in for a long night. A steady rain filled potholes in the parking lot, reflecting light from the single bulb above the back door. Several cars came and left while my pants got soaked and my shoes filled with water.

At 2 a.m. a car drove in and parked behind the store next to Phillip's car. The person inside didn't get out. The person inside lit a cigarette and sat inside with the motor running. His cellphone lit the side of his face as he put it to his ear. He wasn't the suspect I was looking for. After ending his call, he turned the motor off, but stayed in his car smoking.

It was quiet except for the rain dripping off the overhead leaves, a barking dog and an occasional car passing on the street in front of the store. The light above the back door went off. Phillip came outside and locked the door behind him. He stood under the eaves for protection against the rain and lit a cigarette. The other man got out of his car, walked over to him and handed him some money. Phillip counted it and put it in his pocket. He hit the remote to open his trunk and stepped behind his car. The light from the trunk was enough for me to see what was happening. Phillip shuffled through several envelopes until he found what he was looking for. He handed one envelope to the guy and kept one for himself. The man got back in his car and drove away. I wrote down his license plate number.

Phillip got into his car, started the motor, turned on the overhead light and opened the envelope he had kept. I walked up beside his car. He pulled out several photos of young boys and older men having sex.

His eyes looked like silver dollars when I jerked his door open. He attempted to put the car in reverse, but I hit him in the temple, knocking him halfway across the console. I grabbed him by his hair and pulled him out onto the wet pavement. He cried like a little girl about police brutality as I picked him up and bent him over the hood of his car to cuff him. I called the local police station, gave them my location, and asked them to send a patrol car.

Two Denver police cruisers screeched to a stop a few minutes later. A big black patrol Sergeant named Leo Grubbs shook his head as he looked at the photos scattered on the front seat of Phillip's car. "Fucking pervert." He had the other officer transport my prisoner to the station and we waited for a vice detective to arrive at the scene.

Salvador Padilla arrived with a look of scorn on his face. He resembled the drunks drinking out of paper sacks more than a cop. He wasn't happy that I was working his jurisdiction without notifying him. "What's going on here?" he asked.

After explaining the situation, he calmed down and called to have Phillip's car towed to the station until he could get a search warrant for it. When we got to the police station, Salvador sat in on the interview with Phillip and me.

Phillip's real name was Leon Wilkins. He had done three years in the pen for selling child porn while on parole for exposing himself to a child. He was using a fake name because working at an adult store was a violation of his probation.

The side of Leon's face was red where I hit him. He shook as if he were freezing to death even though the interview room was on the warm side. His lower lip trembled.

I identified myself as a homicide detective and showed him the drawing of my suspect. "Who is this guy?"

He shook his head. "I don't know. I swear."

"Bullshit. You bought photos from him. He's killing little girls and you're buying his photos. We're talking about murder here, partner. What's his name?"

He looked at the drawing for a few moments. "It was a long time ago. He called himself Charlie, but people in this business don't usually use their real names and we don't ask."

"What did he sell you?"

"Photos of a girl having sex with a man."

"How old was the girl?"

"She looked to be about 14 or 15. You couldn't see the face of the guy she was with, but I think it was the same man that sold me the photos because he was black and so was the guy in the photos. I only bought from him once because the girl looked drugged or maybe . . ."

"Maybe what?"

Leon looked down at the table. His hands shook as if he had Parkinson's disease.

"Dead." He looked as pale as a body at a morgue. "The guy contacted me about six months later with more photos of another girl. I didn't buy them because they looked the same way. The guy freaked me out. I never saw him again and that was over a year ago."

"Was the girl white?"

"Yeah."

I showed him photos of the dead girls I was investigating. He pointed to one of them. "That's her. That's the girl in the photos I bought. And that's the same room they were in when the photos were taken. I don't see the girl in the second set of pictures he tried to sell me."

"What did you do with the photos you bought?"

"I burned them, man. I swear it."

I knew he was lying because he tried to sell them to Millsap. And he wouldn't get rid of photos he thought he could make money with.

After the interview, Salvador walked me to my car. "I'll send you a copy of my report after we search Wilkins' car and house. I'll check with our homicide guys to see if we can determine who the other girl was."

On the way home, my mood was as dark as the night. I felt frustrated and useless. Slamming my fist into the steering wheel, I knew I wasn't any closer to finding the suspect now than before I went to Denver. Leon hadn't picked out any of our other murder victims, but from what he had told me, I was sure there was another body we didn't know about.

CHAPTER EIGHTEEN

The morning air was wet and damp. Dark low clouds descended on the city and patches of fog clung to the ground in the lower areas. I woke feeling as gray as the sky with a restlessness clawing at my soul. Hoping we'd get a break on our killer soon, I wanted to get to work. I arrived at my office early, grabbed the keys to my unmarked car and drove to the YMCA located across the street from Acacia Park in downtown Colorado Springs. The fog had burned off and patches of sunlight shone through holes in the clouds. I parked on the east side of the building and entered the Y through the main entrance. The old man at the counter wore glasses as thick as coke bottles. I showed him the drawings of the serial killer. He squinted at them, holding them at arms length and then pulled them close to his face. "I don't recognize this guy but I'll give the drawings to my supervisor if you want."

I left some of my business cards and several copies of the drawings. Before I got to my car, I heard a woman yell. "Sir, you dropped something."

I turned to see who was talking to me. She was with her young daughter who was looking at one of the pictures I had dropped. I went back to get it. The girl had curly red hair and was about thirteen years old. She asked, "Did you draw this?"

"No, I'm a police detective. We hire people to do those."

The girl's mother smiled and said, "I'm Judy Olsen. This is my daughter, Amber."

I offered her my hand, "Storm Harrison."

As Mrs. Olsen shook my hand, her daughter asked, "Why did they draw Ivan?"

I knelt down beside her, so not to be intimidating. "Ivan? You know this man?"

"Yes, he works here."

"Do you know his last name?"

"No, but he's always asking me about my paintings. He's kinda weird and freaks me out."

"What does he do here?"

"He cleans the floors and bathrooms." She handed me the sketch and I showed her the other. "He looks more like this bald man than the one you dropped" she said pointing to another drawing, "but he has a mustache."

"When was the last time you saw him?"

"Just a few minutes ago. He was watching you from the hallway when you were at the counter."

"Can you describe him for me?"

"He's black but has light skin. He's bigger than you."

"What's he wearing?"

"Jeans and a blue t-shirt, I think. And a ball cap."

I handed Judy Olsen my business card. "Take Amber home right away and call me tomorrow."

I notified dispatch by radio that the murder suspect we'd been searching for was inside the YMCA on Nevada Avenue. I gave her his description. She advised all available officers to respond.

Fowler came over the radio. "Storm, hold your position until backup arrives."

"The suspect has already spotted me and could be leaving the building."

"Wait for backup before going in," Fowler barked. "No heroics, you hear me?"

I drew my weapon and held it down to my side and walked towards the Y. Several people came out as I approached. I waived my badge at them and ordered them leave the area. I peeked inside and saw a man matching Ivan's description at the far end of the hallway walking away from me. He looked back over his shoulder as he pushed open the exit door and turned north. I advised dispatch by radio that the suspect was exiting the building on the west end.

I entered the building and ran down the hall. Fowler came over the radio and told me to hold my position. I was halfway down the hallway by the time I heard him. I exited the west doors and looked north but couldn't see the suspect. I ran to an abandoned gas station next door but he wasn't there. After scanning the area, I ran across the street into Acacia Park.

Several patrol officers arrived and set up a perimeter around the building. I asked an old man sitting on a park bench if he had seen a black guy run by. He pointed towards the center of the park. "He ran that way towards those bathrooms."

I relayed the information to dispatch and went to check the bathrooms. They were empty. Several patrol officers helped me search the park but we couldn't locate Ivan. Other officers circled the area looking for him. I ran across the street to the businesses located along the west side of park. I did a quick check of each store until I came to a drug store. I heard some type of alarm going off inside. The employees and customers weren't paying much attention to it. I ran inside to an emergency exit on the side of the store just as an employee was shutting the door. The alarm ceased.

"Did someone just go out that door?" I asked.

"Yeah, people don't pay much attention to signs anymore."

I ran outside to the sound of the alarm following me onto a side street.

"Hey, can't you read?" the employee yelled as he closed the door behind me. I looked both ways but couldn't see Ivan. I ran to the alley behind the stores but still couldn't find him. It appeared I had lost my old nemesis again.

We searched for another five minutes before Sergeant Pomush advised us by radio that the YMCA's director said Ivan's last name was Collins and that he lived above one of the small restaurants on Tejon Street a few blocks south of our location. Several task force detectives arrived on scene. Pomush told them by radio to meet us at Ivan's apartment while the patrol officers searched the area around the park. He picked me up on the west side of the park and we drove to Ivan's apartment, hoping to beat him there.

Two detectives covered the back alley while the rest of us entered the building. We started up a narrow dark stairway with guns drawn. The old wooden steps creaked with every step. I took them two at a time, trying to be as quiet as possible. I located Ivan's apartment but the door was locked. I yelled for him to come out but there was no answer. Charlie Blakely contacted the apartment manager who came and unlocked the door. We made entry with guns drawn but the apartment was empty. It smelled musty and stagnant. The faded wallpaper appeared as if it had been around since the late 1800's. The bedframe supporting the unmade bed looked as if was from the twenties. The rear bedroom window was gray from dust and grime. A fire escape led down into the alley from the window. Looking down, I realized Ivan's room overlooked the area where I encountered him the night he killed Julia

Martin. He probably used the fire escape to avoid capture that night, and may have been watching us searching for him from this very window.

"Storm, come into the bathroom," Pomush said. Newspaper clippings about the girls Ivan had murdered were taped to his mirror. Two more were pinned to the wall. They were old and faded and were about Julia's killing. One had a photo of her and the other had a picture of me.

All these years while looking at the drawing of Ivan on my office wall, he had been looking at my photo in his bathroom. Pomush told the other detectives to secure the apartment while he got a search warrant. He put his hand on my shoulder. "Now we know who he is, his time is running out. Go see if you can find that bastard."

When I got outside, Connie Mason stood on the sidewalk in front of building where Ivan lived. She approached me as the cameras rolled. "Detective Harrison, can you tell us anything about the murder suspect?"

I surprised myself, and her, by looking straight into the camera and saying, "Ivan Collins, I know who you are and I'm coming for you. You won't get a second chance this time!" Connie followed me down the sidewalk asking more questions but I had already tuned her out.

Charlie drove me back to the YMCA to get my car. I figured Ivan was on foot, desperate and dangerous. I needed to find out as much about him as possible before he had time to leave the area. I located a white Toyota truck registered to him parked in the Y's parking lot. Charlie had it towed to our impound lot.

Other detectives had interviewed the manager of the YMCA and found out Ivan was a part time custodial employee. He reportedly worked fulltime as a dental assistant but the manager didn't know which dental office.

A criminal history check showed he had no prior convictions or warrants. It had been a productive, yet frustrating day. I decided to spend the rest of the day helping with the search warrants for Ivan's truck and apartment to see what we could come up with.

When I got to my office, there was a message from Fowler saying he wanted to see me as soon as I got in. I walked into his office. "Close the door." Doing as he asked, I turned to him.

"What the hell were you thinking out there?"

I wasn't sure what he was asking.

Fowler raised his voice. "Well, Harrison, are you going to answer me or not?"

"What are you talking about, Lieutenant? I was doing my job, got lucky and located our suspect."

"I ordered you to wait for other officers before entering the Y."

"I know, and I waited until I saw him going out the other side of the building. Then I went after him."

"I ordered you to stay put when you advised us he was going out the door."

"Yes, but I was already half-way down the hall before I heard you say that. What did you want me to do, turn around and go the other way?"

"What I expect is for you to obey orders at all times."

"You weren't in the best position to be giving orders while sitting in your office. I watched the events unfold and did what I should have done. You're saying I should have stood there and watched the suspect walk away?"

"Are you saying I'm stupid?"

"No, I'm saying things were unfolding too fast for you to understand what was going on. You should let the officers on the street think for themselves."

"Harrison, when I give an order, I expect it to be followed. Is that clear?"

"Perfectly."

Fowler's face turned red. He stood up and faced me. "And what should you have done out there today?" he asked.

"I should have disobeyed you the first time and gone in immediately. I would have caught the son-of-a bitch and we wouldn't be having this conversation."

"You're insubordinate, Harrison."

"That's bullshit and you know it."

Fowler stood up, veins popping in his neck. "You're suspended until further notice, Harrison."

I removed the badge and gun from my belt and tossed them on the table. "Fine, you can keep these if you want it. But you know I'm right."

I walked out and heard Fowler yell, "Get back in here!" I ignored him and kept going. My phone rang before I got out of the building. The caller ID showed it was Fowler. I didn't answer and switched it to vibrate.

CHAPTER NINETEEN

Being temporarily out of a job took me out of my comfort zone. It was up to me to make sure it wasn't permanent. I didn't think they would fire me for not following orders, but I needed time to think and clear my head. Donning gym shorts, tennis shoes, and faded Denver University t-shirt, I drove to the "Garden of the Gods." The sky was clear, the air cool and the sun bright. A busload of retirees exited a bus at the Visitors Center when I arrived. I ran to the large red rock formations and stopped on the Susan G. Bretag trail on the east side. Several large homes sat on a hill to the east of the park.

After fifty push-ups, stomach crunches and leg lifts, the scar on my shoulder turned pink in color as it often did when I worked out. A woman in a red bikini stood near the rear fence of one of the houses on the hill looking in my direction. I wasn't sure if she was watching me or just taking in the million-dollar view. Heading south, I ran back to the visitor's center passing hikers and horses on the way. Heavy breathing and clothes soaked with sweat greeted my arrival. I noted that one tour bus had departed and another pulled in to take its place.

I drove to the house on the hill where I had seen the woman in the swimsuit. There were two large homes overlooking the park at this location. The one at the north end had a For Sale sign.

I called Katy but she didn't answer so I left her a message. I went home to take a shower and change clothes before driving to The Oak Barrel. Pete, the bartender, brought me a beer at the bar. Before I finished it, he brought me another. When I shot him a questioning look, he said, "Courtesy of the guy on the patio in the gray suit."

Searching the mirror behind the bar, I located Charles Woods sitting with an older man with silver hair wearing a blue suit. Woods held up his drink and nodded at me. I recognized the silver-headed man as the guy Katy was with the first time I saw her in here.

I drank the free beer and ordered another one. When Pete sat it down, he said, "All of your drinks are on the man in the gray suit."

My phone vibrated in my pocket when Katy called. "Hi, Katy."

"Hi, honey. Sorry I missed your call earlier."

Katy had never used a term of endearment when talking to me before and I liked it.

"Are you ready to call it a day?" I asked.

"No, I've got a client meeting in half an hour. Where are you? It sounds noisy."

"I'm at The Oak Barrel drinking Charles Woods' beer."

"You're drinking with Chas?"

"No, he's sitting out on the outside patio, but he's buying my drinks."

Katy paused for a moment. "It's kind of early to be drinking isn't it?"

"I thought I'd get an early start."

"What's wrong, Storm? And don't lie to me!"

I explained my day, including getting suspended.

"My meeting is only going to last about thirty minutes," she said. "Stay there and I'll come as soon as I can."

"Take your time. I've got nowhere to be." We disconnected and I ordered another beer on Chas, wondering what the hell he wanted.

While peeling the label off my bottle, someone sat next to me. "Having a bad day?"

"Hi, Doc." I said without looking up. "Can I buy you a drink?"

"Grey Goose martini if you must."

I ordered the martini and tried to pay. Pete reminded me that all my drinks were free.

Doc asked, "Who's buying the drinks?"

"Charles Woods. Katy's old boyfriend."

"Oh, where is he?"

"On the patio, the man in the gray suit sitting with the old guy."

Doc waited for his drink, took a sip, and searched the mirror behind the bar. "Ralph Bremer."

"Who's Ralph Bremer?" I asked.

"The guy sitting with Woods. He's a high profile defense attorney. He owns a huge law firm in Denver with branch offices in a dozen different cities. Mega bucks and smart as they come."

"Bremer was with Katy the first time I met her in here. Do you know Woods?"

"Nope, just heard his name from Katy." Doc paused studying my face "So what's bothering you today?"

"That obvious huh?"

As I retold my story, Doc drank his martini, silently listening to me. When I finished, he said, "Be respectful to your bosses, Storm, but hold your ground. You don't know what Jerry knew or didn't know when he gave you that order. It's probably just a misunderstanding on both your parts."

"Screw him. He can't sit in his office and tell me what the best course of action is on the street when he's not there. Can you imagine how a battle would turn out if some prick in a cushy office called the shots out in the field?"

"It happens more than you think. I know. I've been there. The best course of action for you is to do what you believe is right at the time. I know it upsets you but don't take it personally. Your boss will see things differently when he gets it all sorted out. If his pride gets in his way, his bosses will tactfully guide him back to reality."

"Maybe, but I don't need a pencil pusher telling me when to make an arrest. I bet he hasn't made one in years."

"Probably not, but that's not his job anymore. Jerry is a good man."

"Yeah, I know." I said.

"Thanks for the drink," Doc said as he stood up, " but I've got to run. I've got a date."

"Where are you going? To play bingo?"

Doc smiled, "Yeah, right. Later, Storm."

He strolled over to a tall good-looking blonde who had just walked in. He kissed her on the cheek, put his arm around her waist and walked her out. When they got to the door, Doc turned toward me and winked.

After he left, Charles Woods came over and sat on the stool Doc had vacated. "Hello, Detective Harrison. Remember me?"

" Yeah, thanks for the drinks."

Charles smiled. "I hear you got your murder suspect identified today."

"He's not in custody yet."

"You're celebrating a little early aren't you?"

"Nope, I'm on vacation. How's Ralph Bremer?"

Charles looked surprised that I knew who he had been sitting with. "Good, just making the rounds."

Charles got up to leave. "I have to run. I'll see you in court someday."

Katy walked in as Charles was on his way out. They nodded to each other in passing.

"Exchanging notes?" She asked as she took his seat.

"No, photos."

She frowned and wrinkled her nose. "Not funny. What did he want?"

"Who knows?"

"Did he ask about me?"

"No."

Katy got a puzzled look on her face and glanced back towards the exit. "He never does anything that's not self-serving. Be careful around him."

"Maybe he still has the hots for you."

Katy half smiled, "I doubt it," she said as she took my hand in hers and kissed my cheek.

"Then he's dumber than he looks," I said. "Let's get out of here."

"Not before you buy me a drink. And, I'm driving."

"No problem. Sir Charles is still buying."

"Good, he owes me." Katy ordered a $160.00 bottle of Dom Perignon. "I hope he faints when he sees his bill."

I wondered what she had done for him that he owed her, but I wasn't going to ask. "Doc was here earlier and left with a date. Do you know who he's seeing?"

"No and he won't tell. Some mystery woman I guess."

"I didn't get a real good look at her but she's very attractive."

"Good for him. I hope he gets married. He'll need someone in his old age."

We had a couple of glasses of champagne and left the bar. Katy drove and we went to her house. We took a bath together and I almost forgot about being suspended. I wondered what tomorrow would bring and couldn't get Ivan Collins off my mind.

Jim Pomush's phone call woke me up from a restless sleep. "Hey, what's up?" I said rubbing the sleep from my eyes.

"You're what's up, dummy. How'd you manage to get yourself suspended?"

"Hell if I know. Fowler's just pissed."

"What'd he expect you to do that you didn't do?"

"I have no idea."

"Damned if you do and damned if you don't," Pomush said. "I have a meeting with him in ten minutes. I'll try to run interference for you, but as you said, he's pissed."

"The heck with him. I'd do the same thing again. You can tell him that."

"I don't think so."

Having no interest in Jim's meeting with Fowler, I changed the subject. "What did you find out about Ivan?"

"We located the dentist office where he worked. It's near Ft. Carson. One of his victims was a patient there and two others had visited the YMCA where he worked. He had access to personal information at the dentist office and could have easily picked the cheap lock on the files at the Y."

"Sick bastard."

"Yeah. He doesn't seem to have any real friends or relatives that we can find, but get this. He was a straight A student in high school and studies martial arts. It seems his taekwondo instructors didn't like him either. We found a computer in his apartment with a lot of child porn and he collects newspaper articles mentioning you."

"I wonder what his fascination with me is all about," I said.

"You were the only person who could identify him. By the way, Ivan has two pistols and a rifle registered to him. We found the rifle in his apartment and a pistol in his truck. There's one pistol missing. It's a Smith and Wesson .45 semi-auto. I got to run, Storm. I'll call you later."

"Jim, wait. I want you to check my office phone messages. We need to interview Amber Olsen, the little girl who identified Ivan's photo. We have to get a written statement from her. Her mom, Judy Olsen, was supposed to call me."

"Will do. Keep your cell phone on."

"One more thing. What's the name of the martial arts studio Ivan uses?"

"Kim's Taekwondo on Academy Boulevard." The phone went dead.

Katy came in, kissed me good-bye and left for work. I poured myself a cup of coffee and read the newspaper. Ivan's name and driver's license photo was posted on the front page along with a new drawing. I hoped someone would hurry up and call in the information we needed to locate the prick.

I tried to relax but couldn't. My mind told me to lay low and let the Task Force handle it, but my soul told me to do something before someone else was murdered. Although I was officially suspended, my mind was working overtime. I've never been the kind of person to slack my responsibilities or let someone else carry my workload. Being a spectator to my job didn't sit well with me. I figured a visit to Kim's Taekwondo might shed some light into Ivan's character.

I must have been watching too much TV because Kim wasn't what I had expected. Instead of an old man with long gray hair and beard wearing an orange robe, Kim was young and clean-shaven with a crew cut. He wore camouflage pants and a U. S. Army t-shirt. Turned out he was an army sergeant who instructed hand-to-hand combat at Fort Carson. He ran the martial arts business on the side with his brother.

Kim described Ivan as a loner who never spoke unless spoken to. He never asked questions and was unpopular at the school because he was a dirty fighter. Nobody wanted to spar with him. However, Kim claimed he was well trained, quick, strong, and evidently had a lot of training before joining his club.

"Be very careful around Ivan," Kim said. "I think he's is a very dangerous man. He has the cold black eyes of the devil."

I'd hoped I had spent more time at a gun range than Ivan had at martial art schools. And I wondered how much time he'd spent at a gun range?

CHAPTER TWENTY

Jim Pomush walked into Fowler's office. "Have a seat, Jim. We need to figure out what to do with Storm." When Pomush didn't respond, Fowler asked, "Well, are you going to help me or not?"

"What do you want to do with him?"

"I'm not sure. He doesn't take orders, he's insubordinate and walked out on me yesterday."

Pomush paused for a moment choosing his words carefully. "I think you may be overreacting, Jerry. Storm is a good detective and he's identified Ivan for us."

"He's a loose cannon and can't take orders. I think he is a liability to himself and the department."

Pomush shook his head. "I'm putting him in for a commendation for catching that armed robber and you're ready to fire him."

"I might not have a choice. I can't have my detectives doing whatever they want and disobeying orders."

"They'll have a hearing, you know."

"So what? That's normal procedure," Fowler tapped his pencil on the table.

"Yes, and when they do, they'll take a close look at the order you gave."

"You don't think I should have told him to stay where he was, do you? Fowler asked. "There were children in the Y that could've gotten hurt."

"I'm not making judgment here. I'm sure Storm had the same concerns you did. But, he was in a much better position to judge whether he should go in or not. He could see inside and assess the situation better than you could."

Fowler threw up his hands. "Yes, and it would be my ass if some innocent child got hurt.

"That might be true, Lieutenant. But what do you think will happen when Ivan starts killing again?"

Jerry rubbed his chin, got up and walked to the window and stared out over the city. "You don't think the board would back me if I fire him, do you?"

"I'm not a mind reader, Jerry. But it wouldn't look good for you if the board didn't back you. And, even if they did, what do you think the press will do to us if you fire Storm and more bodies start piling up. They'll put the blame right in your lap and Storm will look like a hero. I'd think twice about this if I were in your shoes."

Fowler glanced back over his shoulder. "You're not just looking out for your old buddy are you, Jim?"

"Yes, I am, Jerry. Both of them."

Fowler turned back to the window. Pomush stood up to leave, "Anything else, boss?"

"Jim, I'm concerned about Storm. I believe he'll kill Ivan when he finds him."

Pomush thought about that for a moment. "I wouldn't like that."

"Neither would I. You'd be investigating Ivan's death and Storm could end up in jail. That's why I ordered him to stay put until other officers got there." Fowler looked down at the floor. "If I hadn't given that order, Ivan could be dead or in jail by now. I'm not sure I did the right thing."

Fowler returned to his desk and sat down. "I don't want to fire Storm. But I want him kept on suspension until he learns to take orders." He picked up Storm's badge and threw it to Pomush. "Find him and tell him he can have this back when he gets his head out of his ass. Keep an eye on him. I want you to know where he is at all times. Is that clear?"

"Clear as a bell, boss." Pomush picked up the badge and started to leave. He stopped at the door, and turned. "Thanks for not firing him, Jerry. I need Storm. We're short-handed as it is."

"We need to catch Ivan Collins soon," Fowler replied, "We can't afford any more bodies."

⥤⥢

"Storm, where are you?" Pomush asked when Storm answered his call.

"On my way home. Why?"

"Well go there and stay there. You aren't being fired but you're still suspended. No more police work until I get you reinstated. Is that clear."

"All right. But keep me posted, will you?"

"I will as long as you keep your nose clean. If Fowler finds out you're still working the case, he'll fire you. I'll do what I can to get you back in the office. Until then, stay home."

"All right, I'll be a good boy. What's your plan?"

Pomush's plan was to track down Ivan's family and gather information that might help him. The problem was, he didn't know who Ivan's relatives were.

Before we hung up, I asked, "Did Judy Olsen call?"

"No. We'll get her daughter's statement later."

I wanted to check on Amber and see if she had any information that might help locate Ivan. After talking to Pomush, we hung up. I drove to the Y and got the Olsen's' address and phone number. It was dark by the time I got to their townhouse. I knocked on the door but no one answered. I heard music inside so I called the phone number the Y had given me. Amber answered, "Hello."

"Hi, Amber. This is Detective Harrison. You picked up my drawing at the Y and identified Ivan."

There was a pause. "Oh, yes. I remember you."

"I just knocked on your door and no one responded. Is your mother home?"

"No. She's at work."

"Is your father there?"

"He doesn't live here."

I didn't like what I was hearing. Amber fit the profile of Ivan's other victims. "Amber, Ivan is the guy that's been killing those young girls."

"I know. We've been watching the news and saw you on TV. That's why I wouldn't answer the door. Have you caught him yet?"

"No, but I'm still outside. Can I come in and talk to you? I want to ask you a few more questions about him."

"All right, I'll open the door."

The apartment was clean but sparsely furnished. A folded American flag in a black triangle shadow box sat on the fireplace mantle below a large photo of an American soldier holding an M-16 rifle. He looked to be about twenty years old. The photo appeared to have been taken somewhere in the Middle East. Two smaller photos were attached to the bottom corners of the frame. One was of a wedding. The other was the same soldier holding an infant.

"Your father?" I asked.

"Yes. He was killed in Iraq."

"I'm sorry."

She stepped closer to look at the photos. "I don't remember him. I was six months old when he died."

"And your mother never remarried?"

"No," she said. "They were high school sweethearts."

"Are your grandparents still alive?"

"Yes. They live in Utah. That's where my parents grew up."

Amber was a lovely and bright young lady. "Can you tell me anything else about Ivan?"

She took a deep breath. "He was always asking me questions about my drawings and personal questions, like where I went to school. I've seen him talking to other girls too, but he only spoke to us when no grown-ups were around. He spent a lot of time cleaning the pool area even when it wasn't dirty. I always thought he was a pervert and avoided him."

I checked the doors and windows of her townhouse to make sure they were locked. I advised Amber to have her mother put a broom handle in the sliding glass door track, get a peep hole for the front door and to buy extra locks for the windows. I told her to not to answer the door unless she was sure she knew who was there and if she receives any strange phone calls, to notify the police right away. I gave her my card and wrote my personal cell phone number on the back and told her to call me if she needed anything or thought of anything else I should know. "Another detective will come by when your mother is home and get a written statement from you. He will call first and make an appointment. Don't tell him I was already here, all right?"

"Okay, I won't. But..."

"But what?" I asked.

"I'm scared."

"Would you like me to stay here until your mom gets home?"

Amber looked at the clock. "No. She works all night. She won't be home until the morning. I'll be all right tonight."

I hugged her. "If you hear anything at all that doesn't sound right, dial 911 right away. I think you and your mom should go live with you grandparents until we catch Ivan."

"I don't think she can afford to be off work very long."

"I hope it won't take us too long to catch Ivan. Then you could come home. Have your mom call me tomorrow."

"I'll talk to her about going," she said. "Thanks for checking on me."

I didn't like leaving Amber alone but I couldn't stay there all night. I was already walking on thin ice. If Pomush found out I was there, I'd be in deep shit.

After leaving Amber's apartment, I called Katy and I told her I had to go by my office and home first and I'd meet her at her place afterwards. I stopped at work and listened to my voice mails. When I got out to the parking lot, I realized I had left my car keys in the office. After retrieving my keys, I stopped by my house to grab some clean clothes, and then headed to Katy's house. My mind was racing. I kept wondering where the hell Ivan was hiding while trying to figure out the best way to catch him without getting fired or killed.

CHAPTER TWENTY-ONE

I had a hard time sleeping and was awake by 5:00 a.m. I made a pot of coffee and read the newspaper. There was a story about a homicide in Manitou Springs where a man was stabbed through the heart. Two cups of coffee later Pomush called. "Storm, you're off suspension. Get your ass to work."

"How did you manage that?"

"It's a long story and I don't have time to explain it right now. Your badge is on your desk. Fowler will tell you where I need you."

"Wait, Jim, who was murder...?" He hung up on me.

Pikes Peak disappeared behind a blanket of thick gray clouds as I drove to work. Darkness slid down the mountain like a veil being lowered over a pristine painting of the Rocky Mountains. It was misting by the time I arrived at the station. The cold morning air didn't chill me as much as seeing that the crime scene van and all the homicide detective cars were missing. Something really bad must have occurred overnight.

Fowler talking on the phone when I arrived at his office. He didn't look happy to see me. I entered his office as soon as he hung up.

"What's going on, boss?"

Fowler turned his chair to face me. "We had three homicides last night. I need you to go across the street to the nursing home and assist them. One of their residents and a nurse were murdered."

"All right. Who's over there?"

"Blain and Charlie." Fowler collected a stack of reports. "I've got a briefing with the chief in five minutes. Get across the street and make yourself useful."

Both Maggie's van and the press had gone by the time I got there. Room 308 had already been processed and the bodies removed before I walked in. The bed sheets were missing and a large bloodstain covered the mattress. Another larger bloodstain covered the carpet next to the bed. Detectives Blain Warner and Charlie Blakely were going over their notes and didn't notice when I walked in. Warner and I had joined homicide about the same time and he was a competent detective. They looked like they had been up all night.

"Good morning, Storm," Blain said when he saw me. "Are you ready to go to work?"

Staring at the bloodstains, I answered, "Yeah. How long have you guys been here?"

"Pomush called us around 8:30 last night. An employee discovered the bodies around 8:00 while looking for a missing nurse who never clocked out. We're about finished here."

I studied the crime scene. "Give me a quick brief and I'll get to work."

Charlie began. "The first victim was an 86 year-old man from India. He's a U.S. citizen and has lived in Colorado Springs most of his life. He was a retired pharmacist, never married, and lived alone until he had a stroke about three months ago. He was almost completely paralyzed on his right side and couldn't speak. Someone stabbed him through the heart with a large knife."

I walked around the bed to get a better look at the floor. "I assume the old man was the one in the bed."

"Yeah. The woman was on the floor next to the bed with her throat cut. She was a 64 year-old retired nurse who volunteered part time to give her something to do. Married, six grown kids and twelve grandkids."

"Suspects or motives?" I asked.

"None, but we have a lead we need you to follow up on," Blain said. "A get-well card was found on the man's nightstand from someone claiming to be his nephew. There was no postage, so it was hand delivered."

"Do we have contact information for this nephew?"

Blain shook his head. "No. The old man didn't have any relatives in the states according to the nursing home. He had a brother in India who has two daughters and he didn't have any nephews according to his paperwork. We have his brother's phone number in India and the old man's address here in town."

"What kind of knife was used?" I asked as I took out my notepad and a pen.

"From the look of the wound, I'm assuming a hunting knife, the kind with a serrated edge on the top. We won't know for sure until the autopsy."

I walked to the window and opened the curtains as Charlie and Blain packed up to leave. I could see into the police parking garage and the exit onto Weber Street. "What time were they killed?" I asked.

Charlie stopped at the door and turned to face me. "The coroner thinks between 1800 and 1900 hours."

"Damn! I didn't leave the office last night until after 7 p.m. The killer was here when I was going home. Do you know what time the other homicide happen?"

"We're not sure," Blain said. "Maggie got the call this morning when she was finishing up here. It was a young girl with her throat slit."

"Was she raped?"

Blain and Charlie shared a questioning glance. "Sorry, we don't know. We didn't hear any of the details. You'll have to ask Maggie or Pomush," Blain said.

I had a bad feeling about these murders but I couldn't put my finger on it. I stared out the window knowing the killer could have been watching me leave work last night. Ivan had used a six-inch hunting knife to kill Julia and I wondered if that was the same knife that killed these people and the girl. The hairs on the back of my neck stood up just thinking about it.

Blain turned on his way out. "Storm, Maggie has the card the nephew left. It said, 'Nice visiting with you, Uncle.' It was signed, Kishorne." He spelled it for me and I wrote it down.

"What kind of name is that?"

"It's an Indian name," Charlie answered from out in the hall-way. "The old man's name was Sivakumar. We're headed back to the office. You coming?"

Looking around the room, I couldn't think of anything else I needed to do here. I walked across the street into the parking ga-rage where I had parked my car last night. Looking back, I could see right into the room where the murders had occurred.

I searched for Maggie but she was still out. I went to my office and fired up my computer to look up names of men from India. There were hundreds of them and they all had a meaning. It took me a while to find the name Kishorne. The name means young. I wondered if it meant, I like them young.

I didn't believe three people killed with a knife in the same night could be a coincidence. Remembering the killing in Manitou Springs having the same MO as the old man, I made a call to John French, an old friend in homicide.

"John, this is Storm Harrison."

"Hey, Storm. What's up?"

"I heard you guys had a homicide stabbing the other day. Have you arrested a suspect yet?"

"Nope. We don't have a suspect or a motive."

"What type of knife was used?"

"A hunting knife."

I put my feet up on my desk. "Six inch blade with a serrated edge?"

"Yeah. The victim's name was Bernie Hayden. He was stabbed through the heart. The suspect dumped his body in the bathtub and poured ice on him. We think the perp was in the victim's apartment for about a week. Do you have a suspect for me?"

"Maybe. Your suspect may have killed three more people in Colorado Springs last night. An old man was stabbed through the heart and an old woman and young girl had their throats cut. The weapon used on the old man was a six-inch hunting knife with a serrated edge."

"Sounds like it could be our guy."

I looked at my notes. "Was your victim from India by chance?" I asked.

"No. But it's funny you asked."

"Why's that?"

"Our victim wore the type of clothes men from India wear," John said. "It's a fad for the new age hippies here in Manitou Springs. If you drive around town, you'll see half a dozen young people dressed like that, turban and all. The victim's friends claimed he dressed that way all the time. Why'd you ask?"

"The old man who was murdered was from India. A card was found at the scene from someone claiming to be his nephew."

"And?"

"He didn't have a nephew," I said. I took a sip of my coffee. "Do you have any DNA from your crime scene?"

"Yeah, but we don't have the results back yet. We don't have a lab to process DNA and have to send it to Denver."

Staring at the drawings on my wall, I said, "I think your killer could be Ivan Collins, the guy we're searching for. I think he's the guy that's been murdering all these young girls."

"Why do you think it's him?" John asked.

"Just a hunch. I'm almost positive he killed the young girl last night, but we haven't matched him to the other two homicides yet. Call me when you get your DNA results. Ivan's DNA is in the computer."

"Will do. Thanks for the heads up."

John and I agreed to exchange reports and keep each other informed if we located any suspects. I hung up and called Mr. Sivakumar's brother in India. I think he was sleeping when I called. He hadn't been informed that his brother had been murdered and confirmed his brother didn't have any relatives in America and no nephews. He didn't know anyone named Kishorne. He gave me the address of his brother's house.

I drew up a search warrant for Sivakumar's home but the search came up empty as far as motives, suspects or leads. I found the old man's will. Everything he owned went to his brother in India. There wasn't much to leave. I couldn't find any reason why anyone would want to harm the old man. His phone directory didn't reveal much either. Everyone I called claimed they hadn't seen him since he'd retired. There had to be a motive, but so far I couldn't find one. Unless the killer just wanted to be in that room so he could watch the police station parking lot. The question was, who was he watching and why? If Ivan was in that room, he could have been watching me.

By the time I got back to the station, the rest of the task force and Maggie were long gone. Katy called to remind me we had a dinner date. We met at a small Italian restaurant and avoided talking about work. But I couldn't stop thinking about the three murders. I wanted to know the dead girl's name and the details of her death. I also wanted to know if her murder was connected to the other two slayings.

To say I wasn't very good company would be an understatement. After dinner, we decided to go to my house for the night. It was past 10:00 p.m. when we got there. Everything seemed normal when we walked in. I started to pour glasses of wine while Katy went to the bathroom. I heard a blood-curdling scream, drew my weapon, and ran into the hallway. Katy was backing into the hall with her hands over her mouth, staring into the bathroom.

I pushed her out of the way and entered the bathroom. No one was inside, but a note written in blood on my mirror read: "I know who you are Det. Harrison and I'm coming for you." A small bloody finger lay in the sink. I told Katy to dial 911 and to stay right behind me. We walked backwards into the family room so I could cover the hallway and both doors. We waited for the police officers to arrive before we searched the house for Ivan.

He wasn't there but the back sliding glass door had been pried open. The officers searched the yard and neighborhood but came up empty.

I now knew what the killer was doing in the nursing home across the street from the police station. He had been watching me. The hunter had now become the hunted and he was mocking me. I didn't mind that he was coming for me, but I was very concerned for Katy's safety.

I asked the officers to secure my house after Maggie processed it and to have her call me when she arrived. We drove to Katy's house to spend the night. I made damn sure we weren't followed on the way there. I called and had the beat officers meet us at Katy's house. We checked to make sure it was secure before entering.

My phone rang shortly after we got there and I answered it on the speaker. "Storm."

"It's Maggie. I was told to call you."

"Was the girl that was killed last night missing a finger?"

"Yes."

"What was her name?"

There was a long pause. "Maggie, you there?"

"Storm, I hate to be the one to tell you this, but it was Amber Olsen. I'm so sorry."

I slumped to my knees and dropped the phone. "Oh please, God, no!" I pleaded.

"Storm, what is it?" asked Katy.

I couldn't talk. Tears filled my eyes, my head started spinning and I thought I was going to throw up. Katy placed her hand on my shoulder. "Storm, talk to me."

When I didn't answer, she picked up the phone. "Maggie, this is Katy. What's going on?"

"I'm sorry, Katy. The little girl that was murdered last night was the girl that identified Ivan Collins for Storm."

"Oh my God. Storm was at her house last night."

"Ivan must have killed her sometime after he left."

When Katy hung up, she dropped to her knees and held me. I shook, not from fear, but from rage. "I'll kill that son-of-a-bitch if it's the last thing I ever do. I swear it!"

CHAPTER TWENTY-TWO

I couldn't get Amber out my mind and didn't get much sleep. Any little sound disturbed me. I kept waking up wondering if Ivan knew about Katy or where she lived. I wanted to hurry up and get to work and was up and dressed by the time she woke up. Knowing she had a good burglary alarm system was comforting but I still didn't want her to be alone.

As Katy put on her makeup, I said, "I think you should stay with Doc Martin until we catch Ivan."

She looked at me like I was out of my mind. "Oh, no you don't!" She whirled to face me. "I'm not running. I want to be with you."

"Katy, Ivan is a psychopath and he won't stop until he's been killed or captured."

"I'm not afraid of Ivan or anyone else."

"Well, you should be." But I could see there was no use arguing with her. "Do you have a gun?"

She walked over to the bed and pulled a .32 pistol from under her pillow. I took it from her. It was a loaded semi-auto. "Has this thing been there the whole time?"

"I never sleep without it."

"You do at my house."

"Yes, but you have your gun at your house."

"I'm going to buy you a real gun," I said while examining the weapon. "A .32 caliber is too small."

"It worked fine the last time," she said.

It occurred to me that this was the weapon she used to kill the man who attempted to rape her. "It's a good weapon but I'm going to get you something with a lot more knock down power. I couldn't stand to lose you."

"Suit yourself, but you're stuck with me and don't forget it."

I handed the pistol to Katy and she put it back under her pillow. She showered and got dressed. After securing her house and setting the alarm, she drove me back to my house so I could get my car. A beat officer was sitting in my driveway when we arrived.

"Morning, Storm."

"Morning. Anything new?" I asked as I looked around.

"Nope. Been real quiet around here. None of your neighbors heard or saw anything last night."

I followed Katy to her office and then drove to work, making sure no one followed us. The task force had convened a meeting when I arrived. Conversation ceased when I entered the room. I looked at Pomush. "What's going on?"

"Have a seat, Storm," Pomush said. "We're discussing the murders."

Once I was seated, Jim continued. "As you know, Ivan Collins killed another girl last night."

No shit, Sherlock. "Yeah I know. He left her finger in my sink."

"The MO in this killing isn't the same." Pomush said. "He pried her window open to gain entry, but he didn't rape, strangle, or sodomize her. He just slit her throat and cut off her finger."

Charlie asked, "Why in the hell would he do that?"

Ted Wohler spoke up. "To make a statement in blood."

Charlie looked confused. "What kind of statement?" he asked.

I already knew what was coming next.

"He killed her because she identified him and he wanted her finger to leave Storm the message at her apartment."

This was news to me. "What did it say?"

Ted looked to Jim, who hesitated and scanned the other detectives in the room. None of them would make eye contact with me. I raised my voice. "Damn it, what did the message say?"

Pomush took a deep breath. "It read, 'Just like old times Det. Harrison.' He used her finger to write the note and took it with him so he could leave another note at your house."

You could have heard a pin drop. No one moved or said anything. Now I understood why I'd been sent to the other crime scene. They didn't want me to know about the note. I felt the veins bulging in my neck and my face heating with rage. I slammed my fist on the table and everyone jumped. I rubbed my forehead and stared at the table in front of me shaking my head. I clenched my fists to stop them from shaking as anger consumed me. I wanted to scream.

Pomush broke the silence. "Gentlemen, let's take a break. We'll resume the briefing in fifteen minutes."

Everyone left the room except Pomush. He walked over and placed his hand on my shoulder. "I don't blame you, Storm. We'd all like to kill that bastard. I'm sorry he's made it personal."

I stared at the table for a long time taking long slow deep breaths to calm myself. Pomush left to get coffee.

I shook my head in disbelief. I felt like I was living a nightmare instead of having one. I knew I had to get ahold of myself. If I didn't Fowler would pull me off the case and order me to go see Doc Martin. I'd have to get Doc's permission before going back on duty. That was the last thing I needed right now.

Jim came back and handed me a steaming cup of hot coffee. I took a sip and a couple more deep breaths to calm myself. My legs shook. "Jim, I think Ivan killed the old man and the nurse before he killed Amber."

"What makes you think that?"

"I believe he was in the old man's room so he could watch me leave work. Then he followed me home to find out where I lived. He left to kill Amber and came back later to kill me. When I wasn't there, he left me the note and Amber's finger."

Jim thought about that for a few moments. "I don't think so. He wouldn't have had time to get to his car from that room in time to follow you home before you drove away."

"Normally that would be true. But when I got to my car, I realized I'd left my keys in my office. I had to go back to get them. He would have had plenty of time to get to his car and follow me home."

Pomush looked up at the ceiling and nodded. "Do you think you were followed?"

"I don't know. I wasn't paying any attention. I had too much on my mind."

Jim rubbed his chin and thought for a moment. "It could have happened that way."

"How else would he have known where I lived?"

Pomush walked over and looked through the glass walls at the detectives in the break room. "Now that I think about it, you're probably right."

"That's not all," I said. "There was a guy in Manitou Springs who was stabbed through the heart with a six-inch hunting knife with a serrated edge. It occurred the same day I chased Ivan. The suspect hung out in the victim's apartment for a few days after killing him."

Pomush nodded. "That could explain where Ivan was hiding. And that is the same MO used to kill the old man."

"Yeah. And the guy he killed in the Manitou Springs dressed like he was from India. Ivan is very light skinned and could easily pass for someone from there. No one would have given him a second thought posing as the old man's nephew."

Pomush turned to face me. "I think this guy is a lot smarter than we've given him credit for."

"I think you're right and that makes him a lot more dangerous," I said. "I'm worried about Katy. He might know who she is."

"Can you send her on a vacation?"

"No way. She's in the middle of a trial and she wouldn't leave anyway. I'll never forgive myself, Jim, if she gets hurt."

Pomush paced back and forth. I could almost see his wheels turning as he considered what we'd said. Finally he nodded. "I'll get the guys back in here. You can explain why you think all three killings are connected."

"Four murders. Don't forget about the guy in Manitou Springs."

"Yes, plus the other four girls." Pomush said. "That makes eight total that we know of."

The other detectives returned to the conference room and I told them what I suspected. Everyone agreed it made sense that the last three victims were killed by the same person. Pomush asked Agent Ted Wohler what he thought. Ted stood up and addressed the meeting.

"I think Ivan knows his time is limited and has changed his MO. He's not thinking about sex anymore, he's thinking about revenge. The reason he slit the girl's throat and cut her finger off was symbolic. He killed her because she told Storm who he was and he took her finger because she fingered him. He wanted to leave Storm the message with her own blood. He is much more dangerous now. He wants to kill Storm and go out in glory." He looked at me, "There's no life in prison for this guy if he can help it. He'll keep killing until he's dead and he has his sights on his old nemesis. He'll kill you, your family and anyone that's close to you if he can."

Pomush asked, "Storm, do you have any relatives in Colorado Springs?"

"No. They all live out of state. But, he'll go after Katy if he knows we're dating and we have to assume he does."

"That's right," came a voice from the door. Lieutenant Fowler walked in and made his way to the front of the room. "Gentlemen, we are making the front pages of newspapers all across the country with the murders of these little girls, and the press doesn't know Ivan's responsible for killing the old man and woman or the guy Storm believes Ivan killed in Manitou Springs. If the press finds out about these other killings, the whole town will be in a panic. We have to find this guy. I'll try to keep these newest details out of the press as long as I can." He looked at Pomush. "Notify the court that Katy Taylor may be a target and ask for extra security. Make sure they have Ivan's photo posted in the lobby check-in area. I'm going to have patrol assign a marked car to escort her back and forth to work." He looked back at me. "We can't afford to have one of our beautiful young prosecutors get killed."

I felt better knowing he was covering Katy's back. I assumed he must not be mad at me anymore. Fowler walked over to Pomush. "Jim, I know you guys are doing everything possible to catch this guy and I appreciate it. I'll try to keep the press off your backs as long as I can."

Fowler left the room. Pomush assigned anyone not already buried in paperwork to return to the last two murder scenes. He wanted them to try to locate any witnesses who may have seen a man matching Ivan's description or any suspicious vehicles.

I wanted to be with Katy when she wasn't in her office. I knew Ivan couldn't get past the court security officers with a weapon but I wasn't willing to take any chances when she wasn't at work.

The rest of my day was consumed by paperwork. Maggie confirmed that the finger found in my bathroom sink belonged to Amber Olsen. She also found Ivan's DNA in the old man's room. Charlie Blakely located a witness at the nursing home who stated she had seen a man wearing a turban and matching Ivan's description walking into the building. He had a leather case with a strap on it. She said she thought it might have been a camera or binocular case.

As a police officer, I was used to hunting other men. Knowing I was now being hunted made me uneasy. I found myself watching everything and everyone all the time. We didn't have a possible suspect vehicle. I wasn't sure what I was looking for except for a dark skinned male I now know as Ivan Collins.

While I drove to Katy's office, I looked at every car around me to make sure I wasn't being followed. When I picked her up from work, a marked unit was in the parking lot waiting for her. We went to Wally's Indoor Shooting Range. The marked unit followed us and waited for us in the parking lot. I waited a couple of minutes before entering the store, scanning the area. I didn't see anything or anyone suspicious before entering the store.

The shooting range was owned and operated by Wally Sanders, a retired police officer who specialized in helping civilians and retired officers with their concealed weapons permits. He was also the retired Range Master for the Colorado Springs Police Department. He oversaw the department's state mandated qualifying and active shooters training. Wally sold all types of weapons and ammunition and he gave law enforcement officers huge discounts. I purchased a Glock semi-auto Model 27 pistol and two boxes of .40 caliber hollow points from him.

Katy watched me intently as I laid the pistol, magazines and ammunition on the carpeted table inside the range. I ran the target holder up to our location and pinned a black silhouette of an upper torso on the target. The target had a small circle in the center with an X on it and an outline indicating the kill zone not including the head. It was the standard target used by the police department during our shooting qualifications.

I opened a box of shells and showed Katy how to load the magazines, then laid them on the table. I handed her the pistol. "This weapon has more kick than your .32 but will put a man down twice as fast. These hollow point rounds will spread out on impact causing a lot more damage." Katy felt the pistol and pointed it down range.

I picked up a magazine and showed Katy how to insert it into the weapon, then slammed the bottom of the magazine to make sure it was secure. After racking a round into the gun, I told her the pistol was ready to shoot. I ejected the magazine, removed the chambered round and put it back into the magazine. Katy loaded and unloaded the gun flawlessly. I showed her the proper way to hold the weapon, warning her not to let her hand get too high on the grip because the slide would come back and injure her thumb.

She took the weapon, wrapped the fingers of her right hand around the butt of the weapon, wrapped the fingers of her left hand around her right hand and placed her thumbs to the side.

"That's perfect," I said. "I'm going to fire a few rounds and then I'll let you fire it, okay?"

"All right."

She handed me the gun and watched me without asking questions. I ran the target down range to the twenty-yard line. After giving Katy earplugs and safety glasses, I put mine on and picked up the weapon while giving verbal instructions. "Turn slightly to your right with your left arm slightly bent and your right arm straight out like this. Bring the weapon up to your line of sight and focus on the front sight. The front sight should be level with the back sight and the space on both sides of the back sight should be the same."

I lowered the gun and pointed to the front and rear sight making sure Katy understood what I was telling her. She looked uncertain as she took the pistol, held it in the proper position and brought it up level to her eye. "Like this?"

"Yes. That's good." I took the Glock from her and put one round in the X ring and one round just left of the X ring. "Do you think you can do that?" I asked.

"I think so."

I handed her the weapon and told her to fire one round. Katy raised the weapon and focused on the target. She fired one round and it hit the silhouette in the face.

"Your front sight is too high. Lower it until it's even with the rear sight and try again." Katy brought the weapon up and fired another round. She hit the target at the same height and to the right about four inches.

"Your front sight is still too high. Try to center the front sight between the rear sight this time and make sure the front and rear sights are the same height."

Katy fired another round and it hit dead center in the face on the target but two inches lower. "That's better. You hit a little lower that time but it was in the center. This time, concentrate on leveling the top and rear sights on the X while squeezing the trigger."

Katy raised the weapon and quickly fired six rounds. All the rounds hit the target in the head. Katy looked at me and grinned. Then she fired the rest of the rounds. I watched the X ring disappear into a small hole about the size of a quarter. Katy ejected the magazine, inserted another one and chambered a round. She emptied the second magazine and all rounds hit what was left of the X ring. Then she put the pistol down on the table and asked, "Like that?"

I pulled the target up and marveled at the shot pattern. I was looking at a smiley face in the head and no X ring in the body. Feeling like a fool, I knew I couldn't shoot that well if my life depended on it.

"Well, what do you think?" she asked, a challenging smirk on her face.

"I think I'm a hell of an instructor."

Katy tried to conceal her spreading grin. "You're good, Storm, really good."

I cleared the weapon, picked up the boxes of ammunition and handed the gun to her. "I think your lesson is complete."

Wally grinned from ear to ear when we walked back into the store. "Were you able to teach him anything, Katy?"

They both laughed.

"I assume you two know each other."

"Hell yes," Wally said. "Katy and Doc Martin come in at least twice a month."

I grinned, shook my head and bought Katy a holster for her Glock. When we got outside, I checked the parking lot. The marked unit was still there. The officer inside waved. I looked around and didn't see anything out of place. When we got to my car, Katy said, "Thanks for the lesson, honey. Can I buy you dinner?"

"Sure. But tell me how you learned to shoot like that?"

"My dad taught me when I was just a kid. He gave me the .32 when I was six years old." She reached over and kissed me on the cheek. "Thanks for the big girl gun. I really appreciate it."

I saw her reflection in the side window as she turned away attempting to keep from laughing. We went to a small diner and the marked unit followed us. After dinner, we drove back to Katy's office to get her car. I followed her home and our police escort followed me. He didn't leave until we were safely inside Katy's house and I signaled him that we were all right.

Knowing Katy could handle a firearm and was such a good shot was a huge relief. Now it was my responsibility to find Ivan before he found us.

CHAPTER TWENTY-THREE

K aty had hinted she had something special planned for my birthday. I hoped it was a quiet weekend in a log cabin with a hot tub and no phones. After locking my office, I left work to meet her. When I got to the employee parking lot, Charlie had his head under the hood of his old truck. "Need a jump?"

"No, it's not the battery. It's the starter." He pulled his head from under the hood.

"Have you called for a tow truck?"

"No. I've been tapping the starter with a hammer but it's not working. I'm going to have to replace it."

"Need a ride home?"

"I'd sure appreciate it." Charlie slammed the hood. "It's our fifth wedding anniversary and I'm already late."

We got into my car. "What are you doing for your anniversary?"

"I was supposed to take Jenny to dinner," he said as he fastened his seatbelt. "But that's not going to happen now. This is our only vehicle."

"That's a bummer."

"Yeah. Jenny has a babysitter lined up for Emily. She's going to be very disappointed."

"Bullshit. You're taking your wife to dinner. You can use my car. I'll get out at Katy's office. I won't need it this weekend."

"Are you sure?"

"Katy has something planned for my birthday and I'm going to spend it with her."

We stopped by a small florist shop on the way so Charlie could buy a dozen roses for his wife. I bought some for Katy while we were there.

Charlie dropped me off at the rear of Katy's office complex. I opened the trunk and removed a small suitcase and my golf clubs. Charlie asked, "Going on a trip?"

"A short one," I said with a smile.

"Any place exciting?"

"I don't know. Katy planned it and said to bring my clubs. Have fun, Charlie."

I grabbed my suitcase, golf clubs, and flowers. I left the suitcase and clubs with the security guard who asked no questions after seeing my police ID.

Katy's office was on the third floor with a view overlooking the Pioneer Park Museum. This was the first time I'd seen it. Her furniture was dark rosewood and the paintings on the walls were originals. It didn't look like a typical government office and none of the other offices had such luxurious furniture. Katy was at her computer and didn't see me arrive. I stood in the hall, hid the flowers behind my back, and tapped on the door. "Nice office, lady."

Looking up, she asked, "What are you doing here, sailor? You lost or something?"

"No. I loaned Charlie my car and was hoping I could bum a ride."

She got up, walked into the hallway and gave me a kiss on the cheek. "Only if you promise to buy me a drink."

"I'll do better than that," I said as I handed her the flowers.

Her eyes lit up and a smile spread across her face. "Oh, they're beautiful, Storm!"

She wrapped her arms around me and gave me a big kiss on the lips. Someone down the hall whistled and Katy blushed. With flowers in hand, she dragged me down the hall and introduced me to all her co-workers. I knew a few of the attorneys from past trials. Her paralegal, Marcee Payton, looked familiar but I couldn't place her. She was in her fifties, tall, thin, and classy-looking with long blond hair. When Katy introduced us I asked, "Do I know you from somewhere? You look familiar."

"We've never met but I've heard all about you. Nice to meet you, Storm," She shook my hand. "I hope you know what a wonderful person you're dating."

"I'm a very lucky man," I replied while trying to remember where I had seen her.

Katy made a quick phone call, turned off her computer, and locked the door. She drove us to the Broadmoor hotel where she had reservations for the weekend.

"You've never bought me flowers before," she said as we walked to our room. "Why today?"

"Because I'm the luckiest man in the world. And, because I love you very much."

Katy smiled and kissed me. "This is going to be a very special weekend, Storm."

The doorman opened our car door upon arrival and Katy gave the valet the keys. The hotel was magnificent. I'd visited there many times but never stayed overnight. The hallway was lined with photos of famous people who had visited in the past. Bob Hope, John Wayne and Douglas MacArthur were my favorites.

Our room was more elegant than any I had ever stayed in. It smelled of class. Katy opened the curtains to a magnificent view of the lake lined with old oaks and pine trees. Geese swam in the lake as guests watched from the bridge and benches along the walkway. It was nice to see how the rich and famous lived. Katy seemed to belong here. I didn't but I could get used to it. She took my phone, turned it off and put it in a drawer with hers.

We ate in the hotel's main dining room. After dinner, she took me to a small clothing shop in the lobby. The sales clerk knew her by name. Katy purchased jogging suits for both of us and a new dress for herself. Then she bought me a pair of slacks, a shirt and tie, and a sports jacket and told the lady to put them on her account. I protested manfully and paid with my credit card. We went back to our room and got dressed in the jogging suits. It was already getting dark. "Are we going for a run?"

"We are not. Follow me."

She made a call from the room phone and then led me to the massage parlor. Two beautiful young ladies gave us massages. I melted into the table as one of them rubbed the tension out of me. She was just a little thing but had very strong hands and knew all the pressure points. I hadn't felt this relaxed in years. I almost forgot about Ivan.

After leaving the spa, we walked around the lake, and retired to the bar for cocktails. Then we went to the huge hot tub in our room. The weekend was off to an unforgettable and loving weekend.

Light was shining through the blinds when I awoke the next morning. Katy lay next to me with both palms under her chin watching me.

"Good morning, Ma'am," I drawled.

"Good morning, honey. How did you sleep?"

"Like a baby. And you?"

She smiled and rolled over on her back. "Great."

"What were you thinking?" I asked, captivated by the expression on her face.

"Just thinking how nice it would be to wake up next to you every morning for the rest of my life."

"Oh, you were, were you? Come here." I took her in my arms and held her. I loved the smell of her hair and perfume. I hadn't felt this secure and content in my life. I said a silent prayer thanking God for having this incredible woman in my life. "What's on the agenda today?" I asked.

"Sleep late, which we've already done. Now we take a shower, have brunch and then golf. No phone and no TV."

"Wonderful," I said, and pulled my pillow over my head. She yanked it away and hit me with it. Laughing, I watched her naked body sway towards the shower. As soon as I heard the water running, I joined her.

Soft music played in the background as we ate brunch in the hotel's dining room. Every kind of pastry and fruit you could imagine covered a long table adorned with a large ice carving of a swan as a centerpiece. The food was outstanding. After breakfast, we headed to the golf course where a cart had been reserved. We strapped on our bags and took off. Crisp cool air filled a blue cloudless sky. Leaves of every color imaginable lined the course. It looked as if we were teeing off into a postcard with the Cheyenne Mountain as the background.

Having never played golf with Katy before, I wondered if her game was as good as her shooting. Her first drive told me she was no stranger to the game. I had my work cut out for me if I didn't want to embarrass myself. Our scores were tight. Katy only beat me by seven strokes. My ego was a little deflated, to say the least. She had a wonderful swing in more ways than one and that more than made up for my injured pride. We returned to our room and took a nap. That evening, she wanted to get dressed up. Since we used clip-on ties for work, Katy had to help me tie the one she chose for me.

When we walked into the main dining area, she handed the maître d' her business card. He escorted us to a conference room located near the dining hall. The words, "Surprise" rang in my ears when we opened the door. Most of the Task Force and several other police officers were there along with Maggie, Doc Martin and Katy's paralegal, Marcee. Maggie led everyone into singing happy birthday. Katy was all smiles, quite pleased with herself. She hugged and kissed me, inspiring hollers and catcalls from a dozen uncouth police officers.

She whispered in my ear, "Happy birthday, Storm."

Beer and wine flowed freely as the waiter took our orders. Maggie got me a pillow for my birthday. She said it was for my office and got lots of laughs. Most of the presents were either gift cards or pranks and I appreciated them all. Charlie thanked me for the use of my car and said he and Jenny had a wonderful anniversary thanks to me. When almost everyone had left except Katy, Doc, Marcee and me, Doc handed me a gift-wrapped box.

"I hope you like this. You are a hard man to buy for."

I unwrapped the package. Inside was a chestnut colored leather belt. The hand engraved sterling silver buckle had an eagle carved on it along the initials SH. A mountain scene had been hand-etched into the background. It was very unusual. A lot of work and thought had gone into this gift and I was touched.

"It's beautiful," Katy said.

"It sure is," I said as I continued to admire the workmanship.

Doc said. "Try it on and see if it fits."

It was perfect. "This is great, Doc. I've never seen a buckle like this before."

"It's more than just a buckle. Let me show you how it works," When he pulled on the buckle, a small knife blade slid out. "This is razor sharp so don't cut yourself."

The one-inch blade was held in place by a magnet. I slid it back inside the buckle. You couldn't tell it was a knife until the blade was pulled out and it separated easily with a slight pull with one finger.

"This is really cool, Doc. Thanks."

"You never know when you might need something like that," he replied. "It's great for cutting seatbelts in case of an accident."

"I can think of many uses for it. I'm always losing my pocketknives."

I placed my old belt in the box. We loaded all the gifts in a bag while Katy paid the bill. I couldn't imagine the cost of having a party at the Broadmoor. I felt both guilty and blessed. When we got back to our room, she handed me a card and told me to open it. The card contained a gift card for an all-inclusive paid weekend for two at the Stanley Hotel, which overlooks Estes Park. The hotel is over 100 years old and very expensive. "Katy, I can't accept this."

"Be quiet and read the card."

I read the card; *I've waited all my life for a man like you, Storm Harrison. Don't even think about telling me you won't go to the Stanley Hotel with me or I'll have to take Doc. I love you. Katy.*

"This must have cost a fortune." I said, looking at the card.

She smiled. "I can afford it."

"I can't."

"Of course you can," she said. "It's all-inclusive." She hugged me. "You wouldn't want me to get stuck there with Uncle Bob would you?"

"No, I wouldn't." I removed a small blue box out of my pocket, opened it to display its contents, and got down on one knee. "Katy you are more special to me than anyone I have ever met in my life. We can go there for our honeymoon if you'll marry me."

Her mouth dropped open and her hands cupped her cheeks. "Of course I'll marry you. I thought you'd never ask!" She wrapped me in her arms and kissed me. I picked her up and carried her to bed. It was the happiest day of my life.

CHAPTER TWENTY-FOUR

A soft knock at the door woke me at 2:57 a.m. I slipped out of bed and grabbed my gun. Katy stirred. "What are you doing?" she asked.

"There's someone at the door. Stay here." I saw a shadow move below the door indicating someone was standing on the other side. I didn't look through the peephole because I didn't want to take a bullet in the eye. They knocked again, this time louder than the first time. "Storm, open up. It's me, Pomush." I recognized his voice.

I left the chain attached and cracked the door open. "What are you doing here, Jim?"

"Your phone's turned off. I had to come."

"What's going on?"

"It's Charlie. He was killed last night."

"Oh, my God! Hold on, I'll let you in." Katy had slipped on her robe and stood beside me as I closed the door, turned on the light, and removed the chain. Jim stepped inside.

"What happened?"

"He was on his way home from the party and stopped at a red light. His wife called him to ask when he'd be home. Someone pulled up on his left side at a traffic light while they were talking. The suspect fired one round from a .45 through the driver's window. The round hit Charlie's left hand, went through his phone, and through his brain killing him instantly."

"He was driving my car, wasn't he?" I asked, already knowing the answer.

"Yes," Pomush said. "I don't think the suspect knew it was Charlie. It would have been hard to recognize him with your tinted windows and the phone up to his ear. That bullet was meant for you."

Katy came and held on to my arm. "Oh, no. Not Charlie. I'm so sorry, Storm."

I felt numb all over. I didn't know what to say. I couldn't imagine how Charlie's wife was holding up. Yesterday was the happiest day of my life and today was one of the worst. "How's Jenny doing?"

"Not well. Her parents are with her at the hospital. They are worried she may lose the baby."

"That fucking Ivan. We have to find him before he kills anyone else."

"That's why I'm here. We got a description of the car he was driving. It was an older white car, possibly a Honda Accord or Civic."

"Damn, there are thousands of cars like that," I said. "But at least it's something if he keeps driving it. I'll get dressed."

"No. Stay here, Storm. We have every officer in the city looking for him. They are stopping every car that even comes close to that description. The task force is checking all the hotels, motels and the airport. The surrounding police departments have been notified and are trying to help us locate him. There's nothing for you to do. Ted thinks Ivan will run now that he thinks you're dead."

"But, I want to help."

"No. We're keeping Charlie's death out of the papers and news. Connie Mason knows your car and has reported she believes you were killed. We want Ivan to think you're dead for now. You need to stay out of sight. We have already notified your parents that you are alive and well. They won't panic if they hear anything in the news."

I wanted to help but didn't know what I could do that wasn't already being done. I felt awful. "What can I do to help?"

"Nothing, and that's an order coming from Fowler. Don't mess this up. He'll suspend you again and I'm going to need you. Keep your phone on and I'll let you know if we find anything."

After Pomush left, Katy and I went back to bed but we couldn't sleep. She held me until the sun came up. I felt worse than I had when Julia was murdered, if that was possible. Once the sun rose, Katy asked if I wanted some breakfast.

I wasn't hungry but after a night with little sleep, I could sure use some coffee.

We got dressed. I held my gun in my hand as I opened the door to check the hall, which was empty. I holstered my weapon and covered it with my jacket. We were walking down the empty hallway when a door opened in front of us. I placed my hand on my weapon. Doc Martin stepped out into the hall with a suitcase. He was talking to someone inside the room. He didn't see us until we reached him. A smiling woman just inside the door held a sheet up around her.

"Marcee?" Katy said with a shocked look on her face.

I now remembered where I had first seen Marcee. She was the woman Doc had left The Oak Barrel with.

Marcee smiled and waved. "Hi, Katy," she said as she ducked back inside and shut the door.

Doc showed no emotion whatsoever. "Well, good morning. I didn't expect you guys to be up so early."

"That's obvious," Katy said while staring at the closed door. "You have some explaining to do."

To change the subject and to get Doc off the hook, I said, "Doc, Charlie was murdered last night on his way home from the birthday party."

"Oh, no!" Doc said shaking his head.

"He was driving my car."

Doc slowly shook his head. "You want to talk about it?"

"Yeah," I said. "We're just heading to breakfast. You want to join us?"

While we were waiting for our food to arrive, I told Doc what had happened.

"What are you going to do?" he asked.

"I don't know. When Ivan finds out I'm still alive, he'll come after me. I'm not concerned about that, but I am worried about Katy. We can't go to my house and I believe he might know where she lives. If he knows about Katy, she'll be his next target. I'd like her to leave town for a while. At least until we catch Ivan."

"I'm not leaving unless you come with me," Katy said.

"Doc thought for a moment, then said, "Why don't you go ahead and get married and go away for your honeymoon until they catch Ivan?"

"That' a wonderful idea," said Katy. "We could spend our honeymoon at the Stanley Hotel and then go visit your parents. I want to meet them."

Doc nodded. "That would sure take a load off my mind."

Katy took Doc by the arm. "You know what would be even better? We could have a double wedding and then you and Marcee could come with us."

He shook his head. "I don't think so. If I wanted to get married, I'd just find a woman I hate and give her my house. Skip the preacher and the lawyer."

"Oh come on, Doc," Katy said. "Marcee is a wonderful lady. She'd make you a great wife."

"Maybe, but I have other priorities right now. I need to contact Charlie's family and see if I can help."

Our dark moods returned with the mention of Charlie. I really wanted to stay in Colorado Springs and help find Ivan, but protecting Katy was more important. I wanted her safe and knew I couldn't live with myself if anything were to happen to her. I couldn't imagine her having to go through what Charlie's wife was experiencing. We agreed we would get married right away and Doc would be the best man, while Marcee could be the maid of honor.

Pomush thought it was a wonderful idea and approved my vacation. He told us to have a good time and to let him know before we came back into town. He promised to call if they got any leads on Ivan.

CHAPTER TWENTY-FIVE

Katy and I were married in a small Episcopalian church located in the Broadmoor area. The back of the church was one giant stained glass window frame with pine trees and the Cheyenne Mountains as a backdrop. The private ceremony consisted of Katy and me, the minister, and Doc and Marcee as our witnesses. I wore a black suit, gray shirt and a bright blue silk tie that Katy had handpicked. She wore her mother's wedding dress and looked astonishing. I couldn't believe a woman could look so beautiful. Saying "I do" was something I thought I'd never say, but it felt right. Katy was the perfect woman for me and I doubt any man could've been happier. I wished more of our friends could have shared this day with us.

We left shortly after the private ceremony to spend our wedding night at the Stanley Hotel registered as Mr. and Mrs. Taylor. On the drive there, Katy surprised me when she asked, "Storm, are you content?"

"I've never been so happy in my life," I said glancing over at her.

She placed her hand on my arm. "Then why are you so quiet? You aren't having second thoughts are you?"

"Not at all. You have made all my wildest dreams come true, Katy. I love you very much and I'm the luckiest man in the world."

She smiled and leaned back in her seat, still looking at me. "Storm, I always want you to confide in me. I need to understand how you feel and what your needs are."

I reached over and touched her cheek. "I will."

"Good. So tell me how you feel right now."

I had to think for a few moments before answering. Expressing feelings are more of a woman's thing and I'm not good at it. She kept looking at me expectantly, waiting for my answer.

"I feel as if I've just survived a hurricane where people all around me were killed. I found the most important person in my life and she's unharmed. We are now safely together in the eye of the hurricane, but the storm isn't over. I want to enjoy this moment and be thankful, yet I know the coming nightmare will have to be dealt with."

She watched the countryside pass by through of the window for a long time before answering. "I understand what you're saying. We can never have peace while Ivan is free to wreak havoc. But let's try to have a few days together to enjoy ourselves before we have to face reality. With luck, they'll catch Ivan before we get back."

"I'll do my best to forget about him. And when this is over, we'll go somewhere far away for a real honeymoon. We'll lie on the beach, drink cocktails and just enjoy each other. Until then we'll do the best we can."

The Stanley Hotel was almost as fancy as the Broadmoor. It had spectacular mountain views. We avoided watching or listening to the TV and spent most of our time hiking, relaxing in the spa and hanging out in the hotel's beautiful bar and dining room. I kept my phone on in case Pomush needed to get ahold of me but let all other calls go to voicemail.

It was a wonderful three-day mini honeymoon and we both felt refreshed. But I couldn't stop thinking about Charlie and Ivan. I felt relieved knowing Katy was out of harm's way and did everything I could to make sure she had a good time.

We were sitting in the hotel bar when Connie Mason came on the evening TV news:

"The other day I reported that Colorado Springs homicide detective, Storm Harrison, had been murdered. That was a mistake. The detective killed has been identified as Charlie Blakely. Our thoughts and prayers go out to his family. Detective Blakely was driving Detective Harrison's car at the time he was murdered. I recognized the vehicle at the crime scene as Storm Harrison's car and leapt to a conclusion. I apologize to both Detective Harrison and the Blakely family for the misunderstanding."

The TV showed a photo of Charlie but none of me. "I think Connie did a good job," Katy said. "Don't you?"

"She did okay."

On the fourth day, we checked out of the hotel and drove to Arizona to see my parents. They were excited to meet their new daughter-in-law. Jim Pomush called several times during the drive to tell me there were no new leads on Ivan.

My parents lived in the Sun City retirement community located northwest of Phoenix. More yards had rocks in them than grass and golf carts outnumbered cars. Katy appeared a little apprehensive as we pulled into their driveway. "What did you tell your parents about me?" she asked without getting out of the car.

"I told them you were the smartest woman I'd ever met, that you are gorgeous and had bad taste in men before you met me."

Katy wrinkled her nose. "I'm not sure it's improved that much." Then she winked at me.

I couldn't argue with her. I didn't know what she saw in me. Mom and Dad came out the front door to meet us and Katy shyly stood to greet them.

"Welcome, Katy. Call me Brenda." Mom gave my beautiful wife a big hug. "I'm so pleased to finally meet you. This is my husband Harold."

"Nice to meet you, Katy." Dad stepped forward and took her hand. "We've heard so much about you. Why don't you girls go on inside and get acquainted while Storm and I get your bags."

Dad patted me on the back. "She's one good looking woman, Son." He turned and looked at the Mercedes, "And this is one nice car. Is it hers?"

"Yeah. Mine is in the impound lot at the police station. I'm going to get rid of it." I hit the trunk release and helped dad with the luggage.

"I thought you loved that car." Dad grabbed one of the suitcases. "But I understand why you no longer want it."

"I wish I had never bought the darn thing. I'm still feeling guilty for letting Charlie drive it. If I hadn't, he may still be alive. I'm going to get a truck next time."

"I don't blame you. Trucks are a lot more practical with all the camping you do."

We took the bags inside and joined mom and Katy on the back patio where they were enjoying a glass of tea. They were laughing and sharing stories like old friends. As time for dinner grew near, Katy and I retreated to our room to freshen up while mom started dinner.

"Your parents are wonderful, Storm."

"I thought you'd like them. They're good people."

We changed clothes and I went to help Mom in the kitchen while Dad and Katy got better acquainted.

"Mom, what do you think of Katy?"

"She's a lovely girl. I'm so happy for you. When are you going to start a family?"

"Whoa, slow down Mom. We just got married."

Mom smiled. "I know. But your father and I can't wait to be grandparents."

Mom is an excellent cook. The roast in the oven smelled wonderful. Mom chopped lettuce, tomatoes and cucumbers for the salad while I set the table. The smell of fresh baked bread made my mouth water. We ate like kings that night and every day during our stay. I realized I didn't even know if Katy could cook, but hoped she could pick up a few pointers from mom while we were there.

Mom and Katy either played golf or went shopping every day at one of the many malls in Scottsdale. They would be gone all day and return with bags full of stuff. Not only were they buying clothes for themselves, they bought dad and me something on every trip. I hoped I could get it all in the car for our trip home.

Dad and I were sitting on the back patio one morning drinking coffee and watching golfers tee off when he asked, "Your wife must have a very good job. What law firm does she work for?"

"She works for the county attorney's office. Handles most of the rape cases."

Dad put the newspaper down and looked at me over the top of his glasses. "Really? They must pay their county prosecutors a lot more in Colorado than they do in Arizona."

"I don't think so. I have no idea how much she makes but I'm sure it's more than I do."

Dad took a sip of his coffee and rubbed his chin. "Have you noticed the price tags on the clothes they're bringing home? That's expensive stuff."

"No I haven't paid any attention. Is mom overspending her limit?"

"Oh no," he said. "Your wife is paying for most of it. She won't let your mother pay for a thing. I'm concerned she may bankrupt you at the rate she's going."

Katy and I had never discussed finances but she never seemed to worry about money. She and mom arrived home that afternoon with bags full of clothes, shoes, belts and all kinds of makeup. They were having so much fun that I didn't want to bring up the subject of cost. "Wow," I said as I watched them removing the items they purchased. "You've certainly helped boost the economy today."

"Don't be silly, Storm," Katy said. "Everything we bought was on sale. And they have great prices here."

Mom looked a little sheepish. "Katy does seem to find the best deals in town."

I dropped the subject. Later that evening, I caught Mom and Katy looking at baby cribs in a magazine. They quickly closed it when they saw me, but I could guess what they were thinking.

Dad's back had been acting up so we weren't playing golf. We sat at the Country Club bar downing Black Velvet, catching up on old times. "What's bothering you son?" he asked when we'd finished reminiscing. "You seem restless."

"Sorry dad. I can't help thinking about Ivan. I keep hoping I'll get the call saying he's has been captured or killed."

Dad raised his hand to signal the bartender. "Let me get the next round."

While half intoxicated and celebrating my newfound happiness, the national news came on a big screen above the bar, darkening my mood. Charlie's funeral was being shown live. I couldn't hear what the reporters were saying but my mind raced as I watched the broadcast.

Police vehicles from all over the state formed the funeral procession that followed a black hearse and two white limousines as they turned into the cemetery. The police vehicles had their overhead lights flashing and the cars that followed had their headlights on as a sign of respect.

The sky was overcast with a light rain covering the city. People stood around the gravesite and little kids held flowers and American flags. The hearse stopped next to a freshly dug plot. Pallbearers in police uniform stood waiting for the casket. Most of them were from the task force. Charlie's wife, dressed in black, held the hand of their three-year old daughter, Emily.

A firing squad fired off a twenty-one-gun salute. Several Apache Helicopters flew over the cemetery. One of them veered off and climbed towards Pikes Peak disappearing into the clouds while the others continued straight ahead.

When the ceremony ended, the flag was removed from the casket, folded and given to Charlie's wife. Their three-year-old daughter walked over put a small bouquet of flowers on top of his casket.

Dad turned towards me. "The police sure know how to bury their heroes don't they?"

I nodded. "Yeah. There's only one thing missing."

"What's that?" Dad asked.

"Me," I said, drowning my cocktail in one big gulp.

Dad placed his hand on my shoulder. "I'm sorry you had to get caught up in this, Son."

I stood up to leave, my mood ruined. "I've got unfinished business."

"Yes, but you also need to think about Katy."

I nodded. "I'm worried about her. I wish I could get her to stay here until it's over."

Dad emptied his drink and stood. "We'd keep her in a heartbeat. She's a real sweetheart and your mother and I love her like the daughter we never had. We're going to hate it when you leave."

"Talk to Mom and see if she can convince Katy to stay for a while. I'd feel much better if she were here."

"I'll see what I can do," Dad said as we left the bar.

The next morning Mom was in the kitchen making breakfast. When I walked in, she smiled, kissed me on the cheek and handed me a cup of coffee. "Good morning, Storm."

"Good morning, Mom. Where's Dad?"

"He's outside doing yard work. He likes to do it before it gets too hot."

I looked through the window and saw him in the rear yard. He was raking mesquite beans and putting them in a big plastic trash bag. There were hundreds of them and thousands more still in the tree.

"Storm, I asked Katy to stay here until they catch that Ivan guy but she refused. She said she had lived in fear once before and wouldn't do it again."

"Thanks, Mom." I kissed her on the cheek, took my coffee and joined Dad in the back yard.

"Why are you raking these beans? There'll be just as many on the ground tomorrow. Why don't you wait until they all fall and then rake them?"

Dad kept raking. "You're right, but I find it best to clean up my messes when they're small. If I let them build up, they're a lot harder to take care of when I get around to it."

I wasn't sure if there was a hidden message to what he was saying or not, but it made sense. "I know I left a big mess in Colorado that I have to go clean up. I should have taken care of it years ago."

Dad stopped what he was doing and nodded. "I know, Son." He laid his rake down and put his hand on my shoulder. "We'll miss you terribly. Let's go see what the women are up to."

Katy and I left my parent's home at 5:00 a.m. the next day. MapQuest said it was a thirteen-hour drive to Colorado Springs. We entered the city limits twelve hours later.

"What are you going to do about your car?" asked Katy.

"Trade it in on a used truck. I can't drive it again."

"I understand. Neither could I." She reached over and took my hand.

Thanks to Jim Pomush, a marked police car sat in front of Katy's house when we arrived. I had called him and told him what time we'd be there. I didn't know the officer behind the wheel that met us.

"Hi, I'm Storm Harrison and this is my wife, Katy," I said as we shook hands. "I don't think we've met before."

"I'm Joe Perkins. I've heard of you and seen you around."

"Don't believe everything you hear."

He laughed. "It was all good."

Officer Perkins helped us carry our suitcases upstairs. Before he left, he turned to me. "I'll be here every morning to escort your wife to work and I'll be there when she gets off work to bring her home."

"I bet you didn't expect to be working as a security guard when you hired on, did you?

Officer Perkins laughed. "I volunteered. They're paying me two hours overtime a day to do this and I need the money. I come in an hour early and leave an hour later. Easy job."

"Be careful and watch your back. We don't need another funeral. This guy is dangerous."

"I know." He turned serious. "I'll do my job and protect your wife. You're the one who needs to watch your back."

I was impressed that the department would pay overtime to protect her. I told him Katy would be moving in with Doctor Bob Martin in a couple of days and that I would be staying here. I wrote down Doc's address for him. We exchanged phone numbers and he told Katy to call anytime she needed anything.

True to his word, Officer Perkins was sitting outside our home when we were ready to leave for work the next morning. He followed us to the police station where I got out. Then he followed Katy to her work.

Jim Pomush gave me a ride to the police impound lot where I had an appointment with the insurance adjuster. On the way there, I asked, "Jim, any new leads on Ivan?"

"Nope. It seems he just disappeared again."

I knew better. "He's still here. I can feel his presence." I didn't think we were being watched at that moment but I knew he was out there somewhere, waiting and planning. "What's the task force doing?"

"We don't have a plan. We just keep searching and hoping someone recognizes him or we find him first."

"If we wait too long, we'll have more bodies. I think we need to rattle his cage and see if we can flush him out."

"What do you have in mind?"

"I'll give Connie Mason a short interview and call him out on TV. His ego will get the best of him and he'll do something stupid."

"It might work, Storm. But this guy hasn't made many mistakes so far. You may end up being his next victim."

"I'll take that chance. Tell Fowler what I want to do and see if he'll approve it."

"What about Katy? He won't approve anything if he thinks it will place her in danger."

"She's going to be staying with Bob Martin until this is over. I'd like someone watching Doc's house if Fowler will okay it. If Ivan knows about Katy, I think he'll know where she lives. I'll stay at her house and see if he comes for me."

"I'll talk to Fowler and let you know what he says."

The insurance adjuster and a tow truck driver were waiting when I arrived at the impound lot. I unlocked the gate and stayed outside while the adjuster checked the damage. When he returned, he said they would give me a rental while my car was being fixed and that my Challenger would look as good as new before they gave it back.

They loaded my car and I signed for its release.

When they left, Pomush asked, "Need a ride somewhere?"

"I want to go by my office and check my phone messages and e-mails. Then if you have time, I'll buy lunch and you can drop me off at Katy's house."

"You're on."

Most of the e-mails were congratulating me for getting married or expressing regret about Charlie's death. There was a message from Connie Mason. I'd normally delete it, but since I might need her, I listened to it. *"Storm, this is Connie. I'm so sorry about Charlie. I can't possibly express how upset I was when I arrived on the scene and saw your car. I thought you had been killed. It reminded me of how much I care for you. Please stop being angry with me. I love you."*

Connie apparently hadn't heard about my recent marriage when she left that message. But I knew she would do the interview, given the chance. As much as I resented her, she was a good reporter. I closed up shop, called Pomush and we went to lunch. "How's Jenny Blakely holding up?" I asked once we'd placed our order.

"Not well. Her blood pressure went through the roof. They're keeping her in the hospital until the baby is born. She's due in about a month."

"It broke my heart watching his daughter place those flowers on his casket."

"There were a lot of tears shed that day," Pomush said. "I'm glad it was raining. You aren't blaming yourself for his death, are you?" I didn't answer, and we ate our meals in silence.

When we arrived at Katy's house, a ruby red Dodge truck was parked in the driveway next to the garage. Pomush continued driving, stopping two houses down. "Do you know whose truck that is?" he asked.

"I've never seen it before. Did you get the plate number?"

"It doesn't have a plate. Just a dealer's temporary drive out sticker."

Pomush radioed the suspicious vehicle into the dispatcher and gave her the description. We drew our weapons and approached the house. I snuck up on the porch and peeked through the window. The house appeared empty and nothing looked out of place. We made our way around to the side where the truck was parked. The coal bin was still screwed shut and the padlock was in place. No one was in the truck. We made our way to the rear door of the house. It was secure and the red light on the alarm system told me it was still set. We checked the rest of the windows and garage. They were secure.

Two marked units arrived and we entered the house. It was empty and it didn't appear anything had been disturbed. We went back to check the truck. A small envelope stuck out from under the windshield wiper. I opened it and found a card with Katy's handwriting: *"Your wedding present, Storm. I hope you like it. The keys are on the kitchen table."*

The two uniformed officers started laughing. One of them cleared the call and the other one said, "Lucky son-of-a-bitch. I wish my wife would buy me one of these."

Pomush had a smile a mile wide. "Congratulations, Storm. Katy is one incredible woman," he said as he admired the truck.

As soon as he left, I called Katy. "Honey, what did you do?"

"I bought you a truck," she said. "Do you like it?" She sounded very pleased with herself.

"I love it, but I can't afford it."

"Oh stop it, Harrison. We're not poor. We can afford it. Get used to it. And I'm buying you some new clothes too. I can't have my husband running around looking neglected."

Apparently, I had some adjusting to do. Not knowing what else to say, I said. "Katy, I love you."

"Love you too. Gotta run. I'll see you after work. Decide where we're going to eat tonight."

I got the keys and took the truck for a test drive. Feeling guilty, I drove it to the supermarket and bought the items I needed to cook Katy a gourmet meal. She didn't know I was an excellent cook and I wanted to surprise her.

She arrived home with Officer Perkins in tow. He parked on the street and walked her to the front door. She stepped inside to a fully set, candlelit table with a complete dinner and a bottle of wine. Katy set her purse down. "Storm, something smells wonderful. What is it?" She walked over and kissed me.

"Peanut butter and crackers."

"Oh, wow! She said as she examined the table. "Peter Pan would be so proud of you. What is it really? It smells delicious."

"It's called, Poulet de Provencal, aka, chicken."

Katy inhaled a deep breath through her nose. "The aroma is wonderful. I feel bad. I'm a terrible cook."

I smiled. "You more than make up for it with yoga lessons." She hugged me and we sat down to enjoy our last meal together in this house as long as Ivan was breathing free air.

CHAPTER TWENTY-SIX

Officer Perkins helped load six suitcases into the back of my new truck. Katy drove to Doc's house and Perkins followed. I hung back in an unmarked patrol car with Pomush to make sure they weren't being followed. After carrying the suitcases into Doc's home, Katy took her car and I drove my truck. Perkins and I escorted Katy to her office. When she cleared security, we drove our vehicles to the police station to start our shifts.

I parked my truck in the visitor's parking lot in front of the police station where the press conference was going to take place. Lieutenant Fowler scheduled the meeting with Connie for 1600 hours. The mayor would speak first, and then the chief would comment on the investigation. I wasn't supposed to say anything until Connie asked me questions. I wasn't sure what I was going to say but I wanted to piss Ivan off enough to get him to come after me. I hoped he would make a mistake that would lead to his capture or death. I preferred the second option.

At 1530 hours the news trucks arrived and set up for a live broadcast. Connie showed up a few minutes later. I stepped out to meet her. "Storm, I'm so sorry about Charlie Blakely and for reporting you had been killed."

"It was an honest mistake and there was no harm done."

She looked relieved and we started walking towards the station. "Are you really going to give me an interview or are you just going to say 'no comment' like you normally do?"

"I'll answer your questions but I need a favor."

She wrinkled her forehead as if trying to figure out the catch. "Sure. What do you want me to do?"

I pointed at my new ride. "See that truck. I want your camera-man to follow me as I get in it and drive away after the interview."

Connie looked hesitant. "Why?"

"I want Ivan Collins to see what I'm driving these days."

"What are you doing, trying to get yourself killed?"

"No, I'm not suicidal, I'm bait."

"You're crazy. Look what he did to Detective Blakely."

"Charlie didn't have a clue Ivan was coming. I do and I'll be ready."

"Storm, I'd feel awful if anything happened to you. I don't want to do this." She started to turn away. I took her by the arm and turned her back towards me. "Connie, if I don't stop this guy, more people are going to get killed. They don't have a chance but I do. Do you want their deaths on your conscience?"

She took a deep breath. "You don't play fair." Reluctantly, she added. "All right, I'll do it but be careful. I don't want your death on my conscience either."

"I will. I promise."

Connie left to tell her cameraman what I wanted.

I joined the Mayor, Chief Henderson, Fowler and Pomush on the steps of the police station as the film crew finished setting up. Six posters of Ivan sat on stands next to us. One was a blow up of his driver's license photo. The other five were renderings of Ivan in different disguises – sunglasses, beard, and a mustache. One had his head shaved and another with him wearing a turban.

Connie gave a thumbs-up, signaling they were ready. A live feed TV screen sat to the side so we knew what the public was seeing. Connie introduced herself, and then directed her words to the mayor.

"Mayor Riggs, can you tell us what you are doing to help catch Ivan Collins?"

"I have authorized Chief Henderson to use as much manpower as he needs to catch Ivan Collins. The city council has approved all of the overtime needed and I have the utmost confidence that Collins will be in custody soon."

Connie turned to the Chief. "Chief Henderson, what can you tell us about the investigation?"

"First of all, let me say we hope everyone keeps Detective Charley Blakely's wife and family in their prayers during this difficult time. We are asking for the public's assistance in locating this coldblooded, merciless killer. I have set up a task force to catch Ivan Collins and they are working around the clock, following up every lead we get. It is only a matter of time before he is apprehended. We have his photo and several drawings of him in his many disguises."

He pointed to the posters and the cameraman panned over to them as the chief continued. "Ivan Collins is out there somewhere and we are asking anyone who sees him to please call 911 or the main police number. Do not approach or attempt to apprehend Mr. Collins. He is considered armed and extremely dangerous."

Connie took two steps to the side and stood next to me. "Detective Harrison, Charles Blakely was driving your car when he was murdered. Would you like to make a statement?"

I looked straight into the camera. "I'm almost positive Ivan Collins believed I was driving my car the night Charlie was murdered."

"What are you doing to catch him at this time?"

"I'm part of the task force following up leads. We will continue checking hotels, motels, restaurants and other places he might be visiting. We are talking to anyone who knew Ivan but it appears he was a recluse and had no friends."

"Is there anything you want to say to Ivan Collins if he's out there watching the news?"

I looked straight into the camera. "Charlie was murdered in cold blood by a cowardly low life scum bag. Ivan Collins, you prey on little girls, old men, helpless nurses and unsuspecting police officers because you don't have the guts to confront me. I'm going to find you and bring you to trial and watch them place a needle in your arm."

"Thank you Detective Harrison," Connie said. She then stepped over to the posters of Ivan and asked the viewers to call 911 if they had any information about him.

I paused for a moment until I saw the cameraman scan back to me. "If you'll excuse me," I said to Connie, "I need to get back to work." I stepped around her, walked out to the street, got into my truck and drove away, hoping the camera was following me.

A block down the street, an older gray sedan with two men pulled out in front of me. I followed them a few cars between us. At the next block, a VW van with two longhaired dirt bags that I recognized as undercover officers, pulled in behind me. They followed me downtown to The Oak Barrel. I parked my truck on the street in front of the restaurant and went inside. It seemed as if everyone in the place watched me walk in. I found an empty stool at the end of the bar and took a seat. Pete slid a cold beer in my direction. "Nice interview, Storm. This one's on me. That's a deadly game you're playing. Watch your six."

The men driving the gray sedan walked in and took a seat in the restaurant. They had a good view of both me and the front entrance from their location. My phone rang and caller ID told me it was Pomush. "Hey, Jim. What's up?"

"Did you pick up your tails?"

"Yeah, two of them are in the bar with me. The two guys in the VW van are outside."

"What's the plan?"

"I'll stay here for a while and then take the long way home. They'll remain close until I'm inside the house. If we don't get a bite tonight, we'll try again tomorrow."

"Call me if anything comes up. I'll let you know if we get any leads."

"Sounds good. How did the chief react to the briefing?"

Pomush laughed. "He said he thought you laid it on a little thick. Fowler told him we needed a lot of cheese in the trap if we were going to catch this rat."

I chuckled. "Later, buddy. I need to stay alert." I nursed my beer for another half hour. Several people came by to offer their condolences or comment on the interview. I laid a $5.00 bill on the counter, signaling it was time to leave. The two men who had followed me in got up and left. I waited a few minutes before walking outside. I stood on the sidewalk in front of the bar looking around. The VW van was still parked in the Pioneer Museum parking lot across the street. I couldn't see anyone inside, but reckoned they were there. I didn't see the other vehicle.

I drove around town for a while, not spotting my tails again. After parking in my driveway, I stepped up on the porch and sat in the swing. A few minutes later the VW drove by and soon after the gray sedan came by in the opposite direction. There was no sign of Ivan. It was getting dark so I went inside, turned the alarm off, locked the deadbolt and reset the alarm. I turned most of the downstairs lights on and then went upstairs and watched the street from the unlit master bedroom. My sixth sense told me I was being watched but I couldn't see anyone or anything suspicious. Maybe I was getting paranoid.

At 2200 hours, I went downstairs, turned the lights off and returned to the bedroom, where I left the lamp on for half an hour before turning it off and going to bed. It was a restless night without nightmares.

The next morning, I took my stainless steel semi-auto into the shower with me. I had shaved and dressed when I got my first text. *Blue Chevy sedan and light green ½ ton pick-up.* Knowing which vehicles were tailing me was a relief. The next text was from Katy. *Storm, are you all right?*

I texted back, *I'm good. Love you and don't worry.* Before I got out of the driveway I received a third text. *Love you too. Be safe.*

The green truck fell in behind me about a block from the house. I never spotted the blue Chevy sedan. These guys were good.

The Kings Chef Diner located on Bijou Street had the best green chili burritos in town. I parked in their lot, went inside and ordered a burro and a cup of coffee. Sitting at a stool at the counter with my back to the door, I watched the entrance in the mirror. One of the undercover guys from yesterday's VW came in and took a seat just inside the entrance. He bought a newspaper and ordered coffee. I made eye contact with him in the mirror, letting him know I saw him.

This diner was busy, as usual. I had been on the news so many times during the last few months that several of the customers recognized me. They stopped to ask if we had located Ivan yet or just to wish me luck. I didn't spot anyone who resembled Ivan, but knew word would get around town that I was at the restaurant. After an hour of eating breakfast and drinking coffee, I folded my newspaper and set it on the counter. The undercover officer purchased four cups of coffee to go and left the diner. Three minutes later, I followed. After parking my car in front of the police station, I entered the main lobby and took the elevator up to the detective offices.

Pomush saw me when I walked in and said, "We're getting a lot of reports about possible sightings of Ivan Collins. The whole task force is busy following up on the leads."

"Good," I said as I entered my office. Jim came in behind and took a seat. I called to the undercover guys and told them I'd let them know if I planned to go somewhere so they could be ready. After I hung up, Pomush said, "Fowler is keeping close tabs on us." When I didn't respond, he added, "I hope Ivan shows his hand so we can end this one way or another."

A call from Katy interrupted our conversation. "Hi, Honey. What's up?" I asked.

"Nothing. But I missed you. Let's do lunch."

"I miss you too. But I'd rather we not be seen together in public until this is over. Ivan might not know about you, and if he doesn't, I want to keep it that way."

"What if I ordered food delivered to my office? Even if Ivan saw you going into the courthouse, he would think it was just business and he certainly wouldn't come inside… Please?"

Katy made sense and I really missed her. "It's a date, what time?"

"How about noon? Is Chinese food all right?"

"Perfect. I'll see you then."

I notified my tail of my plans, left my office and drove my truck to the courthouse. I parked on the street, swiped my credit card in the parking meter and cleared the security area. On the second floor, I stopped at one of the dark tinted windows and looked out at the street to see if I could see anything suspicious.

Everything looked normal until I saw a small white sedan stopped at a green light in the inside lane. Cars behind it honked their horns. The car had dark tinted windows and I couldn't see the driver until he rolled his window down. Those same cold dark eyes I'd seen in the alley so many years ago, stared up at the courthouse. It was almost as if he knew I could see him. A chill ran down my spine. I felt as if I was looking at the devil himself.

The car matched the description of the vehicle driven by the suspect when Charlie was killed. There was no way Ivan could see me through the tinted windows of the courthouse, but just as I was about to broadcast the sighting over my hand-held radio, the driver stuck a pistol out of the window and fired four quick shots at the court building, none of them coming close to where I was. Windows shattered and people started screaming.

I notified dispatch that a person whom I suspected was Ivan was shooting at the courthouse and gave them a description of his car. The undercover guys were monitoring both channels and could hear what I was broadcasting. As soon as I started giving out the description, Ivan busted the light, made a quick right turn and sped away.

The license numbers weren't visible from my vantage point but I could tell they were Colorado plates. It occurred to me that Ivan probably had a police scanner with him and was listening to our calls. A few seconds later, the green pickup truck made the same turn as Ivan and hauled ass down the street. I never saw the other undercover vehicle. I monitored the radio traffic as the officers desperately tried to locate Ivan.

Running down the hall, I found Katy standing outside her office with several other employees, all trying to figure out what was going on. "A man believed to be Ivan Collins just fired shots at the courthouse," I said. "He's gone now."

"Why would he do that?" she asked as she led me into her office. I went to the window to see what was going on down below. A police car sped by with its overhead lights on and within a minute, several other marked cars arrived at the courthouse.

"I think he followed me here and wanted to let me know that he was watching me. I saw him shoot while I was by the window next to the elevator."

We watched the traffic below as police cars drove around the area. Several stopped and came into the building. Ivan would be out of the area by now if he was monitoring our radio traffic. If not, he might circle around and someone might spot him. Several vehicles matching his vehicle's description were stopped in the downtown area. All of them came back negative. My hope of capturing Ivan faded with every passing minute.

"If that was him, you know he's following you," Katy said.

I nodded. "It was Ivan. I'm sure of it. He's taken the bait but I think he outsmarted us by having a police monitor. We're going to have to change our communications."

Katy looked frightened.

"Stay here," I said, "And keep away from the windows. I need to go see if anyone was injured."

One of the courtroom's windows had been struck during a trial and they had evacuated it, but there were no casualties. I called Katy and gave her an update and returned to the police station. There had been no other sighting of Ivan.

Pomush called the task force and my undercover detail in for a meeting. Once they were present, he asked me to relay what I had seen.

"Guys, I'm positive Ivan was driving that car. As soon as I broadcast his description, he busted the light and hauled ass. I think he has a police monitor. He was wearing a long sleeved light blue shirt and a dark baseball cap. I couldn't read the plate number."

Jim addressed the meeting. "I want the task force detectives to contact any stores in town that sell radio equipment to see if anyone recognizes Ivan as having bought a police scanner. And let all the other agencies know that he's still driving that old white car."

The undercover guys and I worked out a few codes we could use to confuse Ivan. If he was listening to us, we wanted to try to use the information in our favor to help lure him into a trap. After the meeting, Pomush told me that Fowler wanted to see us in his office. The frown on his face said this wasn't going to go well.

"Sit down," Fowler said as we entered his office. He looked at me. "Storm, this hasn't worked out like we'd hoped. The mayor is pissed and the courthouse doesn't want you anywhere close to it until Ivan is in custody. The chief doesn't want you going where a lot of people might be, including shopping malls, busy restaurants or bars. Is that clear?"

"Yes sir," Pomush and I answered at the same time.

"If some innocent person gets hurt or killed, this will come back to haunt us all." Fowler stood up and walked to his window and looked down into the break area below. "This is a brave thing you're doing, Storm, and I respect you for it. There's no way any of us could have predicted Ivan would shoot up the courthouse. It's not your fault." He turned and looked at us. "We're just going to have to find him another way. Stick to the dive bars and small out of the way hole in the walls from now on. Sooner or later, we'll find him or he'll find you. Be careful. Dismissed."

With that, Fowler turned his back to us again and stared out the window.

For the rest of the week we duplicated our daily work routine much the same as the first with the exception of the restaurants and bars I went to after work. But so far, Ivan hadn't shown himself. I reckoned eventually one of us would make a fatal mistake.

CHAPTER TWENTY-SEVEN

Dark clouds settled over the Rockies as the first cold spell of the season descended upon Colorado's eastern ranges. Significant snowfall was predicted for the higher elevations this weekend but none in town.

The cat and mouse game lasted all week and Ivan didn't show his ugly face. My gut told me he was planning something that I wasn't going to like. The unknown was killing me. I'd been going over everything we knew about the maniac's profile, trying to get into his head but I just couldn't do it. Ivan was so mentally screwed up that it was impossible for me to predict his next move. Maybe Doc Martin could give me the insight I needed to figure out this nut job.

Katy and I missed each other's company and she wanted to see me in the worst way. We decided I'd meet her at Doc's house and spend the night. The plan was for me to leave my truck in the driveway of her house. When it got dark, I'd set the alarm, jump the fence of the vacant house behind us and have a taxi pick me up on the next street over. I would return the same way sometime on Sunday.

Katy called before I left work. "Storm, I'm leaving the office early. What time are you coming over?"

"After it gets dark so no one sees me leaving the house. Are you waiting for Perkins to come escort you home?"

"Yes, he's on his way."

"Good. I'm leaving work now but I have to meet the realtor at my house. We're going to discuss putting it on the market as soon as this mess is over."

"All right, but be careful. I'll see you at Doc's in a couple of hours."

We hung up and I informed the undercover team I was ready to leave and gave them my home address. When I parked in the driveway, the undercover Volkswagen bus with dark tinted windows was sitting across the street from the cul-de-sac. They had a plain view of the front of my house. I never saw the other undercover vehicle. The realtor showed up and we walked around the outside of my house first, him taking notes while I checked for signs of forced entry. Everything appeared normal. We went inside and he made a few suggestions of things he wanted me to do before we listed the house.

After he left, I called the undercover guys and told them I would be going straight home and not stopping at any bars. I told them I wouldn't need them again until Monday morning.

On the way to Katy's house, I called her. Doc answered her phone. "Hey, Doc, what's up?"

"Katy forgot her phone so I answered it for her."

"Forgot her phone. Where did she go?"

"She went to her house to get some warmer clothes and make up."

"She didn't go alone, did she?" I asked.

"No. Officer Perkins drove her over in his police car. They just left a few minutes ago."

"I wish she hadn't gone without me."

"I told her to wait and you could bring the clothes when you came. She said you wouldn't know what to bring and couldn't climb the fence with them. She also wanted to get back here in time to take a shower and get dressed before you got here."

"Have her call me as soon as she gets back." I hung up without saying goodbye and hit the gas. Being rush hour, traffic was a bitch. I got stuck in stop-and-go traffic for several blocks before turning down a side alley in an attempt to find a way around it. The next street wasn't much quicker. After stopping at a red light, I looked both ways and ran it. Then road construction narrowed two lanes into one. When it opened up again, I floored it. By the time I got to Katy's house, it was completely dark.

Officer Perkins' marked unit sat in the driveway. I parked on the street so he could get his car out. A light was on in the kitchen and another shone from the master bedroom. I snuck around to the rear of the house. Everything appeared normal until I tried the back door. It was unlocked. There didn't appear to be any damage to indicate forced entry. The green light on the alarm system told me someone had turned it off. I expected to hear voices when I entered but the house was eerily quiet.

There was no way Katy or Perkins would have left the door unlocked behind them. Ivan must be here. I pulled my weapon and held it upward. After standing still and listening for a few moments, I tiptoed to the family room. It was empty. I scooted along the wall to the main living room. There was no indication anyone was in the house.

"Katy," I whispered but there was no answer. I moved to conceal my location and called to her again a little louder. "Katy." Again, no answer.

Then the lights went off. The hair on the back of my neck stood up. I backed up into the kitchen. The microwave and the refrigerator lights were also off. Hugging the wall, I waited for my eyes to adjust to the darkness.

The alarm system started blinking green, meaning it was now operating on backup battery power. I could almost feel Ivan's presence but had no idea where he was. I had walked into a trap and didn't know if Katy and Perkins were dead or alive.

I wanted to run upstairs to find them, but my instincts told me I'd be dead before I made it halfway up. I needed to clear my head and think. *Where was the fuse box in this old house? I had no idea, maybe upstairs or possibly in the basement.*

Staying as still and quiet as possible, I removed the receiver from the antique wall phone. Counting the holes with my finger, I dialed 911. Not wanting to give my position away, I eased the numbers back very slowly to keep the sound to a minimum. After dialing, I hung up without saying anything. The call would be traced automatically and the dispatcher would send officers to the house to do a welfare check. I didn't want them here too fast and certainly not with lights and sirens. I needed time to find Ivan before they arrived. I was afraid of what he might do.

Removing my shoes, I made my way back into the family room. The drapes were pulled closed but I could still tell that the streetlights were on and there was no power outage in the area. I eased into the entryway at the bottom of the main stairway and peeked up the dark staircase. I thought about charging up the stairs as fast as possible, hoping Ivan would miss his shot and I could kill him before he killed me. However, my chances were slim to none if he were waiting for me. He could be hiding anywhere in the house and I'd be a sitting duck. But I had to get upstairs somehow. Then I remembered the secret stairway with the sliding chair that led upstairs from the kitchen.

Katy had left the key for the padlock of the door to the hidden stairway on top of the refrigerator. Sliding my hand around, I found the key and removed the lock. I held my Glock in my right hand and jerked the door open. My heart jumped to my throat and I almost shot the person sitting in the mobile chair in front of me. It took a moment before I realized it was Perkins. He was slumped over in the seat with his head resting on his chest. Blood ran down the side of his face and dripped on the floor. I wasn't sure if he was dead or alive.

I placed my hand on his chest and felt his breathing. It was shallow. He was alive but unconscious. Placing two fingers on his carotid artery, I checked his pulse. It was strong. Using the light of my cell phone, I saw a large knot and cut on the side of his head.

Staring into the dark stairwell leading down to the basement and up to the master bedroom, I wondered if Ivan had gone upstairs or down, and whether Katy was even alive.

Using the limited light from my phone, I checked the narrow stairwell leading to the basement and up to the master bedroom. It was empty and the doors at either end were shut. Fresh blood spots were on the steps leading up. Ivan had apparently hit Perkins with something, tied him in the motorized chair and sent the chair down to the main floor.

Perkins' holster was empty and his weapon was missing. I had to find Katy before the police got here. Thinking Ivan would expect me to use the main stairway, I decided to go up these stairs.

I squeezed past Perkins and took each step slowly, trying to minimize the creaking sounds by walking on the outside of each step. A hail of bullets could come raining down on me at any moment and I'd have no place to hide. My socks soaked up blood, and stuck to the steps. When I reached the second floor, the door leading into the master bedroom stood open about an inch. I waited a moment, listening, trying to detect movement. My palms were sweating. It was as quiet as a morgue at midnight. I peeked through the crack to my left and saw Katy lying in the bed. She was nude, gagged and tied spread-eagle to the bedpost. Her head was turned in my direction but she gave no indication she had seen me. I felt she must be looking in Ivan's direction. He had to be somewhere to my right, probably guarding the main stairway.

Grabbing the door handle with my left hand and holding my Glock in my right, I started to open the door. I heard the sound of a car and thought it might be the police. I had to make my move now. As the door started to open, Kate saw me and started shaking her head violently back and forth trying to warn me not to open the door. But it was too late. The door's loud creak gave my position away. I pushed it open and turned to my right, expecting to see Ivan with his back to me.

Something crashed down on my right wrist, causing me to drop my pistol. A sharp pain shot through it and I felt as if my arm was broken. Ivan said something at me. Before I had a chance to respond another blow struck me in the side of the head and I fell to my knees. I reached for my weapon with my left hand. He struck my head again and everything went from color to black and white. Several more blows struck my head and shoulders causing my ears to ring. I struggled to stand but a boot came crashing into my face. As I fell backwards, I passed out.

I awoke to a man's voice. My whole body ached and my right eye was swollen shut. I was a bloody mess. Every inch of my body hurt. The electricity was back with a light shining in the bathroom. The echo in my ears began to fade as I regained my senses. Someone was talking in a cold quiet voice.

"I bet you were a beautiful girl when you were younger. Before you got all this hair. Harrison will be surprised when he wakes up and finds it's gone." He paused for a moment and continued. "But he'll like you better. You wouldn't want him to miss the party, would you?"

I was tied with a rope to a high-back chair. My elbows were secured to the arms of the chair and my wrists had been tied together in front of me and my ankles were tightly bound together. My right wrist throbbed. I attempted to open my left eye but couldn't because blood had run into it, sticking it shut. My mouth was dry and tasted of blood. Burning pain came from a busted lower lip and my nose felt like it was broken.

Forcing my right eye open, I lifted my head just enough to see Ivan sitting on the bed next to Katy with his back to me. She was still tied and bound to the bedpost, her gaze fixed on Ivan. I couldn't see what he was doing to her. Two handguns and a big hunting knife lay on the bed next to him.

I wondered why the police hadn't responded to my 911 call. I now hoped they wouldn't come. If the police showed up, Ivan would kill us both and make his escape.

Katy's eyes were filled with tears and she was shaking her head back and forth. She noticed me looking at her and gasped. Ivan heard her and looked back towards me. I dropped my head and faked unconsciousness. He walked over to me, grabbed me by the hair and jerked my head upward. "Are you awake, Mr. Harrison?" I didn't answer and acted as if I were still out. "Come on," he said as he slapped me across the face. "Wake up, Stormy. The party is about to start and you wouldn't want to miss the show your girlfriend has for you."

I wanted to rip his tongue out. But, I knew the only chance Katy or I had of surviving was to stall and think of some way to get us out of this mess. It seemed hopeless at the moment. I didn't know how long I had been out. I figured Doc Martin would have called the police if we weren't back by now. I needed to think of something fast.

Ivan walked around behind me. I heard him opening the curtains. He was apparently checking the street to make sure it was clear. I raised my head slightly and looked at Katy. A can of shaving cream and a razor lay on the bed next to her.

She stared at me. Using her left forefinger, she pointed at my face and then downward. She did this several times trying to tell me something, but I didn't know what it was.

Hearing the curtains close, I lowered my head back to my chest. Ivan stepped back in front of me, yanked my head up and then dropped it. "If you don't wake up soon, Detective, you'll miss your own execution." He walked back to the bed, sat down with his back to me and continued shaving Katy.

I put pressure on the ropes, trying to get them to loosen up, but it was useless. They were tight and dug into my arms, wrist and legs. It suddenly occurred to me what Katy was attempting to tell me. She was reminding me of the belt buckle knife that Doc had given me for my birthday. I twisted my arms slightly so I could feel the buckle. The knife slid out without making a sound. I almost dropped it trying to get the blade open. My right hand was swollen and pain shot through it with every heartbeat. While attempting to slide the small blade between the ropes, I cut my wrist. Blood ran into my lap but I kept cutting and soon felt the rope lose its tension. Holding the ends together with my hands, I reached over and cut the ropes securing my elbows to the chair. Katy's eyes shifted from me to Ivan and back again. I leaned forward and cut the ropes securing my feet.

Finally I was free, and in the dimly lit room Ivan probably wouldn't notice the bindings had been cut without close inspection. He might hear me if I tried to stand up and I couldn't take that chance. I needed him to come to me. Grasping the small knife with both hands to conceal it, I moaned.

He turned and looked at me. I tilted my head back and forth as if I were waking up. Ivan walked over and stood in front of me, my pistol in his hand. "Are you awake, Harrison?" His voice was angry.

"I have a little surprise for you." He bent over, grabbed my chin and lifted my head so he could look into my eyes.

As he did, I used every bit of my strength to launch myself upward. I caught him under his jaw with my head, forcing him up and backward. Following his momentum, I shoved the small blade into his groin area and ripped it upward as hard as I could, splitting him open. The knife stopped when it hit his sternum. I pulled it outward and continued my upward thrust, hoping to slit his throat. I missed the throat but caught him under his chin, laying it wide open. He fell back against the wall and slid to the floor. He dropped my weapon and reached for it, but I kicked him in the face. His head bounced off the wall and blood poured from his nose and chin. I grabbed my gun and kicked him again and again until he slumped forward.

I grabbed the bedpost to steady myself. My head hurt, my eyes watered and my right wrist throbbed. Ivan tried to stand. As he did, his guts spilled out into his lap. His eyes grew wide with panic as he grabbed his intestines with both hands and tried to keep them from falling to the floor.

My whole body ached and I started to tremble. My eyes wouldn't focus and at times I saw two images of Ivan, which would then blend back into one person. Unable to stand on my own, I sat back on the bed and held on the bedpost. Katy thrashed about, jerking on her ropes and yelling at me through her gag. I couldn't understand what she was saying. Nothing was making any sense.

My phone was lying on the bed next to Ivan's .45 semiautomatic. I picked it up and dialed 911. When the dispatcher answered, she sounded like she was yelling from the end of a long tunnel.

My voice was coarse and raspy when I tried to talk. "This is Detective Harrison. I've got Ivan Collins."

"Sir, can you speak up, sir?" said the dispatcher. "I can't understand what you are saying."

I cleared my throat and tried again. "This is Detective Storm Harrison. Can you hear me now?"

"Yes, Detective Harrison, I can hear you. What do you need?"

"I've captured Ivan Collins. He's in our home."

"Are you okay?"

"No, but I'll live. My wife's gagged and tied to our bed. I need paramedics and an ambulance." It took me three tries to give her the correct address.

Ivan began yelling at me while I was speaking to the dispatcher, making it even harder for her to understand me. I repeated the address while Ivan continued ranting in the background. "Harrison, you piece of shit. I'll kill you and that cunt of yours."

I kicked him in the face again. His head hit the wall so hard it made a hole in the drywall behind him. More of his guts spilled out onto his lap.

Stumbling over to the head of the bed, I cut the rope binding Katy's left hand and handed her the small knife so she could free herself. I sat on the bed holding my ribs, which hurt so badly I could hardly breathe. I feared I might pass out again.

The dispatcher was yelling at me. "Detective Harrison, what's happening?"

"Nothing," I said trying to catch my breath. "I'm trying to shut this asshole up so you can hear me."

"Are you all right?"

"Hell no. We need the paramedics and an ambulance."

Ivan started laughing. "You fucking coward! I knew you didn't have the guts to kill me."

"Shut up Ivan or I swear I'll blow your brains out," I yelled.

He laughed even harder. "You're so full of shit, Harrison. All talk. Big man on TV but when it comes time to pull the trigger you can't do it. You couldn't do it in that alley and you can't do it now. You're all talk, pussy!"

The sound of the weapon rang in my ears as Ivan's left kneecap exploded. He screamed at the top of his lungs. The second round shattered his right kneecap. Bone and meat hung from the wall around him. His face twisted in pain. He stared at me. The next round hit him in the groin. It lifted him completely off the floor and more of his intestines spilled out in front of him. His head slammed back against the wall. His howling now sounded more animal-like than human. Then his voice dropped off and I could barely hear him. He was very much alive but most sound had left him.

We stared at each other and I smiled. His face contorted in pain as he tried to speak, but he couldn't make any sounds. It felt good seeing him like this. The next round hit him in the center of the forehead. His brains spewed out on the wall behind him. He jerked once and then slumped forward, his face hitting the floor in front of him.

"Oh no, Storm, don't," Katy said.

The dispatcher was screaming at me over the phone. "Storm, what's going on? Are you all right?"

"Yeah, we're OK," I said. "Send the paramedics for Officer Perkins. He's unconscious downstairs in the kitchen. Send the coroner to get this piece of garbage out of our house."

I disconnected the call and passed out. The next thing I remembered, Katy was helping me down the stairs. We went to my truck and she helped lift me into the seat. The pain in my ribs was so bad I thought I was going to black out.

We passed several police cars with lights and sirens while we drove to the hospital. I faded in and out and neither one of us spoke. Physically, I felt like death warmed over. Mentally, I felt wonderful. Katy looked very scared and concerned. I reached over and touched her arm. "It'll be all right, honey." *That is, if I didn't spend the rest of my life in prison for murder.*

CHAPTER TWENTY-EIGHT

I don't remember arriving at the hospital but Katy had parked at the emergency entrance, opened the truck door, and was attempting to help me out. The pain intensified when I tried to move so I stopped her.

"Honey, don't. It hurts too much."

"Hold on, I'll be right back." She disappeared into the hospital.

The next thing I remember, I was in a hospital bed with a doctor standing over me. My right eye was swollen shut but I could see him through the left one. The bright lights hurt my one good eye. An IV had been inserted into my arm. I had a soft cast on my right wrist and my left was bandaged. When I licked my lips, I felt stitches in the bottom.

"Katy," I said in a weak voice.

A man's voice answered. "Are you awake, Mr. Harrison?"

"Kind of," I said trying to clear the cobwebs from my brain. "How long have I been out?"

"About an hour. I'm Doctor Brambly. How do you feel?"

"It's hard to breathe."

"That's because you have several cracked ribs, a broken nose and a concussion. I've given you a painkiller. I'll give you some oxygen, which should help too."

"Can I talk to my wife? It's important."

"I'll let her come in for a few moments."

Katy came in and placed her hand on my shoulder. "Storm, I'm here."

I opened my good eye and saw the most beautiful woman in the world standing over me. Her mascara was smeared and the right side of her face was swollen. "Are you okay?" I asked.

"I'm fine. Ivan knocked me out but nothing is broken."

"Come close. I want to tell you something." She leaned over and placed her cheek next to mine. "Don't say anything to anyone. Tell them we don't want to make any statements until after we recover and I am off medications."

"Okay, Storm. But I'm so scared. What are we going to do?"

"We'll be all right. I love you. Promise me you won't tell them anything." I squeezed her hand.

"I promise." She leaned down and kissed my forehead. "I love you too."

A nurse walked into the room. "Mrs. Harrison, we need to get a couple more x-rays. You can wait here if you want."

Katy squeezed my hand then released it. The last I remember, I was being wheeled down the hall. I woke up in a bed in a darkened room. A sliver of light shone from the bathroom. A heart monitor beeped in the background. Someone sat in a chair next to me. I couldn't see who it was because the pole holding two IV bags blocked my view. My mouth tasted of dried blood and I needed to pee. A sharp pain shot through me when I attempted to sit up. I moaned and someone stood up from the chair. "Storm, are you awake?" Katy asked.

"I need to go to the bathroom." I held my ribs.

"Hold on." She lifted the covers and placed a plastic urinal between my legs. A nurse came in, saw what Katy was doing and left. I didn't know anyone else was in the room until I heard Doc's voice. "Is there anything I can do?"

"Not right now," Katy said. "The nurse went to get the doctor."

Doc walked over and stood next to us. "Hello, Storm."

"Thanks for being here, Doc. Have the police tried to contact you?"

"No, not yet."

"If they do, don't talk to them. We'll work through this together."

"Are you sure? There's an easier way to handle this you know."

"I know what I'm doing, Doc. They don't know what happened and we aren't going to tell them. Don't answer any questions and this will turn out OK."

"Storm, I'm scared," Katy said. "They'll prosecute you. That 911 call was recorded."

"We'll beat it, Katy. Trust me." To change the subject, I asked, "How long have I been asleep?"

"About six hours,' Katy said. "It'll be light in a couple of hours."

The doctor came into the room. Katy removed the urinal and covered me back up. "Mr. Harrison, how's your breathing this morning?"

"Better as long as I don't move. It feels like two linebackers blindsided me."

"You have a lot of injuries but none life threatening." He picked up my chart and started writing on it.

"My face sure is swollen."

"Yep," said Doc Martin. "He stomped you pretty good. You must have really pissed him off." He stood next to Katy, holding her hand.

"He was going to do a lot worse than that," I replied. "Katy and I are lucky to be alive. How's Officer Perkins doing?"

The doctor answered. "He's going to be fine. We thought we were going to have to operate to relieve the swelling in his brain, but it's going down on its own. He should make a full recovery."

The doctor put my chart back on the bed. "But you have four cracked ribs, two concussions, a stress fracture on your right wrist and bruising all over your back, arms and legs. You have stitches on your head, wrist and lip. Your eye socket has a stress fracture below the right eye. My main concern is blood clots. I put you on a blood thinner which will make the bruises look worse. An eye specialist will be coming by later to check on you. What's your pain level from 1 to 10?"

"Somewhere between 6 or 7, unless I try to move, then it's 8 or 9."

"I'll increase your pain medication. You'll likely feel better within the next couple of days except for the ribs. They'll be very painful for a while longer. Stay in bed and try not to move any more than you have to. We'll give you something to help you sleep at night if you need it." He gave the nurse instructions and they both left.

Katy came over and kissed my forehead. "What can I get for you, honey?"

"Water."

She poured a glass of water and held it to my lips. It hurt where the stitches were. I took several gulps before she suggested I use a straw. I was then able to drink with minimal pain.

"If you're hungry I can get you something soft to eat," she offered.

"Hungry but mouth is sore."

"I'll call the nurse and get you something."

"Have the police been here yet?" I asked.

"Jim Pomush stopped by while you were being x-rayed."

"What did he want?"

"Mainly just checking on you and Officer Perkins. But he asked me to sign a consent form to search our house."

"Did you sign it?"

"Yes. Was that all right?"

I thought about that for a moment. "It doesn't matter. If you had said no, he would have gotten a warrant anyway. But if anyone asks any more questions, just tell them we want a lawyer."

"I've already hired Ralph Bremer to represent us."

I turned my head to look at her and pain shot down my arm. Doc saw me wince. "Are you OK, Storm? What can I do?"

"I'm all right, Doc, but I want Katy to fire Ralph Bremer. I'll get a public defender to represent me."

Katy looked at me and then at Doc. Doc rolled his shoulders and held out his hands palms up. "Haven't you told him?"

"No, we haven't discussed our financial situation," Katy said.

Doc scratched his head. "Well, I think this might be a good time to do that. I'm going to head down to the cafeteria and find some coffee while you two talk."

Doc left and Katy pulled her chair around so it was close to the bed. "I suppose I should have told you this before we were married, but it happened so fast I never found the right time. Besides, you never questioned me about money."

"What should you have told me?"

Katy took a deep breath. "We would never qualify for a public defender. We are what they call, *comfortable.*"

I wasn't sure I understood what she was saying. "What exactly does that mean?"

"We're worth a lot of money. My parents had million dollar life insurance policies that paid triple indemnity if they were to die on a commercial airline. The chartered flight they were on when it crashed was considered commercial. Since I was an only child, I inherited everything. They would never assign us a public defender." Katy looked at him anxiously. "You're not mad at me are you?"

"No, I'm not angry. I understand. Someone might try to marry you for your money. I'm glad I didn't know." Katy squeezed my hand. "But why marry a guy like me?"

She gently placed her hand on my chest. "Oh, stop it, Storm. I married you because I love you and I want to spend the rest of my life with you. I want to have your children and grow old with you. That's why I married you."

I didn't know what to say. We had never discussed money or children. "That's exactly what I want too, Katy."

"Oh, Storm, I'm so glad to hear you say that," she said. "Because we haven't discussed children either." She bent over and kissed me gently on the cheek. "I love you so much."

The nurse came back in and set a tray of food on the swing out table. "We have soup, mashed potatoes, vanilla pudding, and ice cream," she said as she pushed the tray closer to my bed and left. Katy spoon-fed me.

Doc came back in the room. "Did you tell him?"

"Yes," said Katy.

"All of it?"

"No."

"Well you should add that good news too while you're at it," Doc said.

I gave them a puzzled look. "What news."

"Well." Katy paused.

"Go on," Doc said. "He deserves to know."

I looked at Doc and then at Katy. "Deserves to know what?" I asked.

Katy took a deep breath and blurted out, "I'm pregnant. You're going to be a father."

"I . . . I'm going to be a father. Like in a dad?"

"Yep." Doc said with a big grin on his face. "You're going to be a wonderful father and I'm going to be a great uncle. Congratulations, daddy!"

I felt lightheaded and didn't know what to say. Katy looked anxious as she awaited my reaction. I couldn't think for a moment. I feigned a smile. "I'm going to be a father. Isn't that wonderful?"

Katy bent down, hugged me and gently kissed me on the good side of my lips. "I'm so happy," she said.

My smile grew larger and so did my pain as I considered what I had learned over the past half hour. I'm married to the most beautiful woman I've ever met, we're wealthy and I'm going to be a father. Life couldn't get much better than that. *That is, if I can avoid going to prison.*

CHAPTER TWENTY-NINE

Light shone through the window and cottonwood tree leaves blew back and forth in a gentle breeze, casting shadows into my room. Katy was asleep on a small couch next to the window. I would have slept better that night if the nurse hadn't come around every two hours to check my blood pressure. She opened her eyes and saw me watching her. She yawned, sat up and stretched her arms high above her head. She looked tired. "You should go home and get a good night's sleep," I said.

She ignored my comment, walked over and kissed my forehead. "How do you feel this morning?"

"Sore and bored. I want to get out of here."

The nurse came in to take my blood pressure and change my bandages. When she was done, Katy told her that we didn't want any visitors, except Doctor Martin, unless she approved it. I wasn't sure what that was about, but I didn't disagree. I needed rest and time alone with my wife. The nurse left and came back with a sign that read, *All visitors report to the nurses' station,* taped it to our door, and left, closing the door behind her.

The room phone rang about an hour later and Katy answered it. She said she would be right out, hung up the phone and started to walk out. "Where are you going?"

"There's someone here to see us. I'll be right back."

Katy left and I was almost asleep when she returned. A young woman in a wheelchair holding a newborn baby in her arms was wheeled in by a nurse, a little girl following close behind. It took me a few seconds to realize it was Charlie Blakely's wife, Jenny and her children. "Hi, guys. Come in. What are you doing here?" I asked.

"I had my baby yesterday. We're being discharged today and I wanted to come see you before we left."

Katy pushed Jenny closer to me so I could see the baby swathed in pink.

Assuming that meant she'd had a girl, I took a chance and said, "Oh, she's beautiful." I couldn't take my eyes off the tiny infant, realizing it wouldn't be long before I'd be holding one of my own.

Her three-year-old daughter, Emily, came to my bedside holding a drawing in one hand and flowers in the other. "Hi, sweetheart. How are you?"

"I'm all right, Mr. Stormy," she said as she handed me the bouquet. Her big eyes looked sad and tired. She looked at the IV tubes in my arm and touched one of the plastic bags with her finger. "What happened?"

"I had an accident."

"Does it hurt?" Her little voice was full of concern.

"Just a little. It looks worse than it is. I'll be all right in no time."

"I drew this for you," she said as she handed me a crayon drawing. Even though they were stick people, I could tell it was her family. A lady held a baby in her right hand while holding the hand of a little girl with the other. The father had wings and stood on the other side holding the little girl's hand. She pointed to each figure. "That's daddy, that's me, that's mommy and that's Katy," she said as she looked back at me. "My daddy's not here anymore. He's in heaven."

My heart was breaking. I had a lump the size of an apple in my throat. I looked at my wife, fighting to hold back the tears.

Katy could see I was struggling. "Who's Katy?"

"My baby sister," Emily said while pointing at the infant.

Jenny spoke up. "I named her after you, Mrs. Harrison. For what you and your husband did for us."

"Oh, that's so sweet, Jenny." She walked closer to the baby to get a better look at the child. "She's absolutely precious." Katy picked up the baby's hand and little Katy wrapped her tiny fist around her big finger. Her eyes began to mist. "Oh, look, Storm. She took my finger and stole my heart."

"I know this is something you weren't expecting," Jenny said, "and you don't have to give me an answer right away. But, I was wondering if you and your wife would consider being Katy's godparents."

"Oh my gosh, of course. We would love to be her godparents," Katy said. "Wouldn't we, Storm?"

"It would be an honor, Jenny."

"I want godparents too," Emily said.

"Who are her godparents?" I asked.

"She doesn't have any. But with Charlie gone, I know the baby should have someone in case something would happen to me."

"Well, if it's all right," I said, "we'd like to be godparents for both the girls, wouldn't we, Katy?"

"Of course we would," Katy said as she hugged Emily. "I've always dreamed of having daughters."

"What is a godparent?" asked Emily.

Katy knelt down to Emily's level. "That means we will be your parents too. We will always be there to take care of you if you need us."

A big smile spread across Emily's face. "I'd like that. I miss my daddy a lot." Emily started to cry.

"I think we should be going," Jenny said.

Katy hugged Emily. "Come on, honey. I'll walk you out. I'll be back in a minute, Storm."

After they left, I couldn't hold back the tears. Knowing Charlie would still be alive if I hadn't loaned him my car bothered me more than I wanted to admit. I was glad Ivan was dead and that he died in a great deal of pain. But nothing could make up for the loss of a little girl's father or the daughter that Charlie would never see.

Katy came back and saw my tears. She didn't say anything but held my hand and cried with me. It eased my pain. Katy told me she was going to start an educational fund for the girls.

The next few days were a blur, each bringing more medical tests and a little less pain. The IV was removed and I could walk to the bathroom and back. I only had to use the bedpan at night. The nurses insisted on being in the room any time I was out of bed for safety reasons. They woke me up every few hours to take my blood pressure and monitor my medications. The eye doctor said I would heal without the need for surgery. I slept with difficulty because of the broken ribs and I wanted to go home.

We received so many flowers and cards from both friends and strangers that we had some of them delivered to patients who didn't have any.

Katy stayed with me most of the time and only left for a few hours when Doc was there. I was never alone. Katy purchased round trip airline tickets for my parents so they could visit me. They spent three days before returning home.

My cell phone had run out of power and I didn't bother charging it. On the fourth day, we received a call from the nurse's station announcing Jim Pomush was here and wanted to see us. We told them to send him in.

He arrived with a notebook and pen in hand. Clearly, this was not a courtesy call.

"Hi, Storm, Katy, Doctor Martin," he said as he entered the room. He shook mine and Doc's hand and hugged Katy. Doc excused himself to go find some coffee and give us some privacy. Pomush took a seat.

"We completed the search of your home and I've brought you a list of items we removed."

I took the list, examined it and then handed it to Katy. They had taken all the items I expected, including our weapons and the chair I had been tied to. They took the bed sheets and pillows from our bed and the can of shaving cream. They took everything belonging to Ivan, including the rope we had been bound with, his knife, straight razor, the nunchucks and his guns. It was all very professional.

"How are you doing?" Jim asked.

"I think we're all right," I said. "You tell me."

He looked uncomfortable. "I hate to ask this, Katy, but did Ivan sexually assault you?"

"No," she said. "But that was his intent, I'm sure."

I thought he should have asked that question a lot sooner. He waited for us to say something but we didn't.

"Storm, I know you're aware of your rights, but I have to advise you of them anyway." He took a Miranda rights card from his pocket and read me my rights, then asked, "Do you understand your rights?"

"Yes, Jim, we know our rights," Katy said. She handed him Ralph Bremer's business card. "We're not going to make any statements and all questions about your investigation in the future should be directed to our attorney."

Jim read the card and smiled. He was off the hook and there would be no interview today. "All right," he said, making a note regarding the reading of my rights and our notification to contact our lawyer for any further questions. He looked at Katy. "May I keep this card?" Katy nodded and he placed it in his front pocket.

CHAPTER THIRTY

Ivan screamed but I couldn't hear his words. His head exploded and he fell forward, half his brains remaining on the wall behind him. The smell of gunpowder and blue smoke filled the room around me. Katy stood next to the bed with her hands covering her mouth. I couldn't make out what she was saying.

I woke up on the same couch where I'd spent many hours discussing how screwed up I was with Doc Martin. It was dark and I was breathing hard, sweat beading my forehead and heart racing. I wasn't afraid and didn't feel bad about Ivan's death. I hadn't slept with Katy, knowing my tossing and turning would keep her awake most of the night while I tried to find a way to ease my aches and pains.

The clock read 7:12 a.m. I hobbled to my feet, made a pot of coffee, and went out on the back patio with my morning cup. It had rained overnight and the air smelled of fresh pine, damp earth and dead leaves so sweet it was almost addictive. Drops of water clung to red, yellow and orange leaves in the trees and squirrels chased each other up a tree and then along the top of the neighbor's fence. A robin pulled a worm out of the dirt and flew away. The cold damp air of an early winter felt good in my lungs. A red glow filled the eastern sky announcing a new day and steam rose from my coffee.

"Good morning, Storm," Katy said as she walked out to join me, a cup of coffee in hand. She wrapped her arm around my waist and gently pulled me towards her. "It's cold and wet out here. Why don't you come inside before you catch a chill?"

Doc sat at the kitchen table drinking coffee and reading the newspaper when we went inside. He studied me over the top of his reading glasses. "How'd you sleep last night?"

"All right, I guess."

"No bad dreams?"

"Dreams, but not bad ones," I said.

Doc narrowed his eyes as if he didn't believe me but went back to reading the newspaper. I refilled my coffee and sat next to him. Katy brought the yellow pages to the table and joined us.

"What are you looking for, honey?"

"A good contractor." She turned the pages. "I need someone to repair the drywall in our bedroom and remove the electric seat from the hidden stairwell. I want the coal bin removed and sealed up with bricks. I also need a professional cleaning company to clear up the mess so I can list the house."

I couldn't blame her. I didn't want to live there either. But I also didn't want to buy another house before we found out what was going to happen with the State Attorney's investigation. I hoped we wouldn't wear out our welcome with Doc Martin. I felt like a homing pigeon with no home to fly to.

Katy stayed in contact with the lawyer I didn't want. The wait-and-see game was taking its toll on her, our uncertain future weighing heavily on her mind. I felt restless with a sense of uncertainty in my soul, wondering if I would ever work as a law enforcement officer again.

To kill time, I spent the day losing chess matches to Doc. We were on our second evening cocktail and he was humbling me at another game when lightning rattled the windows and rain pounded the roof.

"Storm, Doc, come in here," Katy yelled from the family room. "Connie Mason will be talking about the Ivan Collins case as soon as the commercial ends."

Just the mention of Connie's name stirred mixed emotions. We took our drinks and joined her in the family room. I had a bad feeling about the pending report.

The commercial ended and Connie began her broadcast. *"Special Prosecutor, Paul Miller is asking for a grand jury to determine if Colorado Springs Detective, Storm Harrison, should be criminally charged in the death of serial killer, Ivan Collins. The announcement earlier this afternoon sparked protests in both Colorado Springs and Denver."*

The TV showed protesters at both the county and state courthouses holding signs supporting me. Connie continued to speak during the videos. *"Paul Miller stated that even though Ivan Collins was an alleged serial killer of both young girls and police officers, he believes Detective Harrison took it upon himself to be both judge and executioner. Mr. Miller said he would have sought the death penalty for Ivan Collins if convicted of these horrible crimes, but he deserved a fair trial."*

I wasn't sure if it was Connie or the fact that they were convening a grand jury that upset me the most. I hit the remote, turning the TV off. "I get so tired of listening to her bullshit."

"That's being a little hard, Storm," Katy said. "Connie has been more than fair in reporting this case."

"Whatever! I need another drink." I got up to leave the room.

"Me too," Doc said as he followed me. "Can I get you something, Katy?"

"A club soda for me."

She trailed us to the bar and I made the drinks.

I felt restless and needed to get out of the house. The rain had stopped and the walls were closing in on me. I'd been cooped up way too long. My ribs were still sore and I had a soft cast on my right wrist. The swelling in my eye had gone down but a yellowish color remained. The stitches had been removed.

"Let's go to Wong's," I said. "I'm craving Vietnamese food."

Doc looked at Katy and shrugged his shoulders. "I'm game if you're up to it."

"I am," I said. "How about you, Katy?"

"Sure. I don't want to be here alone. But are they open this late?"

I called Wong's and a recording said they closed at 10:00 p.m. We decided to go to The Oak Barrel instead. A few people sat at the bar watching TV when we arrived but the dining room was almost empty. We were seated and placed our drink orders. Katy nudged me and nodded towards a table where a man sat with his back to us. His half-eaten plate sat in the center of the table and he was doing paperwork. "Who's that? I asked.

"Chas Woods."

"Why don't you go say hello?" I said. "Maybe we'll get free drinks again."

"I don't think so after that last bar bill he got from us. And knowing him, he'd get Paul Bremer to add it to your legal fees."

As our meals arrived, so did Connie Mason. She wore the same clothes she had on during the broadcast. She approached our table and both Katy and Doc stood up. I didn't. Connie kissed them on their cheeks as if they were long lost friends. "I'm so sorry you and Storm are having to go through this," she said. "I'm just glad you both were able to survive such an ordeal. How are you holding up?"

"We'll be all right," Katy said in a not too convincing tone.

"How about you?" Connie asked, looking at me. "How're you doing?"

"I'm fine. . . just hungry," I said hoping she'd get the hint and leave.

"You did a nice job of reporting tonight," Doc said.

"Thanks, Doctor Martin. I hate to be the bearer of bad news."

"You've been more than fair, Connie," said Katy. "We appreciate you even if my husband has bad manners."

I looked up to see Connie's expression when Katy called me her husband. If this surprised her, she didn't show it.

"Congratulations to both of you," she replied. "I wish you all the happiness in the world." She looked at me and smiled. "He's one of the good guys even if he has bad manners. Perhaps you'll rub off on him, Katy."

Everyone seemed to think that was funny except me. "Please excuse me," Connie said. "I have a date."

Connie walked to Chas' table. He stopped writing when she arrived, stood up and pulled her chair out for her. They spoke for a moment and he turned and glanced back at us. He waved, acknowledging us. Katy and Doc waved back. I didn't.

"Storm, you should be nicer." Katy said. "Connie could do you as much harm as good if she wanted to and I understand her boss, Mr. Fiber, doesn't like you for some reason."

"Screw him," I said. Obviously my mood wasn't getting any better and I wished I'd stayed home.

"Chas works for Bremer and might be part of your defense team," Doc said. "It's not in your best interest to piss him off."

Doc had a point and that got me to thinking. I motioned our waiter over to our table and told him to put Mr. Woods and Miss Mason's food and drinks on our tab. Doc and Katy looked at each other but didn't say anything. I pretended as if it were the most natural thing in the world to do. We ate in peace after that.

Before leaving, I wrote my cell phone number on the back of my business card, walked over to Charles' table and handed it to him. "Give me a call sometime, Chas. We'll do lunch." I looked at Connie and smiled, "Goodnight, Miss Mason."

"What's gotten into to Storm?" Katy asked while walking to our car.

"I don't know," Doc answered. "Either he has discovered his manners or his head injury knocked some sense into him." They both laughed, I smiled. Like I said, it got me to thinking.

⊫┼╂╾

The following morning I received a call from Charles Woods. We made plans to have lunch later that day. He asked if I wanted Ralph Bremer to be present. I told him no because I wanted this to be a private meeting.

Charles sat in a corner booth of a small Chinese restaurant when I arrived. Half of the clientele were foreign and many spoke in their native language. Chas stood and offered his hand. I ignored it, took a seat and picked up the menu. I'm not normally the jealous type but the fact that he had once dated Katy was enough for me not to like him. "What's your role in my defense when I get indicted?"

He seemed a little put off by my disrespect. I'm sure he wasn't used to people talking down to him, but I'm not the type of client he normally represented. He sat back down but didn't answer. The waiter came and took our drink orders.

"I've gone over the police reports, witness list, and checked the evidence to determine what, if anything, we can challenge or dispute. I'm still looking into the backgrounds of the potential witnesses to see if we can discredit them." He stopped and looked at me for a moment. "Of course, we won't put you on the stand unless we have to."

"I won't take the stand under any conditions."

Charles cleared his throat. "Well, that will be Mr. Bremer's call. But he normally doesn't like to put defendants on the stand unless he thinks it's necessary. Of course, he'll want to put Katy on the stand."

"Not going to happen," I said.

Charles took drink of water, sat the glass down and picked up his menu. "I'm sure Mr. Bremer will call her to testify, Mr. Harrison."

"You're fired," I said. I got up and left Charles sitting there with his mouth open.

When I got home, Katy was waiting for me. "How did it go?"

"Good. I fired them."

Katy's eyes widened with surprise. "You what?"

"I fired them."

"Why did you do that, Storm? They are the best defense team in the state."

"I told him we wouldn't take the stand. He said that would be Ralph Bremer's call. I won't have an attorney telling me how I want my defense handled."

"Are you crazy? Defense attorneys don't let their clients tell them how to plan their defense. Besides, the prosecutors will subpoena me anyway. "

"My attorney won't subpoena you. Look, Katy, I've been to more murder trials than most defense attorneys and I almost always beat them no matter how good they are. I know what needs to be done to win."

"I don't like this, Storm. I'll call Ralph Bremer and see if he'll meet with us."

"Fine, but this is my life, Katy. If I can't determine how my defense will be conducted, I don't want them."

Katy placed her hands on her hips and stared at me. "It's not only your life, but mine and that of our unborn child. If you want me to go along with this, I need to be involved in the decisions too." She shook her head and went into another room to make her call. When she came back, she told me Ralph Bremer would fly down in his private plane tomorrow and meet with us at 3:00 p.m. in Charles Wood's office to discuss our concerns.

Not wanting this to be our first fight, I didn't protest the appointment. When Katy left again, Doc looked at me with a grin on his face.

"What?" I asked.

"You're learning," he said as he stood up.

I started to say something but thought better of it.

"Want a drink?" he asked.

I followed him into the bar.

When Katy and I arrived at Charles' law office the next day, Paul Bremer was sitting at Charles' office desk looking at a stack of paperwork. Charles stood next to him pointing to a report. A glass wall separated us. The receptionist escorted us into a large conference room with a long wooden table and seated us on one side. Large oil paintings hung on the walls and the room smelled of lemon oil and cigar smoke. She asked if we wanted anything and we told her no. Water and glasses were already on the table.

Bremer came in, greeted us and took a seat at the head of the table. Charles followed him carrying his reports. He nodded at us, and sat across from Katy. Bremer started the meeting.

"Detective Harrison, your wife has retained our firm to represent you but it's my understanding you have some concerns?"

"I know how I want my defense to proceed, Mr. Bremer. Normally the prosecutor presents evidence and the defense attorney attacks it, attempting to make the witnesses look bad. That's not going to happen in my case. If the evidence is correct and the witnesses are telling the truth, we are not going to challenge their testimony or the evidence. Most juries aren't as stupid as you think they are and see right through the bullshit being thrown at them. It just drags the trial out and the final results are the same. And, neither Katy nor I will testify under any circumstances."

Bremer sat back in his chair, rubbed his chin and looked at Charles but didn't say anything. Tapping his pencil on the table, he looked down at the file in front of him and closed it. He leaned back in his chair and asked, "You aren't considering pleading guilty if you are charged with murder are you, Detective Harrison?"

"You mean when I'm charged, don't you?"

Charles intervened. "We won't know what will happen until the grand jury comes back with their decision. Then we can take the appropriate action."

I smiled at Charles. "Bullshit."

He started to reply but Bremer held up his hand and stopped him. "Can you please explain, Mr. Harrison?" he asked.

"The grand jury is nothing more than a rubber stamp and we all know it. The only reason Miller is presenting this case to them is because it would be unpopular for him to prosecute me. He doesn't want any long-term political repercussions. He can always claim he didn't have a choice after the grand jury indicted me."

Bremer smiled and nodded. "That's very perceptive of you, Detective. Paul Miller used to work for me before he took the job as a prosecutor at the Attorney General's office. He's a cold-hearted unscrupulous son-of-a-bitch." He leaned back and smiled. "That's why I hired him in the first place. He could have made a lot more money working for me, but unfortunately, he had political ambitions. This case will give him national exposure and credibility among his colleagues if he wins it. He will go for your throat and do anything to get you convicted. That's why you need us."

"That may be true," I said. "But if you win, it would greatly enhance your firm's reputation and bring in more high profile cases in the future."

"I see you've thought this through, Mr. Harrison. But. . . all of us must consider the consequences of your actions. You have the most to lose. If you are convicted, you'll spend the next twenty years behind bars. And police officers don't fare well in there I'm told."

"I fully understand what's at stake here, Mr. Bremer. The evidence against me is overwhelming. But since it is my life at stake, I want to have a say in how my case is to be conducted."

Katy interrupted. "Storm, this affects me also and I'm paying for your defense. I think you should let Mr. Bremer handle this case the best way he thinks he can get an acquittal."

I turned my head to look at her. "Mr. Bremer would handle this case pro bono and so would any other big law firm in the state. They want the media attentions as much as Miller does. If Bremer's firm doesn't want to represent me, I'm sure I can find many other firms that will."

Charles cleared his throat and adjusted himself in his chair. He obviously didn't like my last statement. He was about to say something when Bremer spoke. "Well, perhaps it's time to look at your defense from a different angle. A person is innocent until proven guilty, Mr. Harrison. It's our job to make sure you remain innocent."

"You're wrong, Mr. Bremer. A person is guilty as soon as he or she commits the crime. It's the job of the police and prosecutor to prove their guilt in court."

"I stand corrected, Mr. Harrison. Of course you're right. I was only speaking from the legal perspective." He looked at his watch. "Perhaps we should take a break and resume our discussion after lunch. That way, you and your wife can come to terms on your defense strategy while we consider your proposal. Then perhaps we can work something out after you explain how you want us to proceed."

I knew Bremer was stalling. He was disappointed in the way this meeting was going and needed time to think it over. Charles' narrowed eyes and frown clearly indicated he was pissed. Bremer hoped Katy would be able to talk some sense into me while we were having lunch, which was why he suggested an early break. I planned on convincing her that I was right, and gaining her support when the meeting resumed.

During lunch I explained my defense strategy to Katy. She listened respectfully without interrupting. When I was finished, she said, "Storm, I understand where you're coming from, but you're taking a huge gamble. You can never know for sure what the jury will do. Most of them don't understand reasonable doubt. You could end up with a conviction or a hung jury and we'd have to appeal or start all over."

"You're right about jury trials. Miller will do everything in his power to persuade jury members to convict, even if they're sympathetic towards me. The evidence is very strong and I don't want most of it challenged."

"I don't know, Storm. It's such a big gamble," Katy said.

"Challenging hard evidence makes us look as if we are hiding something and would insult the jury's intelligence. I want them to trust me. I don't want the jury members and the press to think we're reaching for straws. Miller will get careless if he believes he'll get an easy conviction. I want to blindside him at the very end. It's what they don't know that creates reasonable doubt."

"I want to trust you, Storm, but you could end up in prison for a very long time. I can't let that happen." She began to cry.

"Katy, look at me," I said as I lifted her chin. She looked up with tear filled eyes. "If I let Bremer proceed the way he wants to, there's still no guarantee I would be acquitted. As a matter of fact, I don't believe I would be. But I think I can win my way and I'm willing to take that chance."

Attempting to choke back her tears, she said, "But, Storm, I can't let you go to prison for…"

I placed my hand over her mouth to stop her. "I want you to listen to me. I need you to support me and take care of our baby. You have to do this. Trust me. It's in our best interest."

She wiped tears away with her napkin. "All right, we'll try it your way. But I won't let you go to prison. I love you and need you. It wouldn't be fair. Go talk to Bremer and tell him what you want to do and see if he'll agree. But, I don't want to be in that meeting."

She called a taxi to take her home. I met Woods and Bremer and explained how I wanted my trial to proceed. When I finished, Bremer leaned back in his chair and stared at the ceiling while pondering my proposal. After a few minutes of silence he said, "I understand what you want to do, Mr. Harrison. But I don't know why you want to do it. Your plan might work, but I think you're taking unnecessary risks." He paused and looked at Charles. "Since I cannot guarantee your acquittal under our plan, my firm will represent you for free if you're willing to live with the consequences of your decision and agree to my terms."

I listened to his proposal and agreed. We shook hands. Even Charles seemed pleased with the outcome.

CHAPTER THIRTY-ONE

Katy and Doc sat at the kitchen table waiting to hear how the meeting went. Her eyes were red and she looked tired. Doc showed no emotion, as usual.

"How'd it go?" Katy asked.

"Great. Ralph Bremer decided his law firm would represent me pro bono."

Katy's mouth dropped open. "He's not going to charge us?"

"Nope, he's even going to send your retainer back."

"And his firm will still represent you?"

"Why?" Her eyes narrowed. "What did you do?"

Katy's forehead wrinkled and her eyes narrowed. "All right, Storm. What did you do?"

"We had a lot of differences but we eventually reached an enthusiastic agreement."

"What kind of differences?"

"Ralph wanted to move the trial to Denver. I didn't. He wanted to hire a few experts. I didn't. He wanted to delay the proceeding. I insisted on a quick and speedy trial. I wanted to pick the jurors and he didn't want me to. I wanted to approve the questions asked during cross-examination and which witnesses we called. He didn't. I told him we would hold the trial the way I wanted it or I'd find another firm to represent me."

"And he agreed?"

"Not completely, but he thinks my plan might work," I lied. "And he'll do it for free as long as I make a few concessions."

Katy glanced at me suspiciously. "What concessions?"

"Charles Woods will be my attorney of record, not Ralph Bremer."

"Storm, you don't want Chas. He's a jerk."

"I know, but I want him. He'll be easier to manipulate than Bremer. And you said Woods has a brilliant legal mind."

Katy shook her head. "He does, but why would you want him instead of Bremer?"

"Honey, Ralph Bremer is a smart guy. He wants his law firm on this case because of the national media attention it will generate. He won't represent me himself because if we were to lose it would damage his reputation as a lawyer. He thinks our chances of winning are slim to none. He was hoping I'd cop to a plea deal. He now understands that won't happen. But he also knows that if we win, it will be a big feather in his cap and his firm. It will generate a lot of business for him in the future."

"But what if you lose?"

"Then Bremer will remind everyone that he didn't charge us. Then he'll point the finger at Woods and get rid of him with little damage to his firm."

"But what will you do if you lose?"

"I'll file an appeal on the grounds that I had incompetent legal representation. Then I'd have my new attorney make a plea of not guilty by means of temporary insanity. With two concussions at the time of the shooting, I'd probably win on appeal."

Katy rolled her eyes, threw up her hands, and turned in a circle. "You're crazy, Storm. Why don't you just plead insanity now? I'd even take the stand and testify to it."

"Calm down and hear me out. You can't take the stand and I can't claim temporary insanity because it would end my career as a cop. And besides, I'll take my chances with the jury with my plan. Paul Miller will think Charles Woods is an idiot and not catch on until it's too late."

Katy looked at me for a few moments, walked in a circle, sat down and put her face in her hands.

Doc asked, "And Charles Woods is okay with all of this?"

"Chas sees only the national stage he'll be standing on. All of his friends will see him on TV and think he's some big shot attorney. He has his eye on the huge promotion Bremer will give him if he wins. He hasn't recognized the downside yet.

"I bet he'll figure it out about half way through the trial," Katy said with a concerned look.

"It won't take him that long. By then, it'll be too late. He'll be committed and Bremer won't let him off the hook."

Katy shook her head in disgust. "Excuse me. I've got to go to the bank." She left the room.

"What do you think, Doc?"

"I think I may have to take the stand and testify that you're insane also."

"Why do you say that?" I asked.

"Because they announced that the grand jury indicted you for second degree murder while you were in your meeting."

I tapped my fingers on the wood table. "Well, we knew it was coming. Look at the good side. It wasn't first-degree murder. And as long as Connie Mason is dating Woods, I'll get positive news coverage."

There was a knock on the door. Doc stood up and looked out the window. "You'll be seeing her sooner than you think. Your police buddies are here."

CHAPTER THIRTY-TWO

Doc answered the door and let Jim Pomush in. He had a gloomy look on his face. "Storm, I'm afraid I have to take you in."

He started to read me my rights, but I cut him off. "I'm not going to be making any statements, Jim. You'll have to talk to my attorney." I turned around and placed my hands behind my back.

"Are you armed?"

"No," I replied. He didn't search me.

"I'm not going to cuff you. Let's go."

"You better. The press will be at the station when we get there and will think I'm being given special treatment. And it's department policy."

"Damn you, Storm. Do you have any idea how hard this is?"

"Just do your job, Jim. Everything will work out all right in the long run."

He reluctantly cuffed me in the front instead of the back. The cuffs weren't tight and I might have been able to wiggle out of them if I wanted to. "You're getting sloppy, Detective," I said. "You'd chew my ass if I cuffed anyone like that."

"Oh, shut up and get in the car. Let's get this over with."

I laughed as we walked out the door.

"I'm glad you think this is funny, because I don't."

Two marked police cars were parked at the curb. "I see you brought backup."

"Hell, they're part of your fan club."

I waved and the officers gave me a thumbs-up before driving off.

Pomush opened the front passenger side front door for me. "Not all the officers feel the way they do. Some think you should be fired."

I opened the rear door and slid in. Jim shook his head, closing both doors. He walked around, got in, and started the car. "You're a pain in the ass, Harrison."

The media was out in force when we arrived at the station. News vans and reporters jockeyed for a place to get the best shots, or close enough for a possible statement. Several uniformed officers held them at bay. Pomush opened the rear door to let me out. I was greeted with flashes from a hundred cameras. Several news stations were represented and all had their cameras rolling. I was glad that I shaved this morning but wished I'd worn nicer clothes. Jim quickly escorted me towards the door to the jail. The reporters shouted questions at me, which I ignored.

Then I heard Connie Mason yell, "Detective Harrison, how will you plead to these charges?"

I stopped and faced her cameraman. "Not guilty." She asked something else but I had turned and entered the station before she finished.

Pomush took my property, including the buckle knife that I used to slice Ivan's stomach open. "You lied to me, Storm. You said you were unarmed. Is this the knife you used to cut your ropes?" he asked as he felt the blade.

I smiled but didn't answer. Jim shook his head. "I'd forgotten about this," he said as he shoved the blade in and out. "I couldn't figure out how you'd done that. I'm afraid this will have to go into evidence, Storm."

I watched him looking at the knife. He shook his head as he placed it into a plastic bag and stapled it closed. He seldom made mistakes and knew I had caught him.

After being mugged and printed, I was placed in a holding cell by myself to keep me away from other inmates. There were no windows, just a small table and three small chairs. I had spent so many hours here that it should have felt routine. But being a suspect instead of an officer challenged my security. I leaned back against the wall and closed my eyes. I thought I knew who I was most of the time, but now I wasn't sure. Sometimes when I saw my own shadow, I wondered who the stranger was that followed me.

Several police buddies stopped by to offer their moral support. Jim came back in an hour to deliver me to Court for my arraignment. When we arrived at the courthouse, protesters had gathered with signs supporting me. They chanted, "Set, Storm free. Set Storm free."

Chas, Katy, and a man I assumed was Paul Miller, were waiting inside the packed courtroom. Chas wore what appeared to be a five-thousand-dollar three-piece dark blue suit. He had a gray shirt with a white collar and cuffs and diamond cuff links. His tie was red, white and blue with a small American flag clasp. His hair was freshly cut and fingernails manicured. He looked more like a candidate running for the White House than a lawyer, or a thespian dressed for his first lead role in a major motion picture.

More reporters than spectators filled the courtroom. When the judge entered, everyone stood. He sat down, slammed his gravel on the bench to quiet the crowd, then told the bailiff to close the doors and not to admit anyone else. "You will remain quiet," he said to the audience. "I don't want to see any camera flashes during these proceedings. If I do, I'll clear the courtroom. Is that understood?" No one objected and everyone sat except those who had their cameras rolling.

Judge Stanton addressed me and I stood up. "Mr. Harrison, you have been charged by the grand jury with one count of second degree murder in the death of Ivan Collins within the state of Colorado on or about October 16th, 2012. Do you understand the charge?"

"Yes, Your Honor. I understand."

"Second degree murder under Colorado law means you knowingly caused the death of another person. Second-degree murder can be a class 2 or class 3 felony depending on the circumstances of the death. Class 2 felonies are punishable by 8 to 24 years in prison and a fine of $5,000 to $1,000,000 per Colorado Revised Statue 18-1.3-401. Class 3 felonies can result in a state prison sentence of 4 to 12 years and a fine of $3,000 to $750,000 per Colorado Revised Statue 18-1.3-401. Do you understand the punishment you could receive if you are convicted of second or third degree murder?"

"Yes, Your Honor. I understand." Although outwardly calm, butterflies fluttered deep inside me. I had heard these instructions given to many men over the years, but they held more meaning when applied to me.

"How do you plead to these charges against you?"

"Not guilty, Your Honor."

Judge Stanton looked at me over the top of his glasses. "If you are convicted of second or third degree murder, the jury will be given instruction on the law regarding the differences between second degree murder and third degree murder and they will have to decide which one you are guilty of during the sentencing phase of the trial, if we get to that point. Do you understand?"

"Yes, I understand," I said as I glanced back at Katy. She showed no expression but I could see fear in her eyes.

Chas stood and addressed the court. "Your Honor, my client would like to exercise his right to a speedy trial. We would like to proceed as soon as possible."

Judge Stanton glanced at me over the top of his reading glasses. "Is this true, Mr. Harrison?"

"Yes, Your Honor."

He rubbed his chin for a moment and addressed the prosecutor. "Do you have any objections to a speedy trial, Mr. Miller?"

"No, Your Honor. The prosecution is ready to proceed at any time."

The judge looked back at me and rubbed his temple. "Mr. Harrison, I know you are acquainted with murder cases. Are you certain you don't need more time to prepare for your defense?"

"No, Your Honor. I want to proceed as soon as possible."

The judge addressed Chas. "You are seeking a jury trial, aren't you?"

"Yes, Your Honor."

"I will set a trial date as quickly as possible after the jury selection has been completed. I have no idea how long that will take." He glanced at me over the top of his glasses. I had never testified before him and didn't know him personally. He shuffled the paperwork in front of him and looked at Mr. Miller. "Does the prosecution have a recommendation for bond?"

"The prosecution recommends a bond of one million dollars." There was a gasp from the courtroom. The judge looked around and pounded the gavel on his desk to hush them.

Chas stood up to object. "Your Honor, my client is not a flight risk or a risk to the public. There is no evidence or indication he would flee if released on his own recognizance. He surrendered peacefully and wanted to be at these proceedings. The defense requests that my client be released without bail. I assure you he will show up for court."

The judge tapped his ink pen on his desk while he studied me. After a few moments, he turned his attention to the prosecutor. "I find your proposal for a million dollar bond excessive, Mr. Miller." Then he looked at Chas. "I do believe your client is not a danger to the public, himself or anyone else. But, second degree murder is a serious charge." Then he looked at me again, he asked, "Can you make a bond of 100,000 dollars?"

"No, Your Honor."

"I can and I will, Your Honor," Katy said from behind me.

Judge Stanton recognized her. "And you want to post bond for this man, Miss Taylor?

"Yes, Your Honor."

"Are you part of his defense team?"

"No, I'm his wife."

Everyone in the room turned their attention to Katy. "I see," said the judge. "When do you think you could post his bond, Mrs. Harrison?"

"Immediately, Your Honor."

The judge peered over the top of his glasses at Katy. "I see. Mr. Harrison, I'm setting your bond at 100,000 dollars. These proceedings are complete unless either of you," he said looking at the two attorneys, "have anything else you want to say." Both stated they had no further motions or questions. Judge Stanton slammed his gavel down officially ending the proceedings.

Jim Pomush came forward to cuff me. Katy joined us. "I'll go post your bond, honey," she said as she turned to leave.

"No hurry," I said.

As I was led from the courtroom, reporters yelled questions at me. I ignored them. Chas stopped in front of Connie Mason, faced the camera, "My client is not guilty and we will prove his innocence in court. But at this time we have no other statements to make. Please excuse us."

By the time I got back to the jail, Katy had arrived with an order from the court stating my bail had been met and that I was be released. Pomush gave me back my property, minus my belt and one small knife that would be added into evidence. He told me to stay out of trouble if possible. We shook hands and I left with my lovely bride. It felt good to be free. But the haunting question was, for how long?

CHAPTER THIRTY-THREE

S ix days after my arrest the jury selection began. Surprisingly, Chas and I had gotten along rather well, due primarily to the fact we hadn't seen each other and only spoke on the phone a few times. I met him at his office to go over my requirements for jury selection before we headed to the courthouse. He was eager and confident but it was my guess that it wouldn't last long.

"I'll take any competent military personnel, male or female, active duty or retired, preferably military academy graduates," I told him. "I'll accept schoolteachers if they are coaches, math, history or science teachers. I don't want liberal arts teachers. Blue-collar workers are welcome on the jury as long as they have at least a high school education. I want as many small business owners and mothers as possible. I don't want clergy or anyone on the very outside fringes of the political spectrum, and definitely no politicians. In other words, I want a cross section of everyday hardworking honest men and women with common sense and the ability to understand what is being said in the courtroom. I don't mind if they're a little on the naive side as long as they have a strong sense of right and wrong."

"I can live with that," Chas said. He hadn't yet come to the realization that his future hinged on the outcome of this case. Thus far, he was still basking in the media light, believing he had been handpicked for his talent as an attorney and not as a scapegoat. I hoped he would have a long and successful career at my expense. I decided to call him Chas to appease his ego, and hoped to keep him happy as long as possible.

When we got in the courtroom, I let Miller and Chas fight it out for the best jurors while I studied the possible candidates to determine if I could see anything from their demeanor that would disqualify them. I found a few undesirables who were quickly dismissed. But for the most part, I accepted the potential jury members within my specific categories.

During this time, Katy searched as many cases of acquittal dealing with reasonable doubt as possible. The more she discovered, the more she believed I might have a chance of winning, but not enough for her to feel comfortable with what I was doing. She had said, "Storm, promise you'll let me hire the most experienced appeals attorney in the country if you're convicted. And, I want you to let the new attorney handle the case the way he wants to." I agreed.

It only took two days to pick the jury. Then I met Chas to go over the discovery evidence. His secretary directed me into the conference room. "Would you like something to drink, Mr. Harrison?"

"Coffee please."

Papers covered the table. Ivan Collins' victim's files sat at one end. I had written many of them and knew what they contained. At the other end sat a tape recorder and evidence reports. The center of the table held the reports involving the death of Ivan Collins. One stack contained 8 X 10 color photos taken at the crime scene. Most were from the bedroom and the hidden stairway. I shuffled through them. One of the pictures showed him slouched forward with a big hole in the back of his head, both knees and groin dark red with blood. Another had been taken at the morgue, probably just before his autopsy. He was ashen colored, naked and all his blood had left him. This photo clearly showed the damage a .40 caliber round could do to the human body. His penis was hanging by a thread and one of his balls was missing. The hole in his forehead showed little damage compared to what the exit hole looked like and both knees were shattered with missing bone.

"Enjoying the photos, Storm?" Chas asked as he walked in the conference room.

"I wouldn't mind having a copy of this one." I held it up for him to see.

"I doubt the jury will enjoy them as much as you do. I'll try to keep them out of evidence."

I glanced at the photo one last time before placing it back on the table. "You can try, but I get photos like this into evidence all the time."

"Yes and they've never helped any of the defendants did they?"

He had a point. Jurors for the most part have a hard time seeing something like this. Many of them have never seen a dead body or a crime scene, let alone a murder victim's mutilated body. These photos wouldn't sit well with them and they wouldn't help my case.

We sat down and went over the evidence. Each piece was marked with the date, time, and location of where it was found. The case number, along with either Jim Pomush's or Maggie Hawthorn's name, was written on them to indicate who had entered them into evidence. From what I saw, everything looked very professional. The last piece of evidence was the small belt buckle knife that I had become very attached to.

I was vague in my answers about some of the evidence and wouldn't answer Chas' questions if they were too intrusive about the circumstances of Ivan's death. Miller had taken depositions from half of the detectives in the department and he seemed fixated on the one question he had asked every one of them. "Did you ever hear Detective Storm Harrison say he wanted to kill Ivan Collins?"

Unfortunately, I had told many people I wanted to kill that prick, including both Maggie and Jim Pomush. None of the officers lied during their depositions. And, I wouldn't want them to.

"It's clear that Miller is going to hammer the point that you said you wanted to kill Ivan Collins into the jury members' heads," Chas said. "That won't play well for you. I'll see if I can get it suppressed."

"Go ahead if you want to, but I think the judge will allow it."

Chas looked concerned. "Well if he does, I'll have to attack their testimony and try to get them to admit they thought you were just kidding and not serious."

"I was damn serious when I made those statements. I doubt you can get them to admit otherwise."

Chas stared at the pile of evidence before him. "I'm sure glad you aren't testifying, Storm. You'd hang yourself."

"I don't want you to make a big deal over the fact that I wanted to kill Ivan. If you do, the jury will think we're trying to hide something. That won't be what convicts or acquits me anyway."

"There's a hell of a lot of evidence here and none of it looks good for you. Especially the recording of you and the dispatcher with Ivan screaming in the background. I can try to create some doubt by asking the dispatcher if she knew what Ivan was doing when she heard him screaming."

Chas looked at me for a reaction. I didn't give him one.

"Maybe I can get the jury to think he was reaching for a gun or something," Chas said, searching for straws.

I didn't respond.

Chas shook his head. "He was reaching for a gun, wasn't he?"

When again I didn't respond, he continued. "Damn you, Storm. I could use a little help here if I'm going to have any chance of getting you off. If we put Katy on the stand, she could tell them he was going for a gun or the straight razor before you shot him."

"I've already told you, Katy is not going to take the stand. As my wife, they can't make her testify to anything that will incriminate me, so you'll have to do this without her testimony. If you can find a way to make the jurors think it was self-defense, do it. But we won't lie. Ivan didn't have a gun when he was shot."

Chas appeared much more worried about this case after seeing the evidence. "How about a knife? You had multiple concussions and were weak and confused. You thought you were going to pass out. Maybe you killed him because you knew he would kill both you and Katy if you passed out. She couldn't have stopped him because she was tied up."

"Good points, although I didn't sound all that confused during my conversation with the dispatcher."

"No, but you passed out at the hospital." He made some notes "I'll arrange for depositions from the doctor and nurses who treated you, stating the severity of your injuries and the risk they posed."

It was clear that my perceived lack of cooperation irritated him.

"Storm, why won't you tell me what happened in that room? Your statements to me are protected under client-attorney privilege and no one will ever know except me."

"It's not going to happen." I picked up Jim Pomush's report to read it while Chas went over the evidence list.

"Here's something," I said, pointing to Pomush's report. "See if you can find a witness statement from a Harold Williams."

"Who's he?"

"The neighbor across the street. He's a retired Army officer. He heard the shots and went outside to see what was going on."

"Let me see that." He quickly scanned the report. "This doesn't say anything we don't already know."

"Mr. Williams said he saw someone driving a large gray or blue car leaving the next door neighbor's house when he stepped out onto his porch."

"But he said he couldn't see who was driving the car and Pomush couldn't connect the car or the man to the crime."

"Keep reading. It also states that the people at the house where the car had been parked heard the shots and thought they were firecrackers. They claim they didn't have any visitors that evening and didn't know anyone who drove a car matching that description. I'll look for their statements."

Chas continued reading Pomush's report. "The lady that lives on the other side of Katy also said she saw the big car drive by when she looked out to see what was going on."

"What's her name?" I asked. "I want to look for her statement too." I took a yellow highlighter and started highlighting points of interest.

"Margret Maxwell. What's the big deal about that car anyway?"

"Who was in that car, Chas?"

"Hell, I don't know. You tell me. They never located the driver. Who do you think it was?"

"It doesn't matter who it was, but you need to call these neighbors and get the jury asking the same question you are."

"You're not suggesting there was someone else in that house are you?"

"I'm not suggesting anything."

After studying my face for a few moments, he resumed reading. It appeared that he was now considering other possibilities. I wanted him to keep thinking about them.

Katy had gone to her office to complete the paperwork for her temporary leave of absence and to brief the attorney who was taking over her caseload. I met Doc at The Oak Barrel for lunch. It was crowded and noisy with the noon rush hour. The smell of burgers, fries, onions and mushrooms filled the room. No one paid any attention to us. Doc was quiet and observant as usual as he studied my face. Finally he asked, "How're the nightmares, Storm?"

"They're gone. I sleep like a baby."

He smiled. "You won't think so after the baby's born. They cry a lot."

"How do you know? You've never had any."

"Not that I know of anyway," he said with a smirk. "But I changed a lot of your wife's diapers when she was a baby. She cried a lot. I hope the baby takes after her."

"Me too, if it's a girl."

"I hope so either way," he said with a grin.

Our food arrived and when the waiter left, I asked, "How's she really doing? She isn't saying much to me."

"This is hard on her because she's worried about you and the baby. She'll be all right if you're found innocent, but if you're convicted, I don't know what she'll do."

"If I'm convicted, I want you to take her and the baby away from here and keep them safe."

Doc changed the subject, "How's the defense coming?"

"Not much to work with unless one of us takes the stand and that's not going to happen."

Doc rubbed his chin. "I'll testify if you want me to."

"No thanks. I don't want you anywhere close to the stand this time around. I may need you if I'm convicted to claim temporary insanity on appeal."

"No problem. I'd swear that you've been insane ever since that incident in Iraq."

It was good to know Doc had my back. If Katy and I had a boy, I wanted to name him Robert after Doc. "How's Marcee?"

"Good. I don't worry her like you do Katy," Doc said as he picked up the tab.

I went back to Chas' office. We finished going over the evidence by 5:00 p.m. Chas looked tired when we left. As the day wore on, he seemed to realize what a mess he's gotten himself into.

CHAPTER THIRTY-FOUR

A pre-trial hearing was scheduled to go over several issues, including the media's request to have cameras in the courtroom. The protesters were out in force, holding signs supporting me when Chas and I arrived at the courthouse. I felt better knowing so many people believed in me, but their support wouldn't have any effect on the outcome of the trial.

Judge Stanton was an old fashioned, hard-nosed judge who didn't like anything disturbing his courtroom and I valued these qualities in him. Miller didn't seem to care if the press had cameras in the courtroom or not, but Chas wanted them. He'd regret that decision if I got convicted, but for now his oversized ego blinded him. The judge ruled not to allow cameras, much to Chas' dismay.

Next, Chas entered a motion to have Katy removed from Mr. Miller's witness list, noting Colorado statute 13-90-107 citing a husband and wife's privilege not to testify against each other.

Miller objected. "Katherine Harrison was a witness to the assault of Police Officer Michael Perkins and she was an assault and kidnap victim herself. She has to testify.

"Your Honor," Chas said. "Ivan Collins is not on trial here." "You can't make a wife testify against her husband."

Miller cut in. "Your Honor, we believe Storm Harrison wasn't even in the house when Officer Perkins was assaulted and Mrs. Harrison was kidnapped. Her husband hadn't committed any crimes yet. Her testimony is not protected during that time span."

"Your Honor, any statements my client's wife makes that would aid in his prosecution can't be allowed. I respectfully request she not be allowed to testify."

Miller started to respond, but the judge held up his hand stopping him. "Gentlemen, I will allow Mrs. Harrison to be called to testify about any incident that does not incriminate her husband. But I want evidence presented to the court that Mr. and Mrs. Harrison were married before the death of Mr. Collins. Mr. Miller, if you ask any questions I think are inappropriate, I'll stop you. To Chas he added, "If you feel he is asking questions that are privileged, you can object and I'll rule on the objection at that time."

The judge looked at both attorneys. "Are there any other matters we need to consider?"

Chas spoke up. "Your Honor, the prosecution has a Mr. Dale Justice listed as a witness. He's a ballistics expert, and I assume is being called to testify that all four shots fired at Ivan Collins came from a .40 caliber Glock handgun belonging to Storm Harrison. The defense is willing to stipulate that the weapon used to kill Ivan Collins was indeed the Glock my client purchased a few months prior to the killing, and that he still owns that weapon. The defense requests that Mr. Justice be removed as a witness to speed up the trial."

Judge Stanton looked at Miller. "Well?"

"I'll remove him from my witnesses list, Your Honor."

Chas referred to his notes. "There's a Doctor Ben Marciano listed as a witness. He is a surgeon who specializes in abdominal surgeries. I assume he will testify that Ivan Collins could possibly have survived the injuries to his stomach if he had been taken to the hospital. The defense will concede that Ivan Collins would have lived if taken to a hospital and not shot in the head. We request Dr. Marciano be excused from the witness list to speed up the trial."

Miller removed him from his list of witnesses.

"Your Honor," Miller continued, "the defense has not given us their complete witness list. I ask the Court to order that information be handed over in a timely manner."

"Your Honor, the prosecution has our complete witness list. We plan to call only four witnesses for the defense.

Judge Stanton removed his glasses. "I find the number of witnesses you are listing unusually short, counselor. Are you considering a possible plea deal before this trial starts?"

"Not at all, Your Honor. My client is innocent and we intend to prove that in court."

"Well," the judge said, "if neither one of you are waiting for DNA or other lab reports, I can't see any reason for not setting a date for this trial."

Neither Mr. Miller nor Chas objected.

"All right gentlemen," Judge Stanton said as he looked at his calendar, "how does Monday, November the 1st look? We may even get this over with before Christmas if we're lucky."

Chas looked at me and I nodded. "That will be fine, Your Honor."

"The State is ready to proceed at any time," Miller said.

"November 1st at 9 a.m. it is then. I'll see you in court, gentlemen," Judge Stanton said as he slammed his gavel, ending the proceedings. We all rose as the judge left the courtroom.

Questions erupted from reporters. I shuffled through the crowd and made my way out of the courtroom, leaving Chas to answer their questions. Doc waited for me in the hallway and we walked outside, past the protesters and into the cool clean air. A cold breeze blew out of the south as we drove away.

"Well, you asked for a speedy trial. Looks like you got one," Doc said.

"Yeah, a little sooner than I expected. The trial starts two weeks from today."

Doc glanced over at me. "Are you ready?"

I took a deep breath. "I sure hope so."

CHAPTER THIRTY-FIVE

A slight breeze greeted us that first cool November morning in Colorado. A few clouds clung to the higher mountain peaks, blending in with the snow-covered mountains. The sun appeared bright in a pearl blue sky. Most of the leaves had fallen but the gray gloom of winter had not yet set in. We'd already had a few dustings of snow but it had melted. It was a good day for a trial.

I chose a gray suit with a blue and black tie. Katy wore a dark jacket over a light blue blouse and a gray skirt. She looked stunning, but tired. She had tossed and turned most of the night. Doc wore casual slacks and a green sweater. His calm demeanor helped to keep both Katy and I relaxed. He would sit with her throughout the trial.

We ate breakfast watching the morning news. Connie Mason stood on the courthouse steps talking about the upcoming trial. A small crowd had gathered with signs, demonstrating against the proceedings.

When we arrived at the courthouse, the outside courtyard was packed with reporters and protestors. Doc dropped Katy and I off at the curb and went to find a parking spot. The protestors started chanting, "Storm, Storm, Storm," when they saw us getting out of the car. There were more signs today than we had seen in the past. Three older women stood on the steps with signs that read, "Thou shall not kill," "Only God can judge," and "Repent." I wondered if these signs were aimed at Ivan or me.

Prior to entering the courtroom, I saw a woman standing to one side with a small sign that read, "Thank you, Detective Harrison! Justice has been done. We love you." I was already inside the doors before I remembered who she was. I took Katy's hand and went back outside.

"Hello," I said to the woman as I took her hand and kissed her on the cheek.

"I just had to be here to support you for all you've done for me," she said as tears welled up in her eyes.

"Katy, this is Judy Olsen, Amber's mother."

Katy cupped Judy's other hand in hers. "I'm so sorry for your loss, Mrs. Olsen. I can't imagine the pain you have felt."

"Thanks to your husband, maybe I can start to heal now. I wanted to be in the courtroom to support him, but it was full when I arrived and they wouldn't let me in. I'm sorry."

I felt relieved that Judy didn't blame me for her daughter's death. "Thanks for coming," I said. "And don't worry about me, I'll be fine. If there's anything I can do for you, please let me know."

She squeezed my hand as if she didn't want to let go. Several reporters snapped photos of us. As we walked away, they gathered around Judy asking her questions. Once inside, Katy gave me a quick hug. "That makes this whole situation easier for me."

I kissed her on the cheek and went to join Chas. By the time Chas and I entered the courtroom, Katy and Doc were seated in the first row behind the defense table. The packed courtroom was standing room only, and buzzed with excited conversation. Two officers stood by the doors and weren't letting anyone else inside.

Three illustrators were making sketches. Connie Mason sat behind Katy and Doc. She gave me an encouraging smile, placing her hands together in front of her breast in the prayer position.

When preparing for a trial, all good prosecutors attempt to predict what the defense will be and what witnesses or evidence they will attack. Then the defense will try to tighten these areas so not to confuse the issues.

Most jury members get their information about trials from TV and almost always have unrealistic expectations before they get into the courtroom. They think all weapons should have prints on them, that the police always get good DNA results, and that all witnesses tell the same story. But that seldom happens in the real world. The suspects wear gloves, prints get smudged or the item the suspect touched has a pattern that distorts the prints. DNA isn't always obtained or may have been tainted with chemicals. Sometimes it belongs to the victim or to a source unrelated to the crime. Additionally, witnesses see events differently depending on where they are, what they heard or didn't hear, or how good their eyesight is. Now I find myself on the defense side of a trial wondering if the prosecution has any surprises for me.

"All rise," said the bailiff as Judge Stanton entered and took his seat. He looked around and in a stern voice, said, "You may be seated."

The scraping of feet, the rustling of clothes and sound of papers being shuffled filled the courtroom as everyone sat. A lump formed in my throat and my palms began to sweat. Being the defendant felt foreign to me. After everyone sat, the judge said, "I don't want any disturbances in my courtroom. Anyone with a cell phone, please turn it off now. If I hear a phone ring, I'll have the owner removed." Several people checked their phones, including Chas. "If the prosecution and defense are ready, I'll have the jury members brought in."

Miller stood. "The prosecution is ready to proceed, Your Honor."
Chas stood. "The defense is ready, Your Honor."

When the jury was seated, Judge Stanton addressed them. "Ladies and gentlemen of the jury, my name is Judge Stanton, the presiding judge in this case. Thank you for taking the time to hear this case. I wish I could tell you how long the trial will take, but I cannot. The defendant in this case is charged with second-degree murder, which is a class two or class three felony depending on the circumstance of the killing. The defendant in this case has been charged with a class two felony. The State has the burden of proving the defendant is guilty of murder beyond a reasonable doubt. The defendant does not have to testify on his own behalf."

Judge Stanton took off his glasses and wiped them clean and put them back on. "After considering all of the evidence in this case, if you decide the prosecution has proved each of the elements beyond a reasonable doubt, you should find the defendant guilty of murder in the second degree. If you decide the prosecution has failed to prove any one or more of the elements beyond a reasonable doubt, you should find the defendant not guilty of murder in the second degree."

The judge paused and looked at the jury. "Are there any questions?" When no one raised their hand, he said, "If the prosecution is ready, you may give your opening statement."

Miller wore an expensive three-piece suit, a silk tie and a bad toupee that didn't match the natural color of his hair. He stood in front of the jury like a king addressing his knights. He introduced himself and thanked the jury. "This is a very unusual trial in the sense that the victim in this case, Ivan Collins, was not an innocent man."

He then went into great detail outlining all of Ivan's evil deeds. I assume he felt it was better for the jury to hear this from the prosecutor than the defense.

I couldn't have described Ivan Collins any better myself and was starting to like Miller. He told the jury about Charlie Blakely's death and that Ivan probably thought I was driving the car when he was killed. I thought he was wasting everyone's time because anyone in Colorado who watched TV or read a newspaper already knew this.

Miller walked to his table, took a drink of water, returned to a position in front of the jury box, turned and faced me. "Ivan Collins hated Mr. Harrison for exposing him and he wanted to kill Mr. Harrison." He talked about the finger left in my sink and the note. He was a true thespian. He mentioned Officer Perkins and told them how Ivan had tied Katy to her bed and assaulted her.

"Objection, Your Honor," Chas said before I could stop him. "Mr. Miller doesn't know what Ivan Collins did, or did not do to Mrs. Harrison."

"Sustained. Mr. Miller, you are taking a lot of liberties in your opening statements. I have only allowed you to continue because the defense has not previously objected. You will confine your statements to the known facts in this case and not venture to theories. Is that clear?"

"Yes, Your Honor."

Miller glanced at Katy and then turned to face the jury. "I'm not asking you to find sympathy for the victim, Ivan Collins. He deserved to spend the rest of his life in prison, or to be executed by the state for his crimes. This trial is not about Ivan Collins' crimes, it's about his death and the way in which he was killed. Like everyone else in this great country of ours, Ivan Collins was entitled to a fair trial."

He glanced over at me and walked to the other end of the jury box. "Ivan Collins' murder denied him the chance to have a trial."

Chas started to stand up, but I placed my hand on his arm, holding him down.

Miller continued, "If Ivan Collins had lived, he might be the one before you today instead of Storm Harrison. So why would Detective Harrison want to kill Ivan Collins, you ask? I'm going to prove that he murdered Ivan Collins for personal revenge. Storm Harrison was a young officer the first time he met Ivan Collins. He could have killed him that night and it would have been justified."

Chas started to stand up to object, but I placed my hand on his arm and shook my head.

"If Storm Harrison had killed Ivan Collins then, we wouldn't be here today. Nine innocent people would be alive today if Officer Harrison had killed Ivan Collins when . . ."

"Objection, Your Honor!" Chas argued. "My client was cleared of any wrong doing in that case and Mr. Miller knows it."

"Sustained!" yelled the judge. "Please sit down, Mr. Woods."

Judge Stanton turned to face the jury. "You will disregard that last statement." He wrote a note to himself and addressed Miller. "Counselor, if you make one more statement like that, I will call for a mistrial and you will not be the prosecutor at the new one. Is that understood?"

Miller's face turned red. He had taken a big gamble saying what he said, but the damage had been done. I wanted to rip his heart out. The jury would now look at me as the man partly responsible for the deaths of all of Ivan's victims. Paul Bremer was correct in saying Miller was a cold-hearted bastard.

Judge Stanton completed a few notes and addressed Miller again. "You may continue your opening statements if you can restrict yourself to the facts of this case."

"Thank you, Your Honor." Miller turned to the jury as if he had done nothing wrong. Half of the jurors were looking at me instead of the prosecutor. A small man with glasses, whom I remembered as being a bookstore owner, wrote more notes. There went the "disregard" part of the judge's instructions.

Miller went on to explain about police officers and their responsibilities. He said police officers could not kill an unarmed person no longer deemed a threat. The prosecution will prove beyond any reasonable doubt that this is exactly what Detective Storm Harrison did on October 16, 2012."

He explained my obligation to render first aid and to give or get medical attention for an injured suspect as soon as possible. Then he said, "No police officer has the right to act as judge . . . jury . . . and executioner." Miller ended his opening statements and sat down.

There were whispers from the audience and the little bookstore owner continued to take notes. I began to regret allowing him on the jury.

Judge Stanton said, "If the defense is ready, you may give your opening statements, Mr. Woods."

Chas stood and addressed the jurors. "Ladies and gentlemen, thank you for serving on this jury. I will do everything in my power to get this trial over with as soon as possible so you can return home to your jobs and families." He paused and looked back to me. "When a police officer has to take a life, they normally do it at a moment's notice. They don't know they're going to kill someone until the split second before it happens. The suspect often makes the decision for the officer by reaching for a knife, a club, or a gun and attempts to kill either the officer or an innocent person. The officer usually doesn't know the suspect's intent until that very last moment before the officer draws his weapon and fires. And, if the police officer doesn't act in time, he or an innocent person may die. Think about that for a minute. Think about having to make the decision to take a person's life within a split second. That is not an easy task for anyone, not even trained police officers. And if the officer makes the wrong decision in that split second, he is likely the one who is killed."

Chas walked to our table and took a drink of water, giving his comments time to sink in. Then he stood in front of the jurors and continued. "The term 'reasonable doubt' is defined as *any* doubt that is reasonable. You will have to consider that at the end of this trial. To convict my client, you must believe without any reasonable doubt that Detective Storm Harrison killed Ivan Collins, and that he didn't kill him in self-defense. If any of the evidence shows that Detective Storm Harrison didn't kill Ivan Collins, or that he killed him in self-defense, you must find him not guilty. Thank you."

Judge Stanton let Miller have the last say. "Ladies and gentlemen, I intend to prove that Storm Harrison," he pointed at me, "killed Ivan Collins in cold blood. If Mr. Harrison didn't have a choice, and had to make a split second decision to kill Ivan Collins, as his defense attorney claims, he would not have shot him four times. The first three shots were not fatal. The fourth shot to the head killed Ivan Collins. That decision was not made in a split second. It was an intentional act and the man Mr. Harrison executed was helpless to defend himself."

Miller used his hand to simulate a handgun and pointed it at the floor. "Bang . . . Bang . . . Bang . . . and then, Bang. That decision was not made in a split second. The 911 recording will show it took almost thirteen seconds from the first shot to the last. That is an intentional killing of an unarmed and helpless man. It was not an act of self-defense, but an act of murder. And no one, not even the president of the United States, has that right. Storm Harrison committed murder and that is what I intend to prove. Thank you!"

I heard whispers and people adjusted themselves in their seats behind me as Miller took his seat. I glanced back at Katy. She showed no emotion. The judge took a few notes and addressed Miller. "The prosecution may call their first witness."

"I call Detective Jim Pomush."

Jim took the witness stand, was sworn in and spent the rest of the day testifying with only an hour break for lunch. Most of the questions centered around what he discovered at our house on the night of the killing and the evidence he collected.

I tuned him out and studied the jurors. The first jury member was a small blonde woman with glasses who wore her hair in a bun on the back of her head. She listened to the testimony carefully with her hands folded in her lap. If I remembered right, she was a housewife. The man next to her had the physique of a Buddha. He looked as if he was going to fall asleep at any moment. Another man, who I remembered as a postal worker, kept blinking as if he had something in his eye. An older black man appeared attentive and alert and showed no emotion. It has always been my impression that most blacks take what police officers say with a grain of salt. But with me being a police officer, I didn't know if that worked in my favor or not.

The concept of a "jury of your peers" came from the Magna Carta, but that phrase didn't appear anywhere in the Constitution. We only have a legal right to "an impartial jury" drawn from the surrounding area. A housewife can have housewives, schoolteachers can have other schoolteachers and bookstore owners can have other bookstore owners on their jury. But I have never seen a police officer selected as a jury member on any criminal cases.

I returned my attention back to the trial. After covering the details on the condition of our house, the location of Ivan's body and his injuries, Jim explained about finding Officer Perkins in the stairwell. When Miller seemed to have run out of questions, he asked, "Sergeant Pomush, have you ever heard Mr. Harrison say he wanted to kill Ivan Collins?"

Chas started to stand up but I grasped his arm holding him in his seat. He tossed his pencil in the air and attempted to catch it, but it bounced off his fingers and onto the floor. The judge gave him a hard stare as he fumbled to pick it up. The little juryman who owned the bookstore smiled and made another entry into his notebook. I had no idea what that was about.

"Detective Harrison never used the name Ivan Collins," Pomush said. "He said he wanted to kill the man he had encountered in the alley twelve years ago. But I never heard him say that until after we discovered the same suspect was killing young girls again. I don't recall the exact words Storm used to make those comments."

"Do you think he was serious when he made those threats?"

Pomush nodded. "Possibly. I think all of us wanted to kill that brutal psychopath."

Miller frowned when Pomush's made that statement. "Just answer the question, Detective."

I appreciated Jim trying to cover for me while also telling the truth. Miller waited a moment, then as an afterthought, asked, "But, you wouldn't have killed Ivan Collins unless he was threatening your life or the life of another person, would you?"

Jim paused and looked at me before answering. "Of course not."

The little bookstore owner entered more notes.

"I have no further questions for this wittiness, Your Honor," Miller said as he returned to his seat."

Judge Stanton looked at Chas. "Your witness, Mr. Woods."

Chas stood. "I have no questions for this witness at this time, but reserve the right to recall him at a later time."

Judge said, "Mr. Miller, you may call your next witness."

"I call Maggie Hawthorn."

Maggie waddled up to the witness stand, raised her right hand and swore she would tell the truth, the whole truth, and nothing but the truth, and took her seat.

"State your full name for the court please," Miller said.

"Margaret Sue Hawthorn."

After Maggie told them where she was employed and explained her job descriptions, Miller asked, "Did you process the crime scene where Ivan Collins was killed?"

"Yes."

"Do you analyze all of the evidence at the police lab or do you send some of it out to be analyzed?"

"We send some evidence out to be analyzed if we don't have the proper equipment or the expertise to do it in our lab."

"Did you send any out from the murder case of Ivan Collins?"

"We sent the .40 caliber handgun that killed Ivan Collins out for ballistic testing. Hair and blood samples were sent out for DNA testing. But that's done here in Colorado Springs by a private company."

"How many guns did you find in the house?"

Maggie told the court about the four handguns, where they were found and who they belonged to.

"Mrs. Hawthorn, did you find any fingerprints on any weapons at that location?"

"Yes. I found Ivan Collin's fingerprints on Officer Blakely's weapon, a knife and a straight razor. I found Storm Harrison's and Ivan Collins' fingerprints on Detective Harrison's service weapon and I found Detective Harrison's fingerprints on his personal handgun. Some of the prints were bloody."

"And these bloody fingerprints belonged to Storm Harrison?"

"Yes."

As Maggie gave her testimony, I found myself staring at the fat juryman with multiple chins. I couldn't tell if he was sleeping with his eyes open, or had died. It seemed as if ten minutes went by before I saw him blink. When he did, he looked around as if getting his bearings. *Damn, I think he's sleeping with his eyes open.*

I heard Maggie say that my personal weapon was used to kill Ivan and that all four shots fired came from my weapon. She testified to taking the photographs shown to the jury and answered questions regarding their content. When Miller asked her who the hair samples belonged to, Maggie said she didn't know. She stated she had DNA from the hairs but there was no match in the DNA database.

"Who do you believe the hairs belong to?" asked Miller.

Chas started to object but I told him to let her answer the question. I wanted the jury to know what Ivan had done to Katy.

"I think they belong to Mrs. Harrison."

Miller stood in front of Maggie but looked at the jury members for his last questions. "Mrs. Hawthorn, have you ever heard Storm Harrison say he was going to kill Ivan Collins?"

It was clear Miller wanted to give the jury one more reason for me wanting to kill Ivan. It worked. I should have let Chas object.

"Yes. But Storm didn't use Ivan's name because we didn't know who he was at the time."

"When did he say he wanted to kill him?"

"The day I told him the DNA from the killer of the young girls matched the DNA from the person who killed Julia Martin twelve years ago."

"Do you recall his exact words?"

Maggie looked at me but didn't answer. I nodded, telling her to go ahead.

Miller looked back at me. "Answer the question, Mrs. Hawthorn. Tell us what Detective Harrison told you."

"Well, he said, 'I should have killed that bastard when I had a chance. I'll kill him nice and slow when I find him.' Those were his exact words."

"Did you believe he was serious?" asked Miller.

"You never know about Storm Harrison. He kids around a lot."

"Did his voice sound serious when he said it?"

Maggie took a slow deep breath and looked over at me. "I suppose so."

"I have no further questions for this witness at this time," Miller said as he sat down.

Maggie's questioning lasted until midafternoon. Judge Stanton asked Chas if he had any questions for Maggie but he didn't.

When Maggie passed my table, she mouthed, "I'm sorry."

I smiled to let her know I wasn't upset.

Judge Stanton glanced at the clock. "We'll adjourn for the day. Be ready to resume at nine in the morning."

Katy, Doc, Chas and I walked across the street to The Oak Barrel and took a corner table inside the dining area. Chas didn't say anything while we ordered cocktails but he kept watching Katy. He looked depressed.

"Are you feeling all right, Mr. Woods?" Doc asked. "You've been very quiet today."

"I'm all right." He said as he rubbed his forehead and stared at the table. "I've never had a client like Storm. He refuses to help me defend him and I have no evidence to prove his innocence. I feel like he wants to get convicted."

Katy and Doc glanced at each other but neither responded. I stopped eating, wiped my mouth with my napkin and placed it on the table. "You won't find any evidence to prove my innocence, Chas, so stop looking. Start thinking outside the box. Think about what no one knows."

Chas wrinkled his forehead. "Like what?" he asked.

"What happened in that room between the time I called 911 and the last shot was fired. Like who was driving the car the neighbors saw. Start looking at the timing of the last shot and the time that car left. And when was Katy untied?"

Chas didn't appear to have a clue what I was saying.

"Come on, Chas, think. You're a smart guy, stop trying to prove my innocence and start thinking about what you don't know. Then think of ways to get the jury to start thinking the same way."

Chas stared off into space, his mind processing the information I'd just given him. "Are you telling me there was another person in the house at the time of shooting?"

Doc and Katy locked eyes and both stopped chewing. "I'm not telling you anything, Chas. But I like the way you think. What other possibilities could there be?"

He looked at Katy. "You're not saying---" He stopped in mid-sentence, locked eyes with me and then shook his head. "Never mind."

CHAPTER THIRTY-SIX

Day two of the trial started out much like the first. The jury was escorted into the room and took their seats. Judge Stanton entered and instructed Mr. Miller to call his next witness.

"I call Jamie Carson, Your Honor."

Jamie Carson was one of our dispatchers. Since we don't work out of the same building, I knew her by name and voice only. She approached the bench, took the oath and sat down. Miller approached her but looked at the jury while speaking. "State your full name for the record please."

Jamie cleared her throat and adjusted herself in the seat. "I'm Jamie Anne Carson." Most dispatchers don't testify in court very often and I thought this was her first time, based on her demeanor.

"Where are you employed, Miss Carson?"

"I work as a dispatcher for the City of Colorado Springs."

"As part of your job description, do you take calls from the public when they call the police?"

"Yes, and for the fire department as well."

"Were you working on the evening of October16, 2012?"

"Yes, I worked the 3 p.m. to 11 p.m. shift on that day."

"Did you take the 911 call from Detective Harrison that evening?"

"Yes, I did."

"Miss Carson, I'm going to play a recording of a 911 call. I want you to tell the court if this is an accurate record of the call you received from Mr. Harrison." Miller pushed the play button and Jamie's voice said, "911, what is your emergency?"

"This is Detective Harrison. I've got Ivan Collins." My voice sounded rusty on the tape.

Mr. Miller stopped the recording and asked the jurors if they could hear the tape. They all acknowledged that they could.

He turned his attention back to Jamie. "Is this the taped recording of the conversation you had with Detective Harrison on the night Ivan Collins was killed?"

"Yes."

Miller continued to start and stop the tape while explaining what was being said, as if the jury members were deaf. I sounded drunk. Miller played the loud banging noise when I kicked Ivan in the face. He paused the tape after I'd said, "Nothing, I'm just shutting this asshole up so you can hear me."

"Miss Carson, do you know what Detective Harrison did to stop Ivan Collins from talking?"

"No, it..........."

"Objection, Your Honor. Calls for speculation," Chas said. "She can't see what is happening while talking on the phone."

"Sustained. You may continue counselor."

Miller restarted the recording. You could hear me saying we were okay and me asking for the paramedics. You could clearly hear Ivan laughing, calling me a coward and saying I didn't have the guts to kill him. Then you heard me yelling at Ivan to shut up or I was going to blow his brains out. Again Mr. Miller hit the stop button.

"At this point, it's clear that Ivan Collins is very much alive and that Detective Harrison is threatening him." The tape resumed to the point where Ivan told me that I hadn't had the guts to kill him in the alley and that I didn't have the balls to do it now. He screamed that I was full of shit and that I was a big man on TV but when it comes time to pull the trigger I was a pussy. Then you could hear the first shot and Ivan screamed.

Miller stopped the tape again. "This is the first shot Detective Harrison fired."

"Objection," Chas said. "It hasn't been proven that my client fired that shot."

Miller started to speak but the judge cut him off. "Sustained."

Miller smiled and continued. When the tape resumed you could hear the second shot, after which was a short pause when all you could hear was Ivan's screams. After the third shot his screams turned guttural, sounding barely human. Some of the jury members wore pained expressions at this point. Low muttering could be heard from the audience behind me. I glanced back at Katy. She showed no emotion whatsoever. I wasn't sure, but it looked as if Doc was trying not to smile. Then the sound stopped altogether. A moment later, the forth shot was heard.

Miller stopped the tape. "The last shot you heard ended Ivan Collins' life." He paused and looked into the crowd. You could have heard a pin drop. "That shot hit Ivan right between the eyes, a shot only someone with a lot of training could have made." He looked directly at me. "This is the aftermath of that shot."

He handed Chas several photos to look at, before handing them to the jurors. One after the other a juror would glance at them before quickly handing them to the person next to them. Each picture was handed off quicker than the previous one, as if they didn't really want to see the damage a .40 caliber hollow point bullet made while passing through a man's brain. The little bookstore owner was the only one that took the time to study the photos. After handing them off, he wrote more notes. Some of the jury members looked pale as if they were going to be sick. The judge must have thought the same thing because once the photos were handed back to Miller, the judge announced a fifteen-minute break.

The jurors quickly left the room and a buzz of conversation swelled from the spectators.

I turned to Katy. "Why don't you go home," I said, concerned by how she appeared. "You don't need to relive this again."

She touched my arm. "I'm all right, Storm. How are you doing?"

My attempt to smile was half-hearted at best. "I'm good."

"I'm so sorry, Storm. You shouldn't have to go through this."

"I'll be all right. I kind of liked hearing that prick scream. I wish I would have shot his toes off."

Chas, still seated at the defense table, put his head into his hands. Miss Carson remained at the witness stand, not knowing if she could leave or not. She had never been dismissed.

After the break, Judge Stanton told Miller he could resume questioning the witness.

"I have no other questions for Miss Carson."

Judge Stanton looked at Chas. "Cross examine, Mr. Woods?"

"Yes, Your Honor." Chas stood up and asked, "Miss Carson, do you have any idea what Ivan Collins was doing while he was screaming?"

"No sir."

"Do you know what he was doing when you heard shots being fired?"

"No."

Then he surprised me by asking, "Do you have any idea what Mrs. Harrison was doing during this time frame?"

"No sir."

"I have no other questions for this witness, Your Honor."

"Mr. Miller?" asked the judge.

"No, Your Honor."

The next witness to be called by the prosecution was Dr. James Galvin, the El Paso County Coroner. He was a meek man about 5' 3" who wore thick Harry Potter type glasses. I'd encountered him at several crime scenes. His hair was always a mess. He thought he was smarter than the cops, but seldom asked an intelligent question.

After being sworn in, Mr. Miller asked him if he'd performed the autopsy on Ivan Collins' body? When he replied that he had, Miller continued. "Would you please describe for the court what you found when you examined Ivan Collins' body."

Galvin described the incision wound in Ivan's lower abdomen that ran the length of the sternum, as well as the cut under his chin and a smaller one on his nose. Miller handed him my small buckle knife. "Is this what caused the cuts you are describing?"

Galvin examined it carefully. "There's no way to tell, but it could have. The cuts could also have been made with a box cutter type instrument. Whatever made those incisions was very sharp like this with a very short blade."

"Would the wounds you described have caused Mr. Collins death?"

"The abdominal wound eviscerated him, which would have proved fatal if he hadn't received medical attention, and possibly even if he had. The other incisions were superficial."

Miller checked his notes. "What else did you discover about Mr. Collins' body?"

Galvin explained about the shattered knees.

"Could Mr. Collins have been able to stand up or walk after being shot in the knees?" asked Miller.

"No. Mr. Collins would never have walked again after sustaining those injuries, at least not without full knee replacements.

And, I'm not even sure that would work. There was a lot of damage to the area."

"What else did you discover during your examination?"

Galvin testified that Ivan's testes were missing and that his penis was only attached by a small piece of skin. Several men on the jury gritted their teeth. One of the women put her hand over her mouth.

Miller checked his notes again. "Was there any chance that Mr. Collins might bleed to death from any of those injuries?"

"Definitely, but it could have taken several hours."

Miller walked to the jury box and looked at the jury members as he spoke.

"Was Ivan Collins alive during this time?"

Galvin looked at the jury and answered, "Yes."

"How do you know he was still alive?"

"Because of the amount of blood around the kneecaps and the groin area. When the heart stops, it stops pumping blood. The body will still bleed out but very slowly. If the heart is beating and a major artery is severed, the heart will pump blood at rate of five liters per minute. The human body only has about five liters of blood and will bleed out in about a minute in that case. The person will become unconscious from loss of blood pressure before he dies and that would happen in about 45 seconds. Mr. Collins did not have any major arteries or veins severed, but he had many smaller ones severed. He would have lived for an hour at most without treatment. But he would have died from these injuries unless he was taken to a hospital."

"What was the cause of Mr. Collins' death?"

"A gun shot to the head. The bullet entered his skull just above the eyes and exited the back of his skull, taking half of his brain with it. He died instantly from that wound," Galvin said as he straightened his tie while looking at the jury.

Miller let a moment pass to allow that information to sink in. Then he asked, "Was there any other way to tell if Mr. Collins was still alive until that last shot killed him?"

"Yes. If you listen to the recording of the four shots, you can hear Mr. Collins screaming while he is being shot. After the third shot, his voice becomes weaker from blood loss and pain, but he is very much alive until the final shot."

"Mr. Collins was in a great deal of pain, wasn't he?" asked Miller.

"Objection, Your Honor. He's leading the witness. Dr. Galvin has no idea what Mr. Collins was feeling."

Judge Stanton rubbed his chin and looked at the doctor. "I think Dr. Galvin would know more about what a person was feeling when injured than most people because of his understanding of the human body. And, I think the answer to that question is rather obvious. I'll let him answer the question. Objection overruled."

Galvin directed his comments to the jury. "Mr. Collins would have been in a great deal of pain, especially from the injuries to the kneecaps and the groin area."

Miller walked back to his table, checked his notes and stated, "I have no further questions for this witness."

"Your witness, Mr. Woods," said the judge.

Chas stood up and approached Dr. Galvin. "Were there any injuries to Mr. Collins' hands or arms?"

"No."

"Even with the injuries to the kneecaps and the groin area, was it possible that Mr. Collins could have picked up a gun or a knife if one was within his reach?"

Galvin thought about the question for a moment and then answered, "I suppose he could have picked up a weapon if one were available."

"And would he have the strength to fire that weapon if he had it in his hand?"

"Yes, I believe he could have."

"I have no other questions for this witness," Chas said. He returned to our table and took his seat.

"Do you have any more questions for this witness, Mr. Miller?" asked the Judge.

Miller stood facing the jury and asked from his table, "Dr. Galvin, were you at the crime scene on the night of the murder?"

"Yes."

"Did you see any weapons in that room?"

"Yes, several handguns, a large hunting knife, a straight razor and a pair of nunchucks."

"Can you explain what nunchucks are for the jury?" asked Chas.

"They are sticks tied together with a chain and are used in martial arts."

"Dr. Galvin, were any of these weapons within Mr. Collins' reach?"

"No. The pistols, razor and hunting knife were on the bed and the nunchucks were on the floor on the opposite side of the bed."

"I have no further questions, Your Honor."

"Mr. Woods?" said the judge.

Chas asked, "Do you know if anyone in that room moved any of those weapons prior to you arriving on the scene?"

"No."

"No further questions, Your Honor."

Miller smiled while the little man on the jury with the glasses made a few more notes in his book. Judge Stanton looked at the clock. "We won't have time for any more witness today. We'll resume again tomorrow at 9:00 a.m."

He tapped his gavel down and dismissed court. Chas picked up his briefcase and quickly walked out of the courtroom, ignoring questions from the press. I could almost feel sorry for him.

CHAPTER THIRTY-SEVEN

To avoid the press, we dined at Doc's house during the rest of the trial. Marcee joined us often and we frequently grilled on the patio. After dinners we made cocktails and watched Connie Mason talking about the trial during her evening report. She claimed the defense was useless and if it didn't change its strategies soon, I would be spending the rest of my life in prison. Neither I, nor Chas was answering her questions anymore, but for me it wasn't personal. Over all, she'd done a good job covering the trial.

"Looks like there's trouble in paradise," Doc said. "I bet Charles Woods didn't expect to be beat up on TV by his own girlfriend."

"I'm not sure what's going on with those two," Katy said. "She's not talking to him anymore. I received an email from her asking me to do lunch."

"I wouldn't go if I were you," I said.

Katy wrinkled her nose the way she does when she has a question. "What happened between the two of you that makes you hate her so much?"

"I don't hate her, I just don't like her."

Katy looked at Doc, anticipating that he knew the answer. He rolled his eyes and left to refresh our drinks, with Marcee hot on his heels.

"Come on, Storm. You and Connie were friends once and she's a nice girl. What happened between you two?"

"Why don't you ask her?"

"If you won't tell me, I guess I'll have to. I'm having lunch with her tomorrow."

"Be careful what you say to her. It might end up in print."

The subject of Connie Mason didn't come up again. I wasn't sure if Katy was serious about having lunch with Connie until the next day when she announced, "You and Doc are on your own for lunch today."

I started to say something, but didn't want Katy to think I had anything to hide. And besides, I figured Connie would only be interested in talking about the trial. Knowing Katy wouldn't tell her anything about the shooting, I wasn't worried. Perhaps they could exchange stories about Chas, women's shoes, or the latest in fashion. I didn't really care. I had more important things on my mind.

Doc and I waded through the crowd of protesters on the way into the court. There seemed to be even more today than yesterday. Signs read, "Free Storm." And "To Hell with Ivan Collins." I didn't recognize any of the protesters but it made me feel better knowing a lot of people didn't care if I killed Ivan Collins or not. They believed he deserved to die and they were right. I had no regrets about his death.

We entered the courtroom and took our seats. Chas didn't look as self-assured as he had in the past. He sat examining piles of evidence records in front of him as if somehow he had missed something and avoided looking at me. That was fine with me because he was in too deep to back out now.

Judge Stanton came in, took his seat on the bench, glanced around the room over his glasses and told us to be seated. After we sat, the judge nodded to the bailiff. The bailiff carried a chair into the courtroom and set it behind the prosecutor's table. He then went out of the side door and walked a woman inside. She was thin, frail and her dress looked like something you would find in your grandmother's closet after she passed. The flower print dress resembled wallpaper from a 1940's farmhouse. Her short hair was gray and thin. She looked to be somewhere between fifty and eighty. Her bloodshot black eyes were lifeless and devoid of emotion. Her short high heel shoes were too big for her and flopped when she walked. She looked at the floor as she shuffled into the room, never looking at me. The bailiff helped her into her chair. The scars on her forearms and the back of her hands indicated a life of drug abuse. I thought she was probably suffering from AIDS.

Miller walked over to her. "Thanks for coming, Mrs. Collins."

The jury members watched her with pity in their eyes. I assumed they didn't know she was a lifetime drug user and prostitute, or that the State of Colorado had taken Ivan away from her at the age of three for child neglect and abuse before she was sent to prison. It was a pathetic attempt by Miller to try to get sympathy from the jurors for Ivan's mother. The little bookstore owner wrote at least three pages of notes about her for some unknown reason.

After Mrs. Collins was seated, Judge Stanton said, "You may call your next witness, Mr. Miller."

"I call Mrs. Katharina Harrison," Miller said.

Chas stood immediately. "Sidebar, Your Honor."

"Approach the bench," the judge said. Woods and Miller went to speak with the judge. We couldn't hear what they were saying but I knew it had to do with what Katy could and could not be asked. When they finished their conversation, Chas took his seat.

Judge Stanton nodded toward Katy. "Mrs. Harrison will you please step forward to be sworn."

Katy was sworn in and took her seat on the witness stand. She looked composed.

"State your name and occupation for the record please," Miller said.

My name is Katharina Harrison. I'm Storm Harrison's wife. I work as a prosecutor here in the county courthouse." There was a buzz in the courtroom. Several jurors looked at each other and the bookstore owner wrote more notes.

"How long have you and Mr. Harrison been married?"

"About six months now. We had been married three weeks before Ivan Collins broke into our home."

"Can you explain for the record what happened on the night you were kidnapped?" asked Miller.

"Officer Perkins was assigned to protect me on my way to and from work. He met me at my office and followed me to my uncle's house where Storm and I were living at the time."

"Why weren't you living at your home or at Detective Harrison's home?" asked Miller.

"Ivan Collins had already broken into Storm's house and left him a death threat. He had also killed Detective Blakely who was driving Storm's car. We believed Ivan thought Storm was in that car. Ivan Collins was spotted near the court building where I work and he shot holes in the windows of this courthouse. I moved in with my uncle for protection. Storm didn't want me to be alone and he couldn't be with me all of the time."

"I see," said Miller. "Go ahead with your testimony."

"When Detective Perkins and I got to Doc's house, Storm was still at work. He and I had dinner plans that night. It had turned cold and I hadn't brought any warm clothes with me, so I asked Officer Perkins if he would follow me to my house so I could retrieve warmer clothes and personal items."

"Why didn't you wait for your husband to get home?" asked Miller.

"He was running late and I wanted to get there and back before it got dark. If I had to wait for Storm, I knew we wouldn't make our dinner reservations."

"Thank, you, Mrs. Harrison. Please continue."

"When we got to the house, Officer Perkins checked the perimeter to make sure the residence was secured. The red light on the alarm system was still on in the kitchen. We entered the front door and I turned the alarm off. He checked downstairs and everything appeared normal, with nothing out of place. We walked upstairs to my bedroom and I entered the bathroom while Officer Perkins waited by the door watching the stairs and hallway leading to the other bedrooms. I had forgotten to tell him about the hidden stairs from the closet downstairs. I heard a noise, as if something had dropped on the floor. I asked Officer Perkins if everything was all right. When he didn't respond, I stepped out of the bathroom and came face to face with Ivan. Before I could react, he hit me on the side of my head with his fist, knocking me backwards into the wall. He struck me again and I blacked out."

"Did you know what had happened to Officer Perkins?"

"Not at the time. When I woke up, Ivan had tied me to my bed. Our bed has large poles at each corner and I was tied to the poles with a rope and my mouth was gagged. The ropes were very tight and hurt my arms and feet. I struggled but couldn't get loose. Ivan dragged Officer Perkins into the small closet that had another set of stairs in it. I didn't know if he was dead or alive."

"Where do these stairs lead?"

"To the kitchen on the ground floor and then to the basement. The previous owner had installed an electric chair because climbing stairs was too difficult for him. Ivan tied Officer Perkins in the seat and sent it downstairs."

"Could you see this from where you were tied?"

"Not all of it. I saw Ivan drag Officer Perkins into the closet but I couldn't see him put him in the chair. I heard the chair going downstairs after Ivan came out of the closet."

Miller nodded his head as if he was satisfied with her answer and asked her to continue.

"Ivan picked up a straight razor and cut my clothes off. He wasn't in a hurry and was careful not to cut me. When I was completely naked, he just stood there staring at me. Then he started talking to me in a cold calm voice." Katy stopped talking for a moment.

"What did he say?" asked Miller.

The bookstore owner was writing as fast as he could.

"He said that I must have been a very lovely child before I grew breasts and hair and how much he would have liked me back then. Then he told me he was going to make me look younger for the surprise party we'd have when my husband arrived. At this point he walked into the bathroom and returned with a can of shaving cream."

Katy looked at me.

"What happened next, Mrs. Harrison?"

"Ivan covered my pubic area with shaving cream and began to shave me. He said that I shouldn't be afraid of death because death is over in a moment. But that moment would be the best moment of my life."

A lot of mumbling could be heard from the courtroom behind me during her testimony. The judge picked up his gavel and people grew quiet again.

"I heard a car drive by," Katy continued. "Ivan went to the window and looked out. Returning to the bed, he got the pistol and went into the hallway. It was quiet after that. I tried to get free from my ropes but I couldn't. My hands were numb and when I tried to twist out of them, the rope cut into my wrists and they started bleeding. Within a couple of minutes, I could hardly feel them at all. I tried to yell to warn anyone who might hear me, but all I could do was make a muffled sound. I couldn't see where Ivan had gone."

She took a moment to collect herself.

"I saw movement at the closet where the hidden stairs were located. I couldn't see who was behind the door but hoped it was Storm. Then Ivan came into the room and stood on the other side of the closet door. He had his handgun in his left hand and nunchucks in his right hand. I started thrashing around on the bed in an attempt to warn whoever might be coming up the stairs, but it was too late. I saw Storm's gun before I saw him, but once he cleared the door, Ivan struck his wrist with the nunchucks. I heard what sounded like breaking bones and Storm's pistol fell to the ground. When he tried to pick it up, Ivan struck him on the head several times with the nunchucks. At this point Storm collapsed onto the floor and Ivan continued to hit him and kick him in the face, in the ribs and on his legs and then he stomped on him several times with his boots. I thought he was dead."

Katy stopped and looked at me with tears in her eyes. I hated seeing her having to go through this. It was so quiet in the courtroom that the only sound was the stenographer recording Katy's testimony. The bookseller stopped taking notes. The judge produced a box of tissue and handed them to Katy. "Would you like to take a break, Mrs. Harrison?"

"No, Your Honor. I want to get through this."

"Whenever you're ready, Mrs. Harrison," said the judge.

Katy took several deep breaths through her nose and continued. "Ivan bound his feet together and tied his hands in front of him. He was unconscious and bleeding profusely. Ivan secured his elbows to the arms of a chair and bound his chest to the back of the chair. Storm's head was bent forward and blood dripped from his nose onto his lap. I wasn't sure if he was alive or not.

"Ivan went to look out of the window again and stood there for a long time. Then he came back and lifted Storm's head by his hair. One of Storm's eyes was black and swollen shut. Blood dripped from his nose and mouth. Ivan dropped Storm's head and it fell to his chest. He came back, sat on the bed and started shaving me again. I thought I saw Storm stir for a moment and look in my direction. His face was so swollen that I didn't know if he could see me or not. Ivan saw me looking at him but by the time he turned to look back, Storm had dropped his head and faked unconsciousness.

After Ivan shaved me, he grew impatient that Storm hadn't awakened. He got up to look out the window again and then jerked Storm's head up by his hair and slapped him to wake him up and said, 'Wake up, Harrison'. You're going to miss the party and your own execution.'

I was terrified and kept looking at Storm, willing him to do something. Storm didn't move or say anything. Ivan dropped his head and returned to the bed and sat. This time he just looked at me for a long time. Then he said, 'I wish I'd known you twenty years ago. This would be much more fun for both of us. Don't you remember how good it was that first time?'

The little man with the glasses had resumed his writing at a furious pace and it was beginning to annoy the crap out of me.

"Storm raised his head again and this time I knew he saw me. I pointed my right index finger at his lap. I was trying to remind him of the belt buckle knife Doc Martin had given him for his birthday. I did this several times. At first I didn't think he understood what I was trying to tell him. But then I saw his hand wiggling and prayed he could get to the knife. After a couple of minutes, I saw the ropes loosening and Storm reach down and cut the ropes securing his feet. I didn't think he would have the strength to stand up and knew he was too weak to fight Ivan."

The little man with glasses was writing as fast as he could, trying to keep up.

"Then Storm put his head back down on his chest. I thought he had passed out again. I prayed he would come to before Ivan discovered the ropes were cut. Then Storm moaned, drawing Ivan's attention away from me. He put the straight razor down and walked over to Storm. Ivan grabbed Storm by the hair to pull his head up. Storm leaped out of the chair, head butting Ivan in the face knocking him back against the wall and then lunged at him. Ivan hit the wall and slid down to the floor. When he tried to get up, his guts started falling out into his lap. He realized what was happening and sat back down trying to hold his intestines inside. Storm stumbled back against the bed."

Katy stopped talking.

"Please continue, Mrs. Harrison," Miller encouraged.

Chas stood up. "Objection, Your Honor. Mrs. Harrison can't say anything else or she will be testifying against her husband."

Miller started to say something, but before he had a chance, Judge Stanton said, "Sustained. You may step down now, Mrs. Harrison, unless Mr. Woods has any questions for you."

"I have no questions for this witness. Thank you for testifying here today, Mrs. Harrison."

Katy stepped down from the witness stand and took her seat. The bookstore owner took more notes. I wanted to rip his head off.

Judge Stanton checked his watch and told us we'd break for lunch and to be back at one o'clock.

Katy left with Connie Mason, so Doc and I decided to go to Wong's.

Twee and Harlum were happy to see us. Twee escorted us to their finest table. "Mr. Hairson, I watch you on TV. You need to fire your lawyer. He no good."

"He's all right, Twee."

"You go prison for long time if you don't get better lawyer."

"He'll get better by the end of the trial."

Twee shook her head. "I don't think so. I don't like him." She looked at Doc. "Who your friend?"

"Twee, this is Dr. Robert Martin. He served two years in Vietnam. Doc this is Twee Wong, the owner."

"Nice to meet you, Twee," Doc said as he extended his hand. Twee didn't take it. She took a step backwards to study Doc.

"So, you were one of those guys that were killing my people," Twee said.

"Not unless your people were communist," Doc replied.

Twee smiled. "No, my people not communist. Communist killed my father after the war because he sold lumber to the Americans." She studied Doc for a few seconds. "My back has been hurting. Can I come see you?"

"He's not that kind of doctor, Twee. He is a psychiatrist. He treats mental disorders."

"Oh, then I send my husband." Twee giggled. "Lunch on me. And you," she said pointing at me, "should have the Doctor see that lawyer of yours. He's crazy."

After lunch we returned to the courthouse. Katy and Connie were talking in the hallway when we approached. Connie kissed Katy on the cheek and smiled at me before leaving. I wondered what that meant.

Lunch hadn't improved Chas' disposition. He didn't even acknowledge me when I sat down.

When court resumed, Miller called Connie Mason to the stand.

Everyone turned to watch Connie as she stepped forward. Miller asked her to state her name and occupation.

"My name is Connie Sue Mason. I'm a news reporter for Channel 10 News."

Some jury members nodded to each other indicating they recognized her. The bookstore owner wrote more notes.

"What was your occupation before you worked for the TV station?"

"I worked for the local newspaper as a writer."

"Miss Mason, did you interview Detective Harrison on the day he found out that Ivan Collins was the man responsible for the recent deaths of several young girls?"

"Yes. Well, it wasn't an interview really. He just made a statement for the cameras."

"And what did Detective Harrison say?"

Connie hesitated.

"Please answer the question, Miss Mason."

She swallowed hard. "He said 'I know who you are Ivan Collins and I'm coming after you. You won't get a second chance'."

"Miss Mason, you knew Detective Harrison had met Ivan Collins once before didn't you?"

"Yes."

"You were aware of the incident in which Julia Martin was killed and you wrote several articles about that case for the newspaper, didn't you?"

"Yes."

"And did you write a follow-up article several years later?"

Connie looked uncomfortable, but her voice was strong when she replied, "Yes."

Miller handed Connie an old newspaper. "Is this the article you wrote at that time?"

Connie looked at the newspaper. "Yes."

"And in the story you wrote, and I quote, 'Detective Harrison is still haunted by the killing of Julia Martin.' How did you know this?"

Connie looked at me apologetically. I knew where this was headed.

She said in a faint voice, "He told me."

Miller leaned in towards Connie and put his hand to his ear. "Speak up, Miss Mason."

"Storm Harrison told me off the record."

"What were the circumstances of that conversation?"

"Objection, Your Honor," Chas said, "The witness has answered the question."

"Your Honor, I'm trying to establish the validity of the information that prompted Miss Mason to write an article stating that Storm Harrison was haunted by the killing of Julia Martin."

Judge Stanton rubbed his chin and looked at both attorneys. He wrote himself a note and then said, "Objection overruled. Answer the question, Miss Mason."

Connie looked at me. It was obvious she didn't want to answer the question. And I wasn't sure if she had told Katy or not. I felt sorry for her.

"Because he had nightmares about it."

"And he told you about these nightmare?" asked Miller.

"No, I was with him when he had one."

The spectators began to murmur as the statement sunk in.

The voices faded away. The jurors looked back and forth at each other and the little man with the glasses wrote more notes.

Miller opened his mouth as if he were going to ask her something else but then decided against it. "I have no other questions for this witness."

"Your witness, Mr. Woods," said the judge. Chas stood up but didn't approach the witness stand. He stared at Connie for a moment. "I have no questions for this witness."

Clearly, he hadn't been aware that she and I had a history, and he didn't look pleased. I was more worried about Katy, however, when I glanced back at her she winked at me. Apparently she and Connie had quite a talk.

"You may call your next witness, Mr. Miller," said the judge.

"The prosecution rests, Your Honor."

I wasn't expecting that. Miller must have been convinced that he had proved my guilt. I couldn't blame him. At this point, I'm sure the public and the jurors felt the same.

The judge looked at the clock. We still had a couple of hours left.

"Mr. Woods, would you like to start your defense now or wait until tomorrow morning?"

Red-faced Chas said he would prefer to resume in the morning. As soon as the judge left the bench, Chas gathered up his papers and headed for the door. We followed more slowly, and when we got outside we saw he and Connie talking. Apparently, the conversation didn't go well because she turned her back on him and walked over to her cameraman who was setting up for the broadcast.

He waited for us to catch up and asked if I would come to his office at seven the next morning to go over our defense strategy. I assured him that I'd be there and with that, he left.

CHAPTER THIRTY-EIGHT

We sat in Chas' office going over his witness list and the questions he wanted to ask. He never mentioned Connie but seemed more focused and determined than ever. I had no problems with what he wanted to do.

The crowd at the courthouse was larger than normal when we got there. We met Katy and pushed our way through the crowd to shouts of, "Free Harrison." Connie did her morning broadcast from the courthouse steps but didn't ask for a statement from Chas or me. I assumed she was avoiding us both.

An unusual buzz filled in the courtroom. The audience was probably speculating about what our defense might be. Everyone stood when Judge Stanton entered the courthouse. He had the jurors seated then turned to Chas. "Mr. Wood, you may call your first witness."

"I call Wally Sanders, Your Honor." Wally came forward, was sworn in and took his seat. "State your name and occupation for the court."

"Wally Sanders. I am the owner of Wally's Indoor Range here in Colorado Springs. I sell guns, ammo and we have six shooting lanes for the public's use."

"What was your previous occupation?"

"I am a retired Colorado Springs police officer. I was their range instructor. I opened my store a year before I left the department."

"Do you know the defendant, Storm Harrison?"

"Yes, we worked together for several years. He comes into my store once in a while."

"Were you his shooting instructor while you were on the force?"

"Yes."

"Is he a good shot?"

Wally nodded. "Storm is better than most officers, but not what I would call a great shot. He'd probably rank within the top ten percent of officers on the force, but not the best by far."

"Mr. Sanders, when you were an instructor at the police department, what was the closest distance you taught officers to shoot from?"

"Two yards or six feet."

"What did you have the officers do from that distance?"

"They had to draw their weapon when the targets turned to face them and fire two shots within two seconds and bring their weapons to the ready." Wally used his hand to demonstrate, pointing the weapon down at a forty-five degree angle.

"Then what?" Chas asked.

"We would turn the targets away from the officers and when we turned them back to face the officers, they were to fire two more rounds within two seconds and go back to the ready."

Chas took a few moments to check his notes before continuing. "Did you sell Storm Harrison any firearms within the last year?"

"Yes. I sold him a .40 caliber handgun."

Chas handed him my pistol and asked him if it was the weapon he had sold me. Wally pulled out a receipt from his pocket and checked the serial number. "Yes. This is the weapon he purchased."

"Did Storm Harrison buy the gun for himself or for someone else?"

"He purchased it for his wife." Again there was a murmur in the courtroom. Judge Stanton's stare hushed them.

Chas continued. "I see. And do you know Detective Harrison's wife?"

"Yes. I've known Katy for about four years now. She and Doctor Martin come into my range and shoot every couple of weeks."

"Have you seen Katy Harrison shoot a pistol?"

"Many times."

"How would you describe her ability to shoot a handgun?"

"She handles a firearm very well. In fact, she's a much better shot than her husband."

More talking came from the courtroom behind me and the jurors were looking at Katy. The little man was taking more notes. When I glanced back at Katy, she grinned.

"Thank you Mr. Sanders. I have no further questions."

"Mr. Miller, do you have any questions for Mr. Sanders?" asked the Judge.

"I have no questions for this witness."

Judge Stanton told Mr. Sanders to step down and told Chas to call his next witness.

"I call Harold Williams."

Mr. Williams was a big chested man with a small waist. His gray hair was cut close in a flattop. He looked like a professional wrestler or drill sergeant. I had never met the man but I'd seen him mowing his yard. After being sworn in, he took a seat in the witness stand.

Chas walked up and stood next to the witness stand. "State your full name and occupation for the court, Mr. Williams."

"Harold Stanley Williams. I'm retired from the Army after thirty-two years of service."

"And what was your rank before you retired?"

"I was a colonel."

"Do you know Katy and Storm Harrison?"

"I've never met Mr. Harrison, but I've known Katy since she was a little girl. Her parents and I were friends."

"Mr. Williams, were you home on the evening of Oct, 16th, 2012?"

"Yes I was."

"Did you hear anything unusual that evening?"

"Yes, I heard shots being fired."

"Can you describe what occurred after you heard the shots?"

"I went outside to my porch and realized they were coming from Katy's house across the street. I was in my undershorts so I went back inside to get a robe. I grabbed a pistol and cell phone and went outside to see if I could tell what was going on. I was calling 911when I saw a car pull away from the curb and drive southbound from the house next door to Katy's. I told the police dispatcher about the shots and the car."

"Excuse me, Mr. Williams," Chas said. "Where was the car you saw leaving parked?"

"In front of the house to the north of Katy's house."

"Thank you. You may continue."

"The dispatcher said the police were already on their way. I was giving her my name and address when I saw Katy help her husband get into the passenger seat of their truck parked in their driveway. It appeared he was injured. As soon as he was inside the truck, Katy got in the driver's side, backed out of the driveway and drove away southbound. She was in a big hurry. When she left, I saw a police car already parked in the driveway but I didn't see any officers. I didn't see or hear anything else until the cops got there, which was a minute after Katy drove off. Six or seven cars pulled up and several officers surrounded the house and some went inside. A little while later, an ambulance came and took someone from inside the house. The detectives were there all night, coming and going. A crime lab van and a couple of cruisers were still there when I got up the next morning."

Chas walked over and stood by the jury box and faced the witness. "Mr. Williams, I'd like to call your attention to the car you saw leaving the area right after the shots were fired. Can you describe it for us?"

"It was a big car, either light blue or gray. It appeared to be a newer model. I'd say a 2010 or newer, but I couldn't tell what the make was."

"How many people were in the car"

"I only saw the driver. It appeared to be a man."

"Do you know who this man was?"

"No."

"Can you describe him?"

"No, it was too dark."

"Mr. Williams, did it appear this man was in a hurry?"

"Well, kind of. He didn't speed away from the curb, but he accelerated all the way down the street until he needed to slow down to make a right turn at the next block. He was going maybe forty before he slowed."

"And you never saw the car or the man again?"

"No. I have no idea who he was."

"How long was it from the time you heard the last shot until you saw the car drive away?"

Mr. Williams rubbed his chin for a second. "I'd say maybe a minute."

"Thank you," Chas said, "I have no other questions."

Judge Stanton looked at Miller. "Do you have any questions for this witness?"

"Yes, Your Honor." Miller stood up but did not leave his table. "Mr. Williams, do you have any idea where this man came from?"

"No."

"Did you see him leaving the Harrisons' home?"

"No. I thought he was at the neighbor's house next door to the Harrisons."

"Was it possible the driver was sitting in the car the entire time?"

"Well, I guess that's possible. He was driving away when I came outside. I didn't see anyone get in the car or hear a door slam."

"I have no other questions for this witness, Your Honor."

"Re-direct, Mr. Woods?"

"Yes, Your Honor. Mr. Williams, do you think you could have heard the car door being opened and closed from inside your house?"

Mr. Williams shook his head. "No, I don't believe I would have."

"I have no other questions for this witness," Chas said.

"You may step down, Mr. Williams," the judge said. "You may call you next witness, Mr. Woods."

"The defense calls Edna Stouffer."

A small woman, who appeared to be in her seventies, approached the bench. Her silver hair sparkled and her flowered dress appeared too large for her thin figure. Her ears were adorned in diamonds. She held a small black purse in her hand. I couldn't recall ever seeing her before. She looked like a child sitting on the witness stand and couldn't have been over five feet tall. Woods adjusted the microphone for her. "Please state your name and occupation for the court." Chas said.

She touched the microphone and it squealed. She jerked her hand away. "Oh my, I'm sorry. My name is Edna May Stouffer. I'm a retired housewife and I'm Katy's next-door neighbor. I live in the white house on the south side of her."

Woods approached the jury box. "Mrs. Stouffer, were you in your home on the evening of October 16, 2012?"

"Yes I was, and I heard those shots too. But I thought they were firecrackers or a car backfiring."

"Did you go outside to see what was going on?" Chas asked.

"Oh no, I wouldn't do that. I checked to make sure my doors were locked and peaked out the window."

"Did you see anything when you looked outside."

"Not really. A car drove by and I saw Mr. Williams standing on his front porch talking on his cell phone. Of course, I couldn't hear anything he was saying."

"What color was the car you saw driving by?"

"It was a light blue or maybe gray color but I didn't pay much attention to it. It looked new."

"Could you see who was driving the car?"

"No. Like I said, I wasn't paying any attention to the car."

Chas walked back to our table. "How many shots do you think you heard, Mrs. Stouffer?"

"Maybe three or four. A couple of minutes after the shots, I saw a red truck drive by my house going the same way as the big car had. I couldn't see who was in it either."

Chas checked his notes and said, "I have no other questions for this witness." He turned to Mrs. Stouffer and thanked her for coming.

Judge Stanton asked Miller if he had any questions for Mrs. Stouffer and he said he didn't. The judge dismissed her and she left.

"You may call your next witness Mr. Woods."

"I'd like to call Doctor Robert Martin to testify."

"Objection, Your Honor. Doctor Martin is not on the witness list," argued Miller.

Chas had not mentioned calling Doc to testify and I started shaking my head no.

"That's true, Your Honor," Chas said. "I didn't have him on the witness list because I didn't think he was a witness at the time. But after listening to the testimony of Mr. Williams and Mrs. Stouffer, I think he may be able to shed some light on this case."

"Sidebar," said the Judge. Both Chas and Miller approached the bench. I couldn't hear what they were saying but I didn't want

Doc to testify. After a few moments, Judge Stanton looked at Doc and asked, "Would you object to testifying in this case, Doctor Martin?"

"I can't testify, Your Honor. Storm Harrison is one of my patients and my testimony is protected by Physician-Patient privilege."

"Well that settles that," said the judge. "Objection sustained. The court will take a fifteen minute break." He slammed his gavel and stood to leave the courtroom.

Chas shook his head all the way back to our table. I grabbed his arm. "What the hell are you trying to pull. I never agreed to have Doc Martin testify."

He pulled his arm away from me. "Oh give me a little credit, Storm. I wouldn't let Doctor Martin testify if he was your only witness." He picked up his briefcase and left the courtroom as Katy and Doc approached me. I watched the last of the jury members as they exited. They were looking back at us with a bewildered look on their faces as they exited the room.

"Who put a burr under his saddle?" asked Doc.

Katy stared after him in disbelief. "Is he nuts? What's he trying to prove by putting Doc on the stand?"

Then it hit me. "He wasn't trying to prove anything. He had no intention of putting Doc on the stand. It was all a ploy to get the jury members to start thinking about Doc."

"Darn," said Doc as he turned and glanced back at the exit. "He may be a lot smarter than I gave him credit for. Do you think he's figured out who owns that car?"

"I don't know, but I'm guessing the jury will be wondering what that was all about."

Once court resumed, Chas called Sergeant Jim Pomush."

Jim came forward and the judge reminded him that he was still under oath. Jim took his seat on the witness stand. "Sergeant Pomush, how many times have you listened to the 911 tape made on the night of Ivan Collins' killing?"

"I don't know. Perhaps a dozen times, maybe more."

"How long is that tape from start to finish?" Chas asked.

"I'm not sure. I've never timed it."

Chas approached the stand and handed him a stopwatch. "I'm going to play that tape again in real time and I want you to time it for me." Chas gave Jim a pencil and a piece of paper and told him to write down the time. He placed the recorder on our table and hit the play button. The tape played from start to finish and Chas hit the stop button. "How long was that tape, Sergeant?"

Jim looked at the stopwatch. "Eighteen point five seconds."

"Ok. I'm going to play the tape again line by line and I want you to tell us what you think is being said and by whom."

Miller stood. "Objection, Your Honor. The jury has already heard that tape several times and they know what's on it."

Chas intervened. "Your Honor, the jurors know what is being said on the tape but they don't know what is occurring while the shots are being fired."

"Objection overruled. You may continue, Mr. Woods."

Chas started the tape and stopped it when I was telling the dispatcher that I had captured Ivan Collins. "Sergeant Pomush, how would you translate the word "captured" in that statement?"

"I take it that Storm Harrison has Ivan subdued," Jim answered.

"But you don't know if that means he has him in handcuffs or tied up or what, do you?"

"No."

"Do you know if Ivan is alive or not."

"Not at this point."

Chas continued playing the tape, stopping it when the dispatcher asked if I was all right and I told her that I'd live and that Katy was gagged and tied to the bed."

"From the tape can we safely say that Mrs. Harrison is still gagged and tied to the bed. Is that correct?"

"I assume that's true. That is what Storm…. Det. Harrison, said and you can't hear her saying anything."

"Is Ivan Collins alive at this point?"

"Yes. When you play the tape, you can hear him yelling in the background."

Chas hit the play button and stopped the tape after Ivan yelled that he was going to kill both Katy and me. "Do you know what Ivan is doing while he is yelling at Detective Harrison?"

"No."

When the tape resumed, you could hear the banging noise when I kicked Ivan in the face. He stopped the tape. "What happed in that portion of the tape, Sergeant?"

"I'm not sure. It sounds as if Storm Harrison either struck or kicked Ivan."

Chas continued the recording up to the point I told the dispatcher that we needed the paramedics and an ambulance. "Sergeant Pomush, do you think Detective Harrison had the intent of killing Ivan at this point?"

"Objection, Your Honor," said Miller. "He can't know what Mr. Harrison's intent is at any point in time."

"Objection sustained," said Judge Stanton. "Withdraw your question or reword it, Mr. Woods."

Chas approached the question from another direction. "Sergeant Pomush, if Detective Harrison intended to kill Ivan, do you believe he would have requested paramedics?"

Pomush thought about that for a moment. "It doesn't seem likely. But, I have no idea why he asked for the paramedics."

Miller wasn't happy with that answer but the damage had been done. I saw the little man with the glasses taking more notes. I wasn't upset with him this time. Chas checked his notes. "Is Mrs. Harrison still tied up at this time?"

"I assume so."

"But you don't know, do you?"

"No."

Chas hit the play button. You could hear Ivan laughing, calling me a coward and telling me I didn't have the guts to kill him. You could hear me threatening to blow his brains out. Then Ivan called me a pussy and said I didn't have the guts to shoot him. Chas let the tape play. You could hear a shot, then another, then the third and then the fourth shot. Chas rewound the tape to the point where the first shot was heard. "Now, Sergeant Pomush, I want you to record the time it took between the first shot to the last."

When the recording stopped, Chas asked, "How long did that take?"

Jim looked at the stopwatch. "Six seconds."

"Thank you, Sergeant." Chas hit the play button again. You could hear Katy say, "No, Storm, don't." Then the phone went dead and the dispatcher could be heard asking if I was still on the line. Then the tape ended.

Chas approached the jury and faced them, "Sergeant Pomush, what was the last thing you heard on that tape before the line went dead?"

Jim thought for a moment. "I heard Katy Harrison say, 'No, Storm, don't.'"

"Sergeant Pomush, can you tell the jurors when Katy Harrison got her gag off and was able to speak?"

Jim looked at Katy. "No, sir."

"Do you know if Mrs. Harrison is still tied to the bed or not?"

Jim thought before answering. "I'm not sure."

"What do you think Mrs. Harrison meant when she said, 'No, Storm, don't?' "

Jim looked at me and then at Katy. Then he looked at me again and again at Katy. Chas didn't rush him for his answer. Jim looked at the jury members and said, "When I heard her say that, I thought she was telling him not to shoot Ivan."

"Why would she tell her husband not to shoot a man who was already dead?"

Jim shook his head. "I don't know."

"Could it be that she had a completely different reason for saying that?"

"That's possible," Jim answered as he nodded his head.

"And what do you think she may have been referring to when she made that statement?"

Jim was now focusing on Katy. "I'm not sure."

"Is it possible that Katy Harrison shot Ivan instead of her husband and that she is saying that because Mr. Harrison was taking the gun from her?"

"Objection, Your Honor. That is pure speculation. There is no evidence to support that statement. Storm Harrison's prints were on the gun that killed Ivan Collins, not Katy Harrison's."

There was commotion in the courtroom. Some of the reporters rushed out with their cell phones in their hand. All of the jurors were looking at Katy.

"Your Honor," Chas said. "If Mrs. Harrison fired the shots and her husband took the gun from her, his bloody prints would have covered her prints."

"Oh, that's nonsense. If...." Judge Stanton cut Miller off by holding up his hand.

"You both make good points. I'm going to let that testimony stand, but I want you to move on Mr. Woods."

Miller shook his head. I think he knew he was in trouble.

Chas approached Jim. "Sergeant Pomush, is it also possible that someone else could have entered the room, picked up the pistol from the bed and shot Ivan without saying a word?"

"I think that is highly unlikely. We didn't find any evidence that anyone else was in the house except for Officer Perkins, and he was still tied to the seat in the stairwell when the police arrived."

"But, if the man who left in the car right after the shots were fired would have shot Ivan, and Mr. Harrison were to take the weapon from him before he left, then there wouldn't be any evidence of this man ever being in the house, would there?"

"Objection, Your Honor. This is total speculation," said Miller. "We don't even know who the man in the car was or if he had anything to do with this murder."

"Mr. Woods," said the judge, "do you have anything to connect this person to the crime?"

"I think I do, if you'll let me continue, Your Honor."

"All right, Mr. Woods, but you better get to the point or I'm going to order the jury to disregard this testimony."

"Sergeant Pomush, if you were to walk from the upstairs master bedroom to where Mr. Williams said he saw the car parked on the street, how long would that take?"

Pomush thought for a few seconds. "About a minute."

"Wasn't that the same amount of time that Mr. Williams said he saw the car leaving after the last shot was fired?"

"Yes, I believe it was."

"Were the neighbors home at the house where the car was parked at the time of the shooting?"

"Yes."

"Did you question them about the car and who it belonged to?"

"Yes, I did."

"What did they tell you?"

"They said they were home at the time of the shooting, but were down in their basement watching TV so they didn't hear the shots. They stated they didn't know anyone who owned a car like the one described leaving the area a minute after the shooting."

"Objection, Your Honor. This is getting us nowhere."

Judge Stanton looked a little taken aback. "Mr. Woods, please get to the point."

Chas walked to our table and picked up a sheet of paper, then approached the witness stand. "Sergeant, Pomush, what is a test called GSR?"

"GSR stands for Gun Shot Residue. It is a test used to determine if someone has fired a weapon or not. It is now called SEM for Scanning Electron Microscopy."

"And what does this test look for?"

"It determines if there is a presence of cordite, nitrocellulose, nitroglycerine, carbon dioxide and other chemicals like lead, barium, zinc or even titanium left over from the discharge of a weapon."

Chas looked down at his notes. "Did you have this 'Gun Shot Residue' testing done on Mr. or Mrs. Harrison?"

"No."

"Why not?

"Several reasons. Mrs. Harrison wasn't a suspect at the time. By the time I saw Mr. Harrison in the hospital, he had a cast on his right hand and his left hand had been cleaned, disinfected, stitched up and bandaged. The nurse said they had cut his shirt off when he got to the emergency room and threw it away. The trash had been picked up from the hospital before I got there."

Chas looked at his notes again. "Are there any other reasons you didn't do the test Sergeant?"

"Yes. Gunshot residue lasts nearly forever. All police officers test positive for GSR. Both Mr. and Mrs. Harrison shoot at the range all the time and would have tested positive for GSR anyway. The FBI quit using the test back in 2006 because of the test unreliability."

Chas paused for a moment and then walked over and stood in front of the jury and asked, "Sergeant Pomush, who killed Ivan Collins?"

You could have heard a pin drop as we waited for his answer. He looked at me and then at Katy. Then he looked at the jurors.

Then he looked back at us. Then he shook his head and answered, "I don't know."

The courtroom erupted into pandemonium. Miller stood to object. Judge Stanton slammed his gavel on his bench. The jury members looked back and forth at each other while the little man with glasses wrote notes. Katy stared at me without emotion. Doc Martin looked as if he were holding his breath. I turned back to face the judge. After a few moments the courtroom calmed down.

"What is your objection, Mr. Miller?" asked Judge Stanton.

Miller was livid and red faced. The veins in his neck showed as he paced back and forth in front of his table. "I object to that last testimony. It is sheer speculation."

"May I remind you, Mr. Miller, that Detective Pomush is your witness. You subpoenaed him. You can't object just because you don't like what he's saying. If you choose to cross examine him, you'll get the chance." Judge Stanton turned to Chas. "You may resume your questioning, Mr. Woods."

Chas approached Jim on the stand. "Did you investigate the possibility that Mrs. Harrison may have killed Ivan Collins?"

"No."

"Why not?"

"I assumed she was tied up during the shooting."

"But you don't assume that anymore?"

Jim stared at Katy. "I'm not sure if she was or not."

"And you still don't know if the person who left in the car was the shooter, do you?"

Jim shook his head. "No. I don't."

"The defense rests, Your Honor," Chas said. "I make a motion to dismiss the charges for lack of probable cause."

Judge Stanton shook his head. "Motion denied, Mr. Woods. The jury has listened to all the evidence and they shall have a chance to determine if Storm Harrison is guilty of murder or not."

He addressed Miller. "Mr. Miller, do you want to cross examine this witness?"

Miller stood up and walked to the witness stand. He raised his hand and started to speak but stopped as if he didn't know what to ask. He lowered his hand, turned to look at me for a moment. "No, Your Honor." He returned to his seat.

The judge scanned the courtroom, then checked the time. "We'll break for a two hour lunch." He looked at Miller and Chas. "When we resume, you can start your closing arguments."

Miller stood. "Can we wait until tomorrow, Your Honor? I need more time."

"No we can't. You have the same amount of time as Mr. Woods has. I would have expected you to have had your closing statements done by now." He struck his gavel on the bench dismissing the court.

CHAPTER THIRTY-NINE

When court resumed, Judge Stanton seated the jury and told Miller to give his closing argument. Miller walked to the front of the jury box and began: "Ladies and gentlemen of the jury, you have sat here day after day listening to the testimony and reviewing evidence. What you didn't hear . . . was any dispute of that evidence. The defense never challenged any of it. Not one single piece of evidence was ever questioned. And, why not? Because the witnesses were telling the truth. And ladies and gentlemen of the jury, evidence doesn't lie. They are facts. And all evidence in this case shows that Storm Harrison," he pointed at me, "shot and killed Ivan Collins."

Miller faced the jurors and looked them in the eye. "I ask that you consider the evidence and the facts in this case. If you do, you will know without any reasonable doubt that Storm Harrison killed Ivan Collins. Not his wife and not some trumped up mystery man who just happened to be driving by. No, you are looking at the killer sitting right there. And remember this, he never denied the killing. Thank you."

Miller took his seat. Chas stood up and walked to the jury box to address the jurors. "Ladies and gentleman, the defense did not challenge any of the witnesses in this case because the witnesses were telling the truth. But, what you never heard any of them say was that Storm Harrison killed Ivan Collins. In fact, the lead investigator testified that he didn't know who killed Ivan Collins. We know it is likely that either Storm Harrison, his wife, or whoever was driving the car that left the area that night, killed Ivan Collins. But we don't know who pulled the trigger."

Chas turned and faced Katy. "You know that Katy Harrison is an excellent shot. Both Storm Harrison and his wife had plenty of reasons for wanting to kill Ivan. Katy Harrison is the one who watched Ivan drag Officer Michael Perkins into that closet and she didn't know if he was dead or alive. She is the one that Ivan knocked out and tied to her own bed. She is the one who had her clothes cut off and watched Ivan almost beat her husband to death. Katy Harrison and her husband both knew Ivan was going to kill them as soon as he finished his sadistic game of torture. She had just as much reason to kill Ivan as Detective Harrison did."

He turned back to face the jurors. "Ladies and gentlemen, I don't know who the third man was or if there was another man in that room. But neither do you. I don't know who killed Ivan Collins because Detective Harrison never told me. And neither do you."

He looked at Katy, then me, and then at the jurors. "You can't convict Storm Harrison of murder unless you know without any reasonable doubt that he committed the murder. Unless you are one hundred percent sure that Storm Harrison pulled that trigger, you must find him not guilty."

When Chas returned to the table, he sat stoically, staring straight ahead.

Miller stood up for his final rebuttal. He walked to the front of the jurors before speaking. "Smoke and mirrors. That's what you're hearing folks, smoke and mirrors. If you can't defend your client, you blame someone else. But the facts speak for themselves. There has been no evidence presented at this trial that points to anyone other than Storm Harrison as the killer. Look at the facts and the testimony and consider the evidence in this case. Then convict the man responsible for Ivan Collins' death, Storm Harrison," he said while pointing at me.

Miller returned to his seat. He didn't have the same arrogance he had shown throughout the trial. I imagined him hearing the air deflating from his airtight case.

Judge Stanton gave the jurors their final instructions, explained the meaning of reasonable doubt, and told them they could review any evidence they wanted to during deliberation. When he finished with his instructions, he had the jurors escorted out of the courtroom for deliberation. He told the attorneys to make themselves available in case the jury came back with a verdict. Then he dismissed the court.

Connie was busy on the courthouse steps preparing her camera crew for her next report as Katy, Doc and I walked across the street to The Oak Barrel. The noon crowd hadn't arrived yet. After we were seated, Chas came in and sat by himself on the other side of the room. I walked over and asked, "Want to join us?"

"Are you sure?" he asked. "I don't want to intrude."

"I'm sure, Chas. You did a good job in there today."

"I'm glad you think so. I'm not as confident as you are."

We had just finished eating when his phone rang. Surely the jury hadn't returned a verdict already. We waited anxiously as Chas took the call. Once he disconnected, he said, "The jurors only asked for one piece of evidence. They want to hear the 911 recording again."

Our food arrived and I was too nervous to eat. My guts were in a knot. Not knowing if this might be my last meal as a free man killed my appetite. Katy picked at her salad and I worried. She needed to eat for the baby, if not for herself.

"Storm, I need to speak with you alone," Katy said.

Chas and Doc excused themselves and went and sat at the bar. When no one else could hear us, Katy said, "Storm, what are we going to do if you are convicted?"

"We'll see if we can get a new attorney to look at the case and see if he thinks we have cause for an appeal."

"No attorney is going to take you on as a client if you are not willing to testify to what happened in that room. You will have to testify."

"I'll go to prison before I testify, Katy. And that's final."

"Storm, that's not fair. You can't do that."

"I can and I will. The most they'll give me is twenty years and that will be cut in half for good behavior. Our child will only be ten years old. I can do that if I have too."

"You can't do that, Storm. It's not your fault. I won't allow it."

"Yes I can, Katy. Listen to me. Our child needs you to take care of it and I'll need Doc to take care of you. Don't worry about me. If I have to, I'll plead guilty. But I'm taking responsibility for what happened no matter what you or Doc say."

Katy started crying. I put my arm around her and held her tight. When she finally caught her breath, she said, "Storm, I love you so much. I don't think I can make it without you."

"Sure you can. Just think of our baby. The time will go faster than you think. We'll still have a lifetime to make it up."

Chas walked over to us with his phone to his ear. We heard him say, "You're kidding me. They must have had their minds made up before they even got in there. All right, we'll be there in a few minutes." Chas hung up the phone and looked at us. "The jurors have a verdict."

"Really?" Katy said as she dried her tears. "That was quick."

"Let's go see what my fate is," I said. "I'm tired of waiting."

Katy held my hand in a death grip as we walked across the street. Connie was giving her afternoon news update, but cut it short to return to the courtroom when she found out the verdict was in. People ran back to their seats. Protesters started coming out of the woodwork carrying their signs when they saw us. By the time we got to the courthouse steps, chants of, "Storm, Storm, Storm," echoed down the street." We made it upstairs and had to push our way through the hallway crowd to get back inside the courtroom.

We took our seats and waited for Judge Stanton to arrive. When he came in, he checked to see that everyone was present and ordered the doors closed and locked for the remainder of the proceedings. He asked the bailiff to bring the jury in. The judge asked the jury foreman if they had come to a decision. The foreman was the little bookstore owner who had been taking notes throughout the trial. He stood and nearly dropped his glasses while putting them on. He glanced at the other jurors, who sat expressionless. A couple of them made momentary eye contact with me before glancing away. I took that as a hopeful sign. The foreman's hands shook as he unfolded the envelope containing my fate.

He never made eye contact with me or even looked in our direction. I took this as a bad omen.

"Yes, Your Honor."

The bailiff took the verdict to Judge Stanton who read it. He wrote something on a notepad before handing it back to the bailiff. I studied the judge's face for any sign that might give me a hint, but there was none. The bailiff gave the verdict to the court clerk who recorded it. It appeared to me as if the bailiff was moving in slow motion as he returned it to the foreman. I stood on unsteady legs as I waited for the verdict to be read.

It was all normal court procedure, something I had seen many times over the years while attending someone else's trial. But knowing my fate was concealed within that verdict made my heart race. My hands were sweaty. I felt light-headed and weightless. I glanced back at Katy. She had her fingers crossed, her head bowed, her hands clasped together in prayer with her eyes closed.

"Please read the verdict," the judge admonished.

The little man stood and adjusted his glasses again. His hands trembled like an earthquake. Just before he read the verdict, he looked at me and smiled. "We the jury . . . find the defendant . . . not guilty."

The court erupted in cheers. Katy ran around the table and hugged me, jumping up and down the entire time. Then she grabbed Chas and kissed him on the mouth. Judge Stanton let the celebration go on for several moments before slamming his gavel on his bench to silence the court.

"Mr. Miller, do you wish to poll the jury?"

A dejected Miller stood, shook his head. "No, Your Honor."

Judge Stanton stood. "I declare the proceeding of this trial complete. Court is adjourned." He slammed his gavel down one more time and it was over.

I put my hands on top of my head, took a deep breath and blew it out. I felt as if the whole world had been lifted off my shoulders. Katy slid one arm through Doc's and the other through mine and said, "Come on, guys. We need to celebrate."

She yelled back to Chas who was standing with his mouth open watching the jury members leave. "Come with us, Chas."

"I think I will," he said as he started gathering his paperwork. "I have a few details I need to get done first. Where are you going?"

"The Oak Barrel, of course."

"I'll join you in a little while."

Katy kissed me. "Do you realize you would have made a great attorney, Storm?"

"Thank you . . . I think. Let's go celebrate."

As we turned to leave, Lieutenant Fowler stepped forward and extended his hand. "Congratulations, Storm."

"Thanks, Jerry." I said as I shook his hand. He shook Doc's hand and stepped aside.

When we got outside, the steps of the courthouse looked like a circus. People laughed and hugged each other. Car horns blew and several news crews were broadcasting at the same time. Connie Mason fought her way through the crowd and yelled, "Detective Harrison, would you like to make a comment on the verdict?"

I smiled and said, "No comment." Connie didn't look disappointed this time. She smiled at me and gave me a thumbs-up. I'd hoped she knew I had forgiven her. Katy hugged her and whispered something in her ear.

"What did you say to her?" I asked as we walked across the street.

"I told her to come celebrate with us. She said she would as soon as she's through filming her segment.

Connie had been more than fair on reporting the trial. I just hoped she and Chas had reconciled their differences. Chas stopped to give her an interview. It was his time to bask in the glory he deserved.

When we entered The Oak Barrel the whole place was filled with old friends and police buddies. Maggie ran up to me and gave me a big kiss. She had tears in her eyes. Everyone clapped as we made our way to our table. I spent the next fifteen minutes shaking hands. Even Chief Henderson came by to congratulate me.

We celebrated well into the evening before Katy drove us home. I'd lost count of the number of beers I'd had and the evening was becoming a blur. What I never forgot was that it was over and that I was a free man.

CHAPTER FORTY

The next day, Katy used Doc's car to drive me to the police station so I could retrieve my personal property while she went to the court to get her bond money back. Jim Pomush met us at the evidence counter and I signed the release forms. He handed me my knife buckle and belt.

"You know, Storm, I really thought you had killed that son-of-bitch right up to the point when Woods asked me who killed Ivan Collins. Then I wasn't sure. Do you want to tell me who killed him now that it's over?"

"You're too honest to handle the truth, Jim. Believe whatever you want."

He smiled, "You're a good man, Storm. When can I expect you back to work?"

"I'm not sure. I haven't been reinstated yet. Besides, Katy has a little vacation planned for us. I'll let you know when we get back from Costa Rica. That is, if I'm reinstated."

He shook my hand, gave me back the rest of my stuff and we left. When Katy got back to the car, I told her I wanted to stop and get a couple of books to read at the beach. I directed her to a small bookstore in the downtown area. The jury foreman with the wire rimmed glasses came from around the counter when he saw us enter.

"Detective Harrison, it's so nice to get to meet you in person," he said as he held out his hand. "I'm Neil Coleman. Whose light blue sedan are you diving?"

"That belongs to Doctor Martin. He's Katy's uncle."

Neil quickly removed a notepad and pen from his shirt pocket and wrote himself a note. We shook hands and Katy left to shop for books while I stayed to talk to Neil.

"I wanted to thank you in person for finding me not guilty," I said. "You were the one person on the jury that I thought would hang me."

"No, not me," he said shaking his head. "Not any of us really. We all knew someone murdered that creep, but the prosecution couldn't prove beyond a reasonable doubt who pulled the trigger. If we couldn't determine who killed him, we sure couldn't find you guilty. We were just doing our job."

"I'd like to ask you something personal if you don't mind," I asked.

"Sure. Go ahead."

"You took more notes than all of the other jurors put together. Frankly, it worried me a lot. What was that about?"

He smiled. "I'm not only a bookstore owner, Mr. Harrison, I'm also an author. I write murder mysteries. I want to write a book about this someday."

"I see. Then I suppose you'll want to know who really killed Ivan Collins."

"No, not at all," answered Neil. "Not knowing is what makes it an intriguing mystery."

ACKNOWLEDGMENTS

As my disclaimer, this book is a work of fiction. Some of the towns and locations are actual towns and places. All characters and events in this book are fictional, created in the mind of the author. Some of the names in this book are real and used with the permission of the person named. Jim Pomush was one of the best detectives I ever worked with and I hope he likes the character I made out of his name.

I'd like to thank my editors, Donna Jandro and Toni Zobel for editing this book. You are both amazing and this book would never have make it into print without you.

I want to thank the Power Road Writers Group, Carlene and Anthony Eye, Craig Mazur, Randy Lindsay, Ruth Chavez and Don Wooldridge. With out them, this book would never have been completed. A part them is hidden between each page of this book.

Thanks to my Beta readers, Carmel Fitzgerald, Guy Meeks, Jim Pomush, Larissa Pixler and Edda Pitharoulis.

I'd like to thank my wonderful wife, Sherrie, for putting up with my imaginary friends and me while I was writing the book. She is my biggest supporter and helps me with spelling, editing, grammar and word choices.

Elvis Bray is an American author specializing in crime and suspense fiction novels, short stories and poetry. He served as a helicopter crew chief during the Vietnam War for two tours and was a police officer and detective of over 35 years. Now retired, he lives in Queen Creek, Arizona with his wife, three horses, two dogs and two cats, but he only claims one.

To contact the author, please go to elvisbrayauthor.com or elvisbray04@gmail.com